'Timlin's South London is well drawn, full of dodgy boozers and villains, dodgier clubs and coppers, cemeteries and second-hand car dealers' — *Face*

'Hard-boiled storytelling with attitude' — *Daily Mail*

'Brit-pulp's tough guy prize goes to work on Mark Timlin's Nick Sharman' — *Evening Standard*

'Grips like a pair of regulation handcuffs' — *Guardian*

'The king of the British hard-boiled thriller' — *Times*

'Definitely one of the best' — *Time Out*

Other books by Mark Timlin

A Good Year for the Roses 1988

Romeo's Girl 1990

Gun Street Girl 1990

Take the A-Train 1991

The Turnaround 1991

Zip Gun Boogie 1992

Hearts of Stone 1992

Falls the Shadow 1993

Ashes by Now 1993

Pretend We're Dead 1994

Paint It Black 1995

Find My Way Home 1996

Sharman and Other Filth (short stories) 1996

A Street That Rhymed with 3 AM 1997

Dead Flowers 1998

Quick Before They Catch Us 1999

All the Empty Places 2000

Stay Another Day 2010

OTHERS

I Spied a Pale Horse 1999

Answers from the Grave 2004

as TONY WILLIAMS

Valin's Raiders 1994

Blue on Blue 1999

as JIM BALLANTYNE

The Torturer 1995

as MARTIN MILK

That Saturday 1996

as LEE MARTIN

Gangsters Wives 2007

The Lipstick Killers 2009

mark timlin

a good year
for the roses

The First Nick Sharman Thriller

NO EXIT PRESS

The first one's for Mum

This edition published in 2013 by No Exit Press,
an imprint of Oldcastle Books,
P.O.Box 394, Harpenden, Herts, AL5 1XJ
www.noexit.co.uk

ISBN 978-1-84344-079-6 (print)
978-1-84344-080-2 (epub)
978-1-84344-081-9 (kindle)
978-1-84344-082-6 (pdf)

Printed and bound in Great Britain by Clays Ltd, St Ives plc

THE TURNAROUND [5/04/1995]
Director - Suri Krishnamma
Writer - Tony Hoare
Co-stars - Bill Paterson, Rowena King, Roberta Taylor, John Salthouse

TAKE THE A-TRAIN [4/11/1996]
Director - Robert Bierman
Writer - Guy Jenkin
Co-stars - Samantha Janus, Roberta Taylor, John Salthouse,
Gina Bellman

HEARTS OF STONE [11/11/1996]
Director - Robert Bierman
Writer - Paul Abbott
Co-stars - Keith Allen, Roberta Taylor, John Salthouse, Julie Graham

A GOOD YEAR FOR THE ROSES [18/11/1996]
Director - Matthew Evans
Writer - Dusty Hughes
Co-stars - Ray Winstone, Adie Allen, Colette Brown, Hugo Spree,
John Salthouse, Roberta Taylor

SHARMAN - EPISODE 4 [25/11/1996]
Director - Matthew Evans
Writer - Mick Ford
Co-Stars - John Salthouse, Adie Allen, Colette Brown, Roberta Taylor,
Danny Webb

SOURCES

Mark Timlin Website
http://marktimlin.co.uk/

CrimeTime – Rise and Fall of Nick Sharman
http://www.crimetime.co.uk/features/marktimlin.php

Fantastic Fiction
http://www.fantasticfiction.co.uk/t/mark-timlin/

Thrilling Detective
http://www.thrillingdetective.com/sharman.html

No Exit Press
http://www.noexit.co.uk/authorpages/mark_timlin.php

I woke up last night from the dream of roses again. It was the same recurring nightmare I've come to know so well.

I lay in the dark with my eyes open, and felt the cold sweat drying on my body. As before, whilst I tried to fall asleep again, my mind went back to those few dreadful days last summer.

1

I opened for business on a chilly morning, in a cool August, in a cold and wet, forgettable summer. The headlines in the newspapers told me that there had been a radiation leak at Sellafield Nuclear Re-Processing Plant, Beirut had been bombed for the third successive day, a fourteen year old girl had been raped and left for dead in Clapham, and England had lost in the final test at Edgbaston. It must have been someone's birthday, or someone's wedding anniversary. Somebody had cause to celebrate. But the Lord Mayor didn't come down and cut a pink ribbon for me. I didn't notice the earth move.

I unlocked my office and looked around the room furnished by a second hand commercial furniture company, slumped down in a second hand typist's chair and propped my foot in the open drawer of a second hand desk. My foot was sore. I'd been shot through it by a bullet from a .38 calibre Colt Detective Special two years previously. Ultimately that slug of lead had brought me to where I was sitting. Although I had made virtually a 100% recovery from the injury, I still limped slightly when the weather was wet or cold, and as I said, it had been both that year. It felt good to take the weight off my old wound. I wasn't a walking miracle.

Starting a new venture left me with a certain feeling of anti-climax. But then I felt anti-climax every morning when I woke up.

I was resting on an overdraft that resembled the national debt of a small South American country, like more successful men rest on their laurels. I was in my peak earning years and worth less than zero.

The office I had rented was situated in a cul-de-sac leading to a railway station deep in South London. I had been born and bred in the area and when I was a baby, my mother had taken me for long walks across the grounds of a riding school which was now a council estate where two thousand souls lived. She'd bought our vegetables from a market garden where a used car lot now stood.

The city had eaten into the suburbs like a giant cancer and gobbled up the little communities one by one. Digesting them into a sprawling mass of shopping precincts, slum flats and rows of houses stretching from the river for mile upon soulless mile. The few remaining green areas surrounded by concrete and brick like a wagon train encircled by Apaches.

To most people, that little manor in which I'd put my roots down again was just an insignificant name on the map, a place they drove through to reach the inner city or out to the green hills of Southern England. The South Circular road cut through Tulse Hill like a wire through mouldy cheese. On one side of the road lived the have-nots, on the other the have-lesses. The sign-posts pointing out were a constant reminder that things could be better.

It hadn't always been like that of course. It used to be a genteel area, full of elderly ladies sipping coffee together in tiny cafes, served by young girls in smart uniforms. Now it had slipped down the charts and was full of shops selling greasy take-away food or cut price furniture. The ladies had died or moved down the line to

Surrey. The girls were married now and lived on the council estate. Things had gone full circle. After my short period away, I'd returned to the kebabs and chop suey and litter on the pavements. I'd cashed in my chance of a ticket out again.

The single shop front I sat in had previously housed a coal-merchants. It was in a hundred year old terrace of buildings that were dark with soot from the railway. The narrow windows of the flats above the shops looked over towards the rutted car park next to the station. The whole block was about due for demolition and it showed.

The interior of the shop consisted of a large, high ceilinged outer office. On one wall was set a cranky old gas fire with broken elements, mounted in the middle of a cracked, brown tile fireplace. The front of the office was almost filled with a plate glass window which allowed me a panoramic view of the street outside. Separated from the window by a slat of white painted wood was a narrow door with a pane of frosted glass set into it at head height. The wall opposite the window held another similar door that led into a smaller, windowless inside room, bare but for a stained stone sink with one dripping cold water tap. A further door led out into a tiny, muddy, high walled yard which contained nothing but an outside toilet. I'd congratulated myself on getting fixed up with premises that featured all mod-cons. But it was cheap and the penthouse could come later. I'd painted the interior of the whole place white and fitted some shelves to hold a selection of leather-bound law books which I hoped looked authoritative and business-like. On the day I'd picked up the keys and checked around my new establishment, a big, old cat had come stalking by to suss me out. He was black and white in colour with a ripped ear and a wall eye that appeared to gaze off into the distance behind my shoulder when he looked at me. I'd thrown him a few scraps from the cheeseburger I'd bought for my lunch. He gobbled them down and came back for more. So much had vanished from my life over the previous months that there seemed no harm in feeding him with the left-overs from the take-out food that made up most of my diet. Cod and chips was his favourite, closely followed by chicken tikka from the tandoori.

I didn't want any long term relationship, so I just called him Cat and refused to pet or stroke him. I think we were both satisfied with the arrangement. When he came to be fed we just sat on opposite sides of his bowl and scowled at each other.

At least having an animal around the place was a good excuse for me to talk to myself without being taken away for treatment. I'd had enough of that to last a lifetime.

So I formed a tenuous kind of attachment to Cat. It was a start and about as far as I was prepared to go for a while.

I hadn't got dressed up for my big day, I was wearing a yellow cotton polo shirt and old blue jeans with soft Italian moccasin shoes. No jacket. I'd been up half the night wandering about the place, putting the finish to the decor, besides, I didn't have a shoulder holster to hide. Not yet anyway.

As a thought, I'd put a tiny advertisement in the local paper that week, just my name, address and telephone number, plus a simple description of my new profession. 'Discreet investigations' it read. I'd received no mail yet, not anything addressed to me anyhow. Just a circular giving me the chance to win a new Volvo and someone ordering half a hundred-weight of smokeless fuel. By ten to eleven boredom had set in and I was really beginning to feel like a cold bottle of beer. I thought about knocking up a sign saying I was in the boozer in case anyone was interested.

Suddenly the sun broke through the clouds. It shone down across the roofs of the buildings on the opposite side of the street and directly through my window into my eyes. The room turned primrose colour and I could feel the chill lift from the skin on the back of my hands. The light was bright and piercing.

I was mulling over those thoughts in my mind with my eyes closed against the glare, enjoying the warmth of the sun on my face, when a dark shadow fell across me. Someone was standing in the open doorway. I squinted upwards and saw the outline of a man in the opening. His face and body were silhouetted by the sun shining over his shoulder. I felt a shiver run down my spine for a moment, as if someone had walked over the place my grave would be one day. Then he moved towards me and I shifted my position on my chair slightly, so that I could see him clearly.

He was tall, over six foot and aged somewhere in his mid-fifties, I guessed. He reminded me of Burt Lancaster going to seed, with sharp handsome features beginning to fade under a coating of excess flesh over his cheekbones. He was pale under a tan, giving his face a yellow, unhealthy look. His hair was thick and newly barbered, with grey speckles salting the youthful style.

He was wearing a smart navy blue suit of conservative cut, a white shirt with a red tie and a pair of polished black, lace-up shoes. In his right hand he carried a black brief-case with chrome locks that sparkled in the sunlight. He looked like the managing director of a successful advertising agency, or a top consultant at a private hospital, or the VAT man.

2

——————

'Is your name Sharman?' the man demanded with rather more vehemence than I thought was really necessary. 'I want to talk to you.'

His accent was basic London town, but the nice part.

'Good morning,' I said politely. 'Do sit down.'

I nodded at one of the two metal chairs facing my desk. He looked at them as if he'd never seen such items of furniture before, and with a moment's hesitation pulled one towards him and sat. I got the feeling he would like to have wiped it down with his hankie before he did so. He fixed me with the sort of look usually reserved for something that has crawled out of a side salad.

'Are you a registered private detective?' he asked.

'Registered with whom?' I asked back.

'Well, you have to register with someone, don't you?' he asked with a puzzled look.

It was my turn to look puzzled. 'I don't know what you mean,' I said.

'That's what you do isn't it, investigations?' He pulled a scrap of newspaper from his jacket pocket and tapped my advertisement.

I began to understand. A little late perhaps, but I was out of practice.

'Yes,' I said, 'that's what I do, but this is not Los Angeles. In London you don't need a licence to undertake investigative work.'

'I didn't know that,' he said. 'Have you got any qualifications?'

Christ, I thought, he wants to see my 'O' Level certificates. And then said aloud, 'I used to be a policeman, ten years on the force.'

'You're too young to be retired. Why did you leave?' he asked almost accusingly.

'I resigned for personal reasons,' I said. 'If it's any of your business.'

'It'll be my business if I'm paying you to work for me,' he said. I shrugged.

'And there's me convinced you were the VAT man.'

Things were beginning to look up. I pulled a shorthand pad and pen from the top drawer of my desk and placed them neatly in front of me. I opened the pad to a fresh page and said,

'Let's start at the beginning. What's your name?'

'Bright, George Bright,' he replied.

'Address, telephone number?'

He gave me the information.

'All right, Mr Bright,' I said. 'Tell me what the problem is.'

'It's my daughter Patricia. She's missing,' he said.

Sitting there with him in that stuffy little room reminded me of the beginning of one of those 1950s black and white detective films that are transmitted in the afternoon, or late at night on TV. I liked it.

'Tell me the whole story,' I invited.

I made myself comfortable as he began. He started slowly, thinking back.

'Two months ago, two months exactly today, Patsy went out for the evening. She left after we'd eaten dinner. She made a salad for us both. A prawn salad,' he looked as if he could still taste it. 'She came and said goodbye as I was watching TV in the library.' I made a mental note that this guy didn't live in a council maisonette. 'She told me she was off to visit a friend,' he continued.

'Where?' I asked.

'In Brixton. I told her to be careful. That's no place for a young girl, alone at night. She promised me she wouldn't be late and she'd catch a cab home.'

'Why didn't you offer to pick her up?'

He gave me a pained look. 'You're joking, she's a very independent girl.' Obviously, I thought.

'But she never showed up,' I said.

'No.'

'When did you begin to get worried?'

'When I went to wake her up the next morning and realised her bed hadn't been slept in.'

'So you didn't wait up?' I asked. I think he took it as an accusation.

'I had no reason to,' he replied quickly. 'Patsy was a trustworthy girl. A little vague sometimes. But if she told me she was going to be home, there was no reason for me to believe she wouldn't.'

'Did she often stay out all night?' I asked.

'No, never; well only if she'd arranged it with me beforehand. A party or something like that. But I always knew.'

'Who was she visiting that night?' I asked.

'What?'

'You said she was off to see a friend,' I said patiently. 'Who was it?'

'I don't know,' he was almost squirming in his seat.

'No idea?' I probed.

'She didn't like to be tied down to anything definite about her movements,' he explained. 'I told you she was a little vague. Most of the time it was on purpose.' His whole attitude hinted at countless arguments about people and places.

'But you always knew if she was going to come home or not?' I asked.

'Yes.' He sounded more definite. I decided to believe him.

'Did she have a boyfriend?' I changed my line of questioning slightly.

'No, she wasn't keen on boys,' he sounded rather defensive at the question.

Fair enough, I thought, you should know. But I scribbled a notation on my pad.

'So it was a girlfriend or girlfriends,' I said.

'I suppose so.'

'You don't seem too sure, Mr Bright,' I said.

'I'm not sure about anything. I sit at night and try to work out if she knew she wouldn't be back. It's been so difficult to cope with her since my wife died. I've tried to do my best -' He didn't finish the sentence, just lapsed into silence and slipped lower down into his chair. 'Then I got this.' He plunged his hand into his inside jacket pocket and produced his wallet. It was black leather, expensive, well worn and fat. He opened it on his knee and removed an envelope. From the envelope he slid out a sheet of folded paper. He leant over and placed the paper in the centre of my desk in front of me. I picked up the paper and unfolded it carefully. It had obviously been read many times. The few words were written in black ballpoint. The handwriting was stylish yet somehow immature. It read:

Dear Daddy,
Don't worry, I'm fine. I need some time
to myself to sort a few things out. I'll be
in touch soon.

> *Love*
>
> *Patsy*

I sat holding the letter in my hand.

'When did this arrive?' I asked.

'About a week after she left,' he replied.

'Is it her writing?'

'Yes.'

'Where was it posted?'

'Stockwell.'

'Well there you are,' I said. 'She'll be back soon. I don't think I can be of much use. We'll both be wasting our time.'

'Let me be the judge of that,' he said.

'I assume you've been to the police,' I said after a moment's silence. He gave me a piercing look from under his eyebrows.

'Of course I have. They filled in all the bloody forms, and that was that. They don't seem to care. She's just a kid,' he added, as if it meant anything.

'How old is she, Mr Bright?' I asked.

'Eighteen.'

'When?'

'Last March, March 24th.'

'So she's an adult in the eyes of the law.'

'What the hell does that mean?' He interrupted in a high-pitched, strangled kind of voice. 'She could be dead.'

'It means she can come and go as she pleases,' I replied calmly. 'The police are too busy to spend a lot of time on cases like this, unless suspicious circumstances are suspected. And you've got this note.' I tapped the paper on the desk to underline the point.

'Fuck the note and the police,' he shouted. Then continued in a more subdued tone, 'Will you look for her too?'

I tapped the letter on the desk again.

'You have shown this to the police, haven't you?'

'Yes of course.' He dismissed my question with a savage, spastic movement of his hand.

'It's the Salvation Army they'll send you to,' I said.

'Or a private detective,' he finished my sentence for me.

The words hung around like unwelcome guests in the warm air of my office.

'When did you inform the police?' I asked.

'The day after I discovered she was missing,' he replied. 'I last saw her on the Sunday evening. On Monday I waited for her at home all day. By late afternoon I was desperate. I hadn't heard a word. No phone call, nothing. I went out and drove the streets looking for her.'

'But you didn't know where to look,' I interrupted.

'I didn't care, I just drove around for hours. Then I went back to the house and sat up all night hoping she'd come back or get in touch at least. She didn't. So the next morning, Tuesday, I went to the police.'

'Where?' I hated to ask.

'Brixton.'

'That makes sense I suppose. Who did you see there?'

'A detective sergeant. Reid is his name. I've got his card in here.' He lifted his wallet.

'I might have guessed,' I said, and felt the cold chill again.

'Do you know him then?' Bright asked.

'Just slightly,' I replied.

3

'What's wrong with him? You don't seem keen I must say. He looked a bit of a hard case to me; is he? ' asked George.

'He's a hard case alright,' I replied. 'It was partly due to him that I left the force.'

'Why?'

'He shot me,' I pointed at my foot that was resting on the open desk drawer again. 'In my bloody foot.'

George Bright looked at me as if he wished that John Reid had shot me in the head. Sometimes I wished he had too. Especially on long dark nights when sleep wouldn't come and the ghosts of my past mistakes circled my bed and haunted my thoughts.

I didn't like the look one bit. He stared at me as if trying to say something without words. Suddenly it dawned on me.

'What is she into Mr Bright?' I asked. 'Something a bit iffy? Thieving? Drugs?'

He didn't answer right away. Then he said, 'I'm not sure. I found some stuff when I looked into her room.'

'What stuff?'

'A box hidden in her wardrobe. Here, you look.'

It was his briefcase. It was a small, shallow, black lacquered box with a hinged lid and a tiny brass lock. It looked quite valuable.

'It was hidden under some sweaters,' Bright volunteered.

'Was it locked?' I asked, for something to say.

'No,' he replied.

I opened it. There was nothing special inside. Just the usual dope smoker's stash. Rizla papers, some broken up cigarettes. Silk Cut king size, I noticed, my old brand. Various ripped up business cards advertising mini-cab firms and Indian restaurants, a scalpel and some tweezers. It was all depressingly familiar to me, I'd had something similar myself for years, until I'd quit. At the bottom of the box, wrapped in silver foil was a lump of hash. Black, pungent smelling, about the size of an Oxo cube.

'It's really no big deal, George,' I said, using his Christian name for the first time. 'It's hardly reefer madness. Everyone has a go at this at one time or another.' He looked shocked. 'Well nearly everybody,' I added. 'Did you tell the police you found this in her room?' I asked as I sat fiddling with the box and it's contents.

'No,' he replied.

'Not very wise was it? They might have shown more interest if you had.' I gave him back the box and he put it carefully in his jacket pocket.

My instincts told me to shut George Bright out, to close him down and send him packing. Instead I kept asking questions about his daughter.

'How did she get to wherever she was going? Did she drive?' It would be easier to locate her if there was a car sitting somewhere parked on the street.

'No, she never learned,' he replied. 'I promised her a car for her next birthday, but she didn't seem to be interested.'

'Was she picked up then?'

'I don't think so. The library is at the back of the house, you see. But no-one called for her. I know that,' he added as an afterthought.

'But someone could have been waiting?'

'Yes, I suppose so.'

'Have you asked your neighbours if they saw anything?'

'I haven't mentioned it to my neighbours,' he replied.

'Why not?' I asked.

'It's none of their business.'

'But they might have seen something.'

'I doubt it,' he said.

'Are you worried what they might think?'

He didn't answer. 'Well are you? Because it doesn't matter what people think.'

He looked at me in a disgusted manner. 'Of course it matters. The world runs on money and what other people think.'

There was no answer to that.

I changed my tack again.

'Do you fancy a drink?' I asked, already halfway to my feet.

He looked at me incredulously.

'Be serious Sharman,' he said. 'This is important.'

'I am being serious. We can talk in the pub. It'll be quiet at this time.' I said. 'Come on, you look as if you could use one.' George got up from his seat reluctantly and I ushered him out of the office.

As I closed the door behind us, I looked at Cat who had been listening to our conversation all the time. I shrugged at him and he seemed to shrug back before continuing the vital task of cleaning his torn ear with a damp paw.

George Bright and I walked across the road and through the door of the pub. The bar smelled of beer and old cigarettes, as all bars do when they first open. I suddenly wanted a new cigarette, but fought back the craving.

'What'll you have?' I asked.

'Anything, I don't mind,' he answered.

I walked over to the counter and ordered two bottles of cold Heineken and looked around the room. There were just a few early drinkers in. I nodded to Hilary and Hubert, a pair of regulars who often popped in for a quick one after their trip to the local supermarket.

They were both bottle brunettes and invariably wore matching black outfits. They were perched on their stools at the bar like a couple of gay old crows on a barn fence pecking at two gin and tonics.

I steered George over to an empty table, and we sat in silence for a while sipping our drinks. From the state of his face, he certainly looked as if he needed a livener. With me it was inevitable. I was drinking too much lately. I decided to cut down. Maybe tomorrow.

'Are you going to help me?' George finally asked.

'I don't know,' I replied. 'When I left the Met. my wife left me. She got almost everything. So I'm starting again. I came into this business because it's what I know. I was a copper for a long time. I've never done anything else. But I'm not a policeman any more, not a real one. What I'll be doing for the main part is working for solicitors and finance firms, serving court orders and other legal papers. Tracing missing relations and looking for people who haven't paid their HP, or nicked the video from Granada Rentals.

'I put that ad in the paper for my own satisfaction. Just to prove to myself that I existed again. I've been away for a while. Out of circulation.'

I'm glad to say that George was discreet enough not to ask where I'd been. He might not have liked the answer.

'You see,' I continued, 'it's a nice little service industry, tracing missing people and debt collecting.'

'But my Patsy's a missing person,' George interrupted.

'I appreciate that,' I said. 'But it's a bit different. I'm not exactly going to blend in with her age group. What I'm talking about is going through the voter's register or checking out newspaper files. A bit of surveillance. A few words in the right ears and no trouble. This is different. There's a definite drug connection, and I can't afford to get mixed up in that sort of thing. Besides the last mob I want to meet again are the Brixton old bill.'

'Too dangerous?' he asked with a sneer.

'There's more than one kind of danger,' I replied. 'For instance, when I was stationed at Brixton, I worked for a while on the drugs squad, undercover. Well, I got too fond of the merchandise. That's another reason I left the job.'

'You were taking drugs when you were a copper?' asked George.

'The police aren't saints, if you cut them they bleed like anybody else,' I replied.

'Christ, you're a right one. But at least you know about drugs, don't you? It could help if Patsy's got involved.'

Who was he kidding? Of course she was involved. I kept a straight face and said. 'I know too bloody much about them, besides that was a while ago. Two weeks can be a lifetime when you mess with dope.'

'But you're looking for work aren't you?'

'Yes, and I'm expensive.'

'How much?'

'Two hundred pounds a day, plus expenses and mileage.'

'You'll be in the upper tax level in no time,' said George drily. I don't think he was impressed.

'Not really,' I said. 'Most of my work will be pro rata. An hour here and there. As you can tell from the fact that I'm sitting here with you shooting the breeze. I'm not exactly overworked. Besides I'm broke.'

George leant over the table.

'Listen, you're my last chance,' he said. 'Help me please. Here, look.' He picked up his briefcase which he had brought into the pub with him. He placed it on the table and opened it up. He produced a large brown envelope and extracted a photograph which he placed in front of me.

'That is Patsy,' he said proudly.

The photograph was an 8" X 10" head and shoulder professional shot of an extremely attractive young blonde girl.

'She was going to be a model,' he said.

He didn't seem to realise that he was speaking in the past tense. I looked at the photo for a while. The subject reminded me of my own daughter, Judith. Although Judith was ten years younger, the likeness was uncanny. Judith always told me that when she grew up she would be a film star.

'Look on the back,' George said.

A piece of white paper had been stuck on the reverse side of the photograph. On it was typed Patricia Bright's vital statistics. Everything from her birthday to her glove size.

'I've got a couple of dozen here,' said George, tapping the envelope. 'You can use them, and I've got money too. I'm not a poor man.' He said with a certain dignity. He produced his cheque book, which he opened and placed on the table in front of him. We looked at everything but each other. Then I noticed that he was crying.

Although I was not fond of the man, I felt intensely sorry for him.

'Alright,' I said, 'I give in. I'll tell you what, give me a kite for a hundred quid and I'll take a look round. I'll talk to the police and get back to you after the weekend, is that alright?'

George pulled out his handkerchief and dabbed at his eyes. I was always a sucker for a hard luck story. Besides, I knew how I'd feel if Judith had disappeared.

'Thank you,' said George. He fumbled around in his briefcase for a pen and wrote a cheque out for the amount agreed, tore it out of the book and slid it in front of me.

'I'll have the box back, too,' I said.

He retrieved it from his pocket and passed it to me.

'What do you do, George?' I asked, leaning back in my chair. 'For a living I mean.'

'Leisure,' he replied. 'I'm in the leisure business. Juke boxes and fruit machines. I'm well known in the trade. I've got a showroom in Herne Hill. I'd better give you my card.'

He produced a printed card from his pocket like a magician. I put it in the envelope with the photographs, then carelessly pushed the cheque into the back pocket of my jeans.

And that was how I obtained my first paying customer on an August morning that neither of us would ever forget.

I should have asked George why I was his last chance.

I should have listened to my instincts.

I should have just let him cry.

4

After George left. I drank another beer. I kept an eye on the office through the pub door, but no one else stopped by with any little jobs that I didn't want. If the telephone rang, I didn't hear it. When I had finished my drink I walked back to the office carrying the photos of Patsy Bright and her lacquered box.

At last the weather seemed to have broken. The sun was still shining brightly. I was grateful. In the warmth I walked with hardly any trace of a limp.

I sat down at my desk and put the box in the bottom drawer and locked it. I kept the envelope on the desk top. I looked at my watch, it said almost twelve.

I thought about the implications of telephoning John Reid. When I was on the force, we'd been as thick as thieves. In my case, quite literally. I'd been going to pieces for a while, drinking up a storm and hanging around with the kind of people police officers shouldn't.

John had covered me for months. He was a few years older than I was, and we had struck up a close friendship as soon as we had met. He liked a drink and we'd had some very good times together. Then I'd gone too far even for him. I ripped off some cocaine from a drugs bust.

I still went hot and cold thinking about it.

I was far down the river of no return at the time. I didn't even care that John was responsible for the evidence that I had misappropriated. The morning after my little heist both John and I had been on a target mission for a suspected armed robber. I was as high as a kite on the coke, drunk and hadn't slept for three or four days.

Perhaps you know what it's like. Everything takes on a translucent look. Nothing is real. Nobody matters, and paranoia scuttles around your feet like a hunchbacked, slimy rat. Too many cigarettes are smoked, too many drinks are drunk and the inside of your mouth is chewed to a bloody mess. Food is forgotten and families are ignored in the quest for speed. Speed is of the essence.

Just as we went in on the raid, who should turn up, but the regional crime squad from somewhere out in the sticks after the same guy on another fire-arms related charge. None of us knew what was going on, what with everyone tearing around dressed like extras from Minder and screaming at the top of their voices. Someone had fired his gun and an inter-officer gun fight started. The only person who knew that everyone was after him was our target. As long as he didn't top his mum, who shared the house with him, he was alright.

He didn't know if we were the law or not, and cared even less. It was like the ending of 'Butch Cassidy and the Sundance Kid'. The villian came out of his bedroom wearing just his Y-fronts, brandishing two single action .45 Colt revolvers. He was blasting at anything that moved. The only thing we knew to our advantage was that he had no spare ammunition. There was no room in his jockeys.

I was stoned, I hadn't even drawn my gun. I was well out of position when it all happened, halfway up a metal fire escape at the

back of the house. The target jumped straight over me from the first
floor landing window. John Reid stepped out from the back porch
and fired upwards. The bullet went straight through the sole of my
Bass Weejun, broke several tiny bones and exited through the leather
upper of the shoe in a shower of blood, skin and Argyll sock. I'll
never forget looking down at the red mess as it burst all over my
trouser leg. I felt no pain at the time. I was too well anaesthetized.
John didn't even stop to see how badly I was hurt. It was another two
officers who prised my fingers from the metal of the ladder to which
I was clinging and carried me to a Transit van and away to hospital.
Luckily, the slug flew off at an angle. If it had carried straight on
it would have blown my balls off too. It was also fortunate that
John was using standard home-office issue ammunition. No Teflon
coatings or dum-dum cuts, and the bullets hadn't been dipped in shit
or strychnine to make the wound go bad.

The target got clean away. Two other policemen were slightly
wounded. The only result that we got was that we did the mum for
receiving stolen goods. Not much to show for three weeks work.

I hadn't spoken to John since that day. He came close to losing
his seniority, if not his job, over the missing drugs. And now, here I
was sticking my nose into something that was strictly his business.
I pulled the phone in front of me and dialled the familiar number.
When the officer on the switchboard identified himself, I asked
for Detective Sergeant John Reid. I recognised his voice when he
answered.

'Reid,' he said.

'Hello, John. It's Nick, Nick Sharman.'

'Fuck me, what do you want?'

'A little help.'

'What's the matter. Lost your walking stick?'

'Very amusing,' I said.

'I must say we never thought we'd hear your name again, but what happens, there you are in the local press this week. Can't you get a proper job?'

'Leave the jokes out, John, I'm not in the mood. I need to know about Patricia Bright.'

I went straight to the offensive. Whether or not that was the right attitude to take, I didn't know.

He was silent for a moment, and I listened to the echos on the line. Then he asked, 'Who?'

'Patricia Bright, she's one of your cases. A missing person.'

I read him some of the details from the back of the photograph.

'I remember,' he said. 'What's it to you?'

'Her father has hired me to look for her.'

He was silent again for so long that I thought he'd cut me off. Finally he said 'Jesus, he must he hard up.'

'If he is mate, it's because he's lost faith in your lot to find her.'

'Don't give me that shit, Nick. The little slut's hopped it to join her junkie mates.'

'How do you know she's a junkie?' I asked. 'Have you seen her?'

'No, but I've collated a report. I'm not stupid, Nick. It's obvious.'

'What put you onto drugs?' I asked. 'I didn't think her father had mentioned anything about them.'

'He didn't, but he did tell me she mixed with a bunch of undesirables. I made some enquiries and found out she was into all sorts.'

'What enquiries?' I asked. 'Who did you speak to?'

'I don't think I should be talking to you,' replied John.

'What you mean is, you haven't pushed yourself to find Patsy. Is that what you're saying?'

'Don't piss me off, Nick. You know what it's like. She wrote him a note sometime later if I remember rightly, saying she'd be back.

Bright brought it in and showed it to me. He admitted it was in her writing. We haven't got time to solve every family row. That's all it was, if you ask me. She's probably with some geezer fucking her brains out right now. If we did find her she'd probably tell all of us, including her old man, to get stuffed.'

'Perhaps he shouldn't be denied the chance.'

'You always were a wanker, Nick. What are you trying to do? Set yourself up on the old boy's savings. You always did have an eye for the main chance.'

'No John, I've taken half a day's fee and that's all. I just thought I'd check on how our police force are spending the rates these days.'

'You're a cheeky bastard Nick,' said John. 'I'm not your personal link into the police computer. You resigned remember? Just before you would have got fired.'

'It was partly down to you, though, John, wasn't it?' I was on sticky ground and I knew it.

Silence again. The line stretched like elastic.

'Perhaps,' he said grudgingly.

'So you owe me.'

'No chance. It was more your fault than mine. If you'd carried on like you were, always out of it, you'd have ended up shooting yourself.'

'I doubt it John, but have it your way if you want.' More silence.

'John?'

'What?'

'Could we meet and discuss the Bright girl. Perhaps you can bring your case notes.'

I was taking a risk asking.

He laughed without humour. 'You've got two chances.'

He meant a dog's chance and no chance.

'Let's meet for a drink then.' I had to keep pushing.

'I don't want to be seen with you.'

'Alright, come to my place tonight.'

'Not tonight, I'm busy.' He seemed to be weakening. 'Maybe over the weekend. Where are you living now? I heard your wife kicked you out.'

'More than that John, we're divorced and she's remarried. I've got a little flat off the Norwood Road now.'

I gave him my home number and told him I had no plans for the next couple of days. In reality I had no plans for the rest of my life.

'Ok, I'll get round if I can,' he said reluctantly. 'But no notes, and I don't have the keys to the evidence lock-up either. Remember? Where we keep the drugs.'

I was beginning to lose my patience.

'I'm clean John,' I said. 'I don't even smoke cigarettes any more.'

'Alright, I believe you,' he said, quite obviously lying.

'I'd appreciate it if you can come,' I said finally.

The statement sounded oddly pathetic in my own ears.

'We'll see,' said John. 'And if I do come, try to be straight, Nick. I don't want to waste my time.'

Before I could reply, he'd hung up. I held the dead receiver in my hand for a moment before replacing it on the cradle.

5

First thing the next morning I decided to pay a visit to the photographer whose address was on the back of the copies of the shot of Patsy Bright that I'd been given. His studio was in Holborn.

I'd met some professional photographers before and I wasn't too keen, but I'll talk to anyone.

I pushed the car through the late rush hour traffic heading towards town. It was a 1972 E-Type jaguar hard top, with an automatic shift. I'd picked it up cheaply not long after I joined the police. It had been used in a smash and grab raid on a jewellers in Tooting. The thieves had underestimated the power that the V-12 engine poured into the drive wheels, and the driver had put it through a brick wall whilst trying to negotiate a sharp bend near Amen Corner. The beautiful bodywork had all but been destroyed in the crash. The owner had taken write-off value and I'd made an offer to the insurance company. At the time E-types were very unfashionable and they'd jumped at the money.

An old friend of mine in the motor trade had put her back into mint condition. She was sprayed in gleaming black cellulose with chrome wire wheels and white wall tyres. The interior was upholstered in red leather and I loved the vehicle to distraction. Although it had occurred to me that if I got into any serious surveillance work using a car, I'd have to invest in a nice little runabout as the Jaguar was, to say the least, rather conspicuous.

I ducked into the driver's seat and pushed a cassette of blue grass music into the jaws of the stereo. I drove off to the sound of Bill Monroe and his band booming through the speakers.

I soared over Blackfriars Bridge and into the narrow streets around Chancery Lane. I invested in an NCP ticket close to my destination and grabbed a cappucchino in a sandwich bar in the shade of the Prudential building. The studio was right next door to the cafe and I blimped several pretty girls carrying little cases and folders of photos as they picked at a light breakfast before work.

I paid for the coffee and strolled round to the old warehouse that contained the studios. There were a dozen or so photographers' names listed on the board on the wall just inside the main entrance. The man I wanted was located on the third floor. There was no receptionist so I walked straight up. The stairs were narrow and hardly illuminated by the bare bulbs mounted in the brick ceilings. No trace of daylight filtered through from outside. The entrance to the third floor was through a pair of black wooden doors held shut by vicious springs. I forced the doors open and slid through the gap. An arrow painted on the wall directed me deeper into the building. It was cold and I shivered. As I walked down the corridor I bumped into a kid with a two-tone fringe and I asked him if Howard Mayles was around. He gestured with his thumb. 'Through there,' he said. I pushed through another set of double doors, this time painted pale blue and I could feel I was in the presence of genius.

The studio was vast, running down about a hundred feet. There were no windows. The room was high ceilinged and the light hardly penetrated, but I could make out water pipes and all sorts of odd pulleys and apparatus attached to the inside of the roof. The end of the studio where I entered was in semi-darkness, but the far end was brightly lit. Spotlights, some mounted on scaffolding, others in holders that looked like giant Anglepoise lamps shone down on to the floor which was covered with thick white paper. A backdrop depicting a Paris skyline was hanging at the back. Three tripods were facing the set. On each one was mounted a camera. Power cables ran across the floor and hooked into various pieces of equipment I didn't recognise. A bunch of people were huddled in conversation around a table which held a coffee machine, a midi hi-fi system and a big tub of ice with the necks of a dozen or so wine bottles poking out.

About halfway down the room on one side was a long table attached to the wall under a horizontal mirror surrounded by tiny light bulbs. The table was covered in cosmetics. In front of the table, sitting on high chairs were perched two models being made up by two girls who looked like they should have been models themselves.

I stood holding the door open for a moment before I let it close behind me with a crash. Every head in the room turned except mine. I just stood in the gloom looking in.

A tall, curly headed young face with a Japanese suit and a Bermondsey accent shielded his eyes against the light and shouted 'This is a closed set.'

I just stood and said nothing. He stepped out of the glare and walked towards me. 'Are you fucking deaf? I said this set is closed to visitors.'

I remained silent. He came up close and said, 'You can't come in, we're working.'

'I'm looking for Howard Mayles,' I said.

'Well you can't see him now. We're getting ready for a shoot.'

'Which one is he?' I asked.

'That's got nothing to do with it. Mr Mayles is extremely busy and can't be disturbed.'

'Which one is he?' I repeated.

'Who are you?' the young face asked. 'If you're from a client you really shouldn't be here. If you're looking for Clive, he's off with a bug and I'm standing in for the agency. I'm sorry about my language before, but it's always a bit hectic at this time.' He was backpedalling furiously. I had something to thank Clive's bug for. Obviously the face thought I was someone I wasn't. And I let him go right on thinking.

'Don't worry son,' I said. 'Everyone makes mistakes.'

I walked past him and left him talking to himself. I went up to where the cameras were waiting to fire. The bunch of people had fragmented into individuals. There were four under the glare of the arc lamps. Three stood in a row facing me. On my left, a large, open pored woman in a check suit carrying a clip board. Her hair was dark, bobbed and greasy and she had a four inch ladder running up her left stocking from the ankle. Sloppy, I thought.

In the middle stood a very tall cat who looked like a chopstick in a business suit.

On my right, a dream in Italian knitwear and faded denim. He had bitten nails and a skin tone that screamed heavy coke habit. The pupils of his eyes were the size of eight-balls, but the dead give-away was the slight dusting on his upper lip where he hadn't wiped his nose after his last toot. He looked like a little boy who'd been at the iced cakes.

The fourth member of the party was a Chinese girl who was doing very complicated looking things to one of the three mounted cameras. She turned and smiled at me and asked. 'Would you like a glass of wine?'

'Delighted,' I replied.

Curly had re-appeared at my shoulder. 'This gentleman's from a client.' He said. Everyone stood to attention.

I was glad I'd slid into something worsted and cut slightly baggy that morning, complete with pastel shirt and paisley tie. I like to look my best when impersonating a rich client. 'Can I introduce you?' Curly was the soul of politeness when he wanted to be.

Open pores was named Kathy something-something and was PR for some shit. Chopsticks was a copywriter, I didn't catch his name. Mister Hundred-A-Day-Habit was my man, Howard Mayles. The Chinese girl was Jackie, she fetched me a glass of cold duck.

Curly was Dominick, junior executive from BBD&W or some such initials. I wasn't listening. I wanted to talk to Howard.

Then we came round to me. I was saved by Prince of all people. Two tone fringe came back carrying a bag of what smelled like bacon sandwiches, dumped them onto the table containing the hi-fi, and switched it on. 'Kiss' boomed out of the speakers and I just smiled at Dominick when he tried to elicit a name from me. Dom stomped off to turn the music down and I sipped at my wine.

I took one of my cards from my inside pocket and presented it to Howard. He blanched at the sight of it. The volume of the music lowered. 'I thought you were from a client,' said Howard.

'I never said that,' I replied.

'Dominick!' he shouted.

'I'd like a word,' I said.

'What about?'

'Patsy Bright.'

'Who?'

I pulled a folded copy of her photograph from another pocket, unfolded it, and handed it to Howard. 'Her,' I said.

He held it up to the light. 'What about her?' he asked.

'She's missing from home.'

'That's got nothing to do with me.'

'Your name's on the back.'

He turned it over and Dominick arrived in a clatter of leather soles on parquet floor.

'Get this man out of here,' ordered Howard. 'He's a detective.'

Old Dom turned a trifle grey. 'A what?' he asked incredulously.

'A detective,' I said, to clarify things for him. 'I just want to speak to Mr Mayles.'

'A policeman?' asked Dominick.

'Private,' I replied.

'Then you're trespassing and I'll call the real police if you don't leave now.'

'Dominick, old buddy,' I said. 'Call them by all means, but I'd guess by the look of Howard here, that there's quite a bit of charlie around this studio, and I'm sure the Old Bill would love to be invited in to sniff around, if you'll excuse the expression. I used to be a copper and if you like I'll call them myself. They've got a wicked little drug squad at Holborn Nick. Dogs, the lot.' It was a shot in the dark but it scored a bullseye.

Howard put his hand on Dominick's arm. 'Forget the police Dominick.'

He said, 'I'll talk to - ' he looked at my card again. 'Mr Sharman, but not right now. We've got work to do. We break at one for an hour or so. There's a pub on the corner opposite. I'll meet you there.'

He looked at me. 'At one on the dot, is that alright?'

I nodded. 'Be there,' I said. 'Don't try to use the time to clear up the coke traces. You'd be amazed where it gets to. Delicious wine by the way,' and handed my empty glass to Dominick. 'One o'clock then,' I said to Howard and picked my way through the cables to the door and away.

6

I spent the rest of the morning browsing around the shops. I even bought some books and magazines, nothing special.

By twelve I was in the pub opposite Mayles' studio. I blagged a table close to the door and made myself comfortable.

The pub started to fill up around twelve-thirty. It was no spit and sawdust establishment. The clientele was heavily mobile in an unpward direction. Lots of stylish whistles and suede jackets. And not the kind of suede you picked up down the lane for £39.99 either.

At one o'clock precisely Howard pushed through the front door. He wasn't alone. He had one of the models who'd been receiving the make-up treatment at his studio earlier in tow.

She was tall, taller than Howard and she was dressed in a leather biker's jacket over a denim miniskirt. Her hair was as wild as a lioness' mane and the colour of honey. I wondered if she was there for my benefit. I wondered if I should pretend to be gay. That'd fool them.

I stood up as they looked round the bar. Howard spotted me and headed in my direction, the girl tagged along behind. Howard introduced us. Her name was Matilda. She looked up at me. 'My, but you're tall,' she said.

I thought about the Chandler line and used it. Why not, someone has to now and then. 'I try to be,' I said.

She giggled. Howard looked at me disgustedly. He'd obviously read The Big Sleep. He went off to get some drinks from the bar. I opted for a pint of lager. Matilda chose Perrier. Howard went for scotch, a double, straight up, no ice, no mix. A real man's drink.

I found an extra chair for Matilda. When she sat and crossed her bare legs I got a flash of white cotton panties. Yeah, I know, I shouldn't have been looking. But when you've been through what I'd been through, and you've been out of circulation for as long as I had, when that much naked thigh is thrust under your nose, believe me brother, you look.

When we were all sitting comfortably, I began.

'Howard,' I said. 'You don't mind me calling you Howard, do you?'

He shook his head. 'Patsy Bright has vanished. She left home two months ago for an evening out and hasn't been seen since.' I placed the photo on the table in front of him. 'Now, from what I can gather from her father, which isn't much, you took some photos of her a while back. Now I'm not suggesting for a minute that you know anything about her disappearance, but you must know something about her. So tell me.'

'Like what?' He asked.

'Firstly, do you know where she is?' There's nothing like getting down to the nitty gritty.

'No,' he replied.

'OK, but tell me, did she have a chance of making it as a model?'

He shrugged. 'Who knows? If I could tell you that, I'd have opened my own agency years ago and long since retired to the sun. She might, she might not.'

'What kind of model?' I asked.

'Not page three,' he said. 'Not enough up top, and I don't mean in the brain department. No tits you see. But maybe advertising or catwalk.'

'Nothing else?'

'What do you mean?'

'Glamour, porn, I'm no expert.'

He looked tired all of a sudden. 'No, Mr Sharman. I don't do that kind of thing, I don't need it.'

'How come you took these shots?'

'She pestered me into it,' he said.

'Do you usually do, what do you call them? Audition shots, is it?'

'Well everyone needs a portfolio to show around,' he replied as if talking to a simpleton.

'But from what I saw this morning, someone of your calibre wouldn't normally do a session like that.'

He loved the flattery. Matilda nearly cracked up. I liked that.

'Did she pay you?' I went on.

'I did it as a favour at the end of another session,' he replied.

'Because she pestered you?' I asked sceptically.

'Yes, in a word.'

'Where did you meet her?'

'At a club. Legends I think it was.'

'What happened?'

'She walked up to me and said she wanted to be a model and asked for my help.'

'Just like that?'

'Just like that.'

'Do you always help aspiring models who buttonhole you in nightclubs?' I asked with even more sarcasm.

'No.'

'Then why Patsy?'

'She had a way about her, a freshness, an appeal.' I left it at that.

'What did you get out of it?' I asked.

'Nothing.'

'Nothing?'

'No.'

'Did she, how can I put it, offer you any favours?'

He laughed, so did Matilda. 'I wouldn't take them if she did. I don't swing that way.'

Jesus, just as well I hadn't put on a limp-wristed act. I might have got more than I bargained for. I think I blushed.

'Sorry,' I said

'Don't be,' he replied.

'So that's it.' I said. 'One session for her book?'

'Exactly.'

'When did you last see her?'

'I bumped into her, maybe three months ago.'

'How was her modelling career going?'

'Not good.'

'Even with photos by you?'

He smiled and didn't take my bait. 'No dedication,' he said. 'Rich daddy, too many late nights, that was her problem. She wasn't hungry enough. Not like Matilda here. Perrier water, a strict vegetarian diet, lots of exercise and early to bed. Right Matilda?'

'Right,' said Matilda. I wouldn't have minded being in on the last two of the four.

'Did she take drugs?' I asked as innocently as possible.

'No, I don't think so, that's my poison as you guessed earlier. She was too young for that sort of thing.'

'I know she smoked dope,' I said.

'That's not drugs,' he replied. 'It's almost legal isn't it?'

I wondered if they'd changed the drug laws since I'd been in the boozer, but said nothing. 'OK,' I said, 'and thanks. I'm sorry about, you know, what happened earlier. It's just that I wanted to get to you quickly.'

'And you did.'

'No hard feelings?'

'None, as long as you keep schtumm about the other.'

'Absolutely,' I promised.

I bought them a drink. Howard was OK. He didn't bear a grudge. Matilda was OK too. I even got her 'phone number before they left, but I doubted if I'd use it, but who knows?

For some reason I felt well depressed after I came out of the pub. I lost myself in The West End and didn't do anything more about Patsy Bright that day. I visited some drinking clubs I know round the back of Tottenham Court Road. I met a few people I knew and a few I didn't. I quit around eight and rescued the car from the garage. I was too drunk to drive home, but I did anyway.

I undressed and hung my suit up neatly. I took a pill to make me sleep and drank two bottles of Moosehead to make me sleep better.

7

I went into the office late the next morning. I drank too many cups of tea, leaning against the cold oven in the kitchen, putting off going.

I walked down from home and bought a paper on the way. It was full of bad news and I tossed it into the trash. I unlocked the front door, and as I opened it, Cat ran from under a parked car, slid through the narrow gap between the door frame and my legs and sat down in front of his empty bowl. 'You're getting to rely on me.' I said to him. 'You'd better watch out or it'll end in tears. Eventually I'll let you down. It always happens.' Cat looked at me reproachfully and I went and checked the larder. It was empty. 'I told you so,' I said. Cat said nothing. I picked him up and tossed him back into the street. 'Go and ponce off somebody else,' I said. Cat spat playfully and took a strip of skin over two inches long off the back of my left hand with his claws as I let him go. I swore and sucked at the tiny beads of blood that sprang from the scratch. Cat stretched and slunk back under the car 'Nine lives,' I said, 'but don't push your luck son.'

I went back into the office and sat down behind the desk. I sucked at the back of my hand again as I stared through the window.

I suppose I sat there for twenty minutes just doing nothing. Eventually I pulled my address book from out of the top drawer. I opened it at 'S' and ran my finger down the page until I found the neatly printed entry for SOUTHALL, TERRY. Another old friend, another face from the past, from the clutter that filled my head.

I wondered if he, too, was still around. As I dialled the number I thought back over my friendship with the man I was telephoning. Terry was ten years older than me, give or take. That would put him at about forty five now. But he looked older and acted younger.

He was born in Hackney or Stepney or Plaistow, or somewhere like that in the East End where good South Londoners never go unless they're lost or have their cab fare home carefully folded and hidden in their shoe. He'd escaped early. Away from the back-to-backs and the bomb sites, up West, where the living was easy. First in the rag trade and then into photography. Now, as I said, I don't much like photographers as a rule, but Terry was different. He'd been an original London mod, a face who'd gravitated into the working class mafia of popstars, designers and advertising people who'd temporarily taken over from the real aristocracy in the sixties.

He'd been a real speed freak in those days he'd told me, living on a diet of purple hearts and french blues washed down with scotch and coke, and his heightened senses demanded excitement that even swinging London couldn't supply. So he'd taken his cameras and gone to the States. Over there he'd fallen with an even faster New York crowd which for a while had satisfied his needs. Then one day whilst watching TV, he'd seen a news report about the war in Vietnam. The story had captured his imagination and he'd conned Time Magazine into sending him over to do a photo report from an Englishman's point of view.

Once there he was hooked. Hooked on the Orient, hooked on the excitement of war, hooked on the easily available drugs and women, and finally, I think, from the way he told it, hooked on the whole macho army bullshit which he'd never experienced in mundane old England. He'd lived a charmed life in South-East Asia, at least for the first couple of years he'd been there. His work had been acclaimed, initially in the USA and then in Europe. He'd lived with the GI's amidst the mud and bullets. Sleeping in their bivouacs and taking part in both overt and covert missions on and behind enemy lines. He'd shared their rations and their joints, chased the dragon and caught VD with his beloved grunts. Then late in '68 it all caught up with him. He was syphilitic, living in a bottle and attached to a Ranger outfit somewhere on the An Hoa Basin. The Rangers had gone in to hit a Viet Cong command post. Terry had gone with them. He'd strapped himself to the outside of a Huey helicopter, festooned with cameras and as the chopper engaged the enemy, shot reel after reel of film. The Huey had come under fire. An incendiary grenade fired from a Russian rocket launcher had exploded inside the aircraft. All the occupants were killed. Terry had been neatly flipped out of his tightly laced combat boots and thrown over fifty feet down into the river they were following. He'd been shaken, but unhurt. The worst was yet to come. Another gunship had crashed nearby. The crew had survived and been captured. The VC dragged Terry from the river and punched and kicked him over to join the other prisoners. Reinforcements of marines had been drafted in. Over twenty choppers came in fast out of the sunrise, their shadows like giant scarabs as they sliced the top branches from the trees with bullets from the Gatling guns mounted on their sides. The Cong had fired their own automatic weapons into the small group of POW's. Terry had been lucky, he was at the centre of the bunch. The bodies of the other men had protected him from the worst of the sporadic fire. One bullet had smashed into the camera that was still hanging round his neck. He also received arm and leg wounds, but he was alive. The other half a dozen men didn't make it. The marine force landed and body-bagged the dead out. Terry ended up in a military hospital. The doctors patched up his wounds and cured his social diseases. Within a month he was declared fit and discharged.

He felt fine, except that every time he picked up a camera he began to tremble. His career was finished. A year later he'd made it back to England. By then he was clean of booze and drugs.

Broke and disheartened he'd become a drug rehabilitation counsellor. Unfortunately he couldn't relate to a team environment, so, funded by the GLC, he'd set up a one-man drug clinic in Stockwell in the mid-seventies, which is where I'd met him.

Whilst he was with the forces in Vietnam he'd developed a strange cockney and western accent, littered with army slang and French and Vietnamese bastardisations. He'd never lost it. Personally I thought it was a load of old bollocks. But I'd never been there, so what did I know.

The phone rang at the other end and I recognised his voice as he answered. 'TS,' he said. That was another thing about him I remembered. He loved initials.

'Hello Terry,' I said. 'It's Nick Sharman.'

'Goddamn,' he said in reply, stretching the second syllable to breaking point. 'Nick, my friend, long time no see.'

'Hi Tel, I wondered if you'd still be around.'

'Around and around as always. But where the fuck have you been? I mean, how long is it? Two years?'

'About that,' I agreed. 'What are you doing with yourself?'

'You got me at the old number. Nothing's changed. Still trying to clean up other people's messes. Same as usual.' That's what I'd hoped.

'But listen, man,' he went on. 'Where the hell are you? And what are you doing?'

'You might not believe it,' I said, 'but I'm a private detective.'

'Oh, but I do,' he interrupted. 'Nick Sharman, PI. Prime time schlock if ever I heard it. It's perfect.'

'I'm glad you're amused,' I said. 'But this is serious. I've been employed to try and locate a young girl who's missing. She seems to be into drugs. That's why I've called you up. With the clinic and all I hoped you might be able to give some information. She's local,' I added.

'Not the only reason I hope,' he said. 'And besides, the last time we met, you were the expert on consciousness expanding substances.'

'Not you and all Terry,' I said. 'Listen, I'm finished with all that. And even if I wasn't, I've been away too long. I need to talk to someone who's up to date with what's happening. I've got some photos of the girl I'm looking for, you might even know where she is. Can I see you?'

'Sure, when?'

'How about today?'

'Why not?'

I looked at my watch, it was eleven thirty. 'How about a pint at lunchtime?'

'Sure.'

'I'll pick you up about one then.'

'Look forward to it,' said Terry.

We made our farewells and hung up.

I hung around the office for a bit and then decided to take a trip down memory lane.

I drove to Stockwell via Brixton. As I cruised through the familiar streets, I could almost feel the oppression and discontent rising through the cracks in the pavements. It had been a long time since

I had ventured there. I'd avoided the place since I'd been back, but now I welcomed the journey. I purposely went down Railton Road, the old front line, to check out the changes. There were a lot. Whole rows of houses had been demolished. Cafes and shops that I had been familiar with had changed hands or were standing empty. A good deal of cosmetic work had been done. New yellow brick maisonettes had been built to cover the sites where petrol bombs had exploded. Some brave attempts to promote local pride had been made, but somehow it didn't seem to have worked. I could still sense a heavy tension in the air. As I drove, I could almost see old momma despair flitting from house to house, peeping through the dirty windows at me and twitching the curtains back as I passed.

The sun shone down on the locals hanging out in the streets. Rastafarians sat on the front steps of the houses, chatting and smoking together. Small groups of smartly dressed youths moved gracefully amongst the pedestrians, boogying along to the sounds coming from the giant tape-players hoisted on their shoulders. The market was as busy as ever. I stopped the car for a few minutes and strolled amongst the stalls. I saw a lot of faces I knew, but made no attempt to talk to anyone, even though I noticed a few looks of recognition as I walked by.

I remembered huddling for shelter, one hot summer's night, just a few years previously, not far from where I now stood, as my uniformed colleagues had been the targets for bricks and Molotov cocktails. I shuddered at the memory and picked my way through the rubbish and back to the car.

I could tell that all was not well on the streets. Life was normal enough on the surface, but I knew the area well enough to guess that trouble was throbbing beneath the surface like an ulcer about to burst and flood the bloodstream with poison. All my instincts told me that one day soon, violence would return to the streets and Brixton would burn again.

I motored on down the main shopping street, past Brixton Police Station where I'd spent so much of my working life and turned left into The Stockwell Road.

I found a parking meter in a quiet back street and left the car. I walked through an estate of old LCC flats towards the clinic which was housed in a shop front close to the clock tower.

I pushed open the glass door and stepped into the clinic. It had been partitioned with plywood into two offices. The front section where I stood was decorated with posters for concerts, unemployment benefits and the Labour Party. An old table was jammed into one corner and groaned with leaflets for various drug programmes and social security schemes. By the door stood an old tin desk, behind which sat a girl, her head bowed over the papers before her. I coughed politely. She ignored me.

'Excuse me,' I said. She slowly lifted her head and looked at me. Her eyes were exactly the shade of lavender blossom. She stared at me but said nothing

'Is Terry in?' I asked, though I was perfectly sure he was. She continued to look at me with those beautiful eyes. Then she looked away. 'In there,' she said, with a sigh that almost broke my heart, and pointed to a door set in the wooden partition. I felt as if I was missing something. 'Just go in,' she went on. I sidled over to the door, knocked and opened it. I looked back at her, but once more her head was bowed over the desk. I stepped into a tiny cubicle and found Terry sitting behind the twin of the desk in the front office, his feet propped up on the top.

He looked the same as I remembered him, only in worse shape. But I suppose none of us are getting any better. Terry was very tall, six foot three or four. His black hair was shot with grey, and hung long and greasy to his shoulders. There was a round, bald spot on the crown. He seemed to have lost weight in the time since I'd seen him and could ill afford to. His angular body was dressed in a battered camouflage suit, topped by an old leather flyer's jacket. On his feet were black, low heeled cowboy boots with silver trimmings on the toes and heels.

He looked up at me as I entered. 'Nick,' he said. 'You're a sight for sore eyes.'

'Hi Terry,' I said. 'Not disturbing you, am I?'

'I'm just meditating my man,' he said in reply. 'Looking into my inner being, on the quest for truth.'

'I've tried it,' I said. 'And discovered you'll find as much truth looking into the inner workings of a chicken sandwich.'

'Quite the cynic Nick. Lighten up a bit. You always were too uptight.'

'Roger and out, Terry. I'll try my best. What's happening?'

'Same old scam. Different players, is all,' he replied. 'The rehab business is not what it was. Once I was treated like Saint Peter laying hands on the junkies and performing miracles. Now you can get crabs by just looking at the little bastards.'

'Is that how you got that?' I asked referring to a large cold sore on Terry's top lip.

'Fucking herpes,' he said with a pained smile. 'I got it from mouth to vagina resuscitation.'

'Your life style is obviously as attractive as ever,' I said. 'Aren't you ever going to grow up?'

'Grow up?' he echoed. 'Look who's talking. Private eye indeed. I can almost see the credits rolling.' He dropped even further into an American accent. 'The city is a bitch,' he intoned.

'Too funny for words,' I said drily. 'I've come to you for help. Are you going to come through or not?'

'With what?' he asked innocently. 'Not drugs surely. As I said before, you used to be the expert on all that shit.'

'Let's get a few things straight,' I said. 'The past is past, I'm clean now. This business I'm involved in is a one-off. I didn't want to take the case, if that's not too fancy a word for it. I'm helping someone who cried on my shoulder a couple of days ago. It's a coincidence that drugs are involved. I need some information. I'm a freelance now, just like you, and I can do with all the friends I can get. But it's a two way street. You help me now, and maybe in the future I can help you. Is that a deal?'

I hoped I didn't have to ask. I was sure I could count on Terry. He owed me a favour from way back.

It had been five or six years earlier. I'd been on the Stockwell Park Estate making routine enquiries about some case or other. Really I'd been killing time until the end of my shift on a hot summer's day, when I noticed a squad car parked in the entrance to one of the basement garages of a tower block. I'd walked down the ramp into the smelly darkness out of sheer nosiness. In one of the empty bays, I saw two uniformed policemen. One was holding Terry in an armlock, whilst the other was giving a black teenager a good kicking. The boy was lying in a pool of brackish water, doubled up in agony. Terry was struggling and screaming at the uniformed men, his words echoing uselessly between the concrete walls. I'd flashed my warrant card and cooled everything out. I got the boy to hospital where he was treated for broken ribs and a fractured jawbone.

Of course charges were never brought against the officers involved. I had to draw the line at giving evidence against fellow coppers. I was a real establishment figure then. Nowadays the squad car would probably be stoned off the estate before the law could lay a finger on the kid. I wondered if that was progress.

I'd kept in touch with Terry after that first meeting and we soon drifted into a wierd kind of friendship. I'd taken to calling into his flat after work for a beer or two or nine. That's where I'd heard his Vietnam stories and seen his photographic work bound in leather books, worn along the edges from constant handling. It was good I knew. Perhaps he wasn't a Bailey or Donovan, but his talent was obvious. 'That seems fair,' Terry said, interrupting my train of thought.

'Do you remember that black kid we rescued from the flats that day?' I asked. 'Have you ever heard from him again? What happened in the end?'

'In the end who knows?' shrugged Terry. 'He went back up north to his parents. I've not heard from him since. Couldn't stand southern hospitality, I guess.'

Terry glanced at his watch. 'Anyway,' he said. 'How about that lunch? There's a pub just round the corner. It's a bit dead, but at least we can talk in private.'

He hauled himself out of his chair, picked up a packet of Marlboro and a lighter from his desk and made as if to leave. I grabbed him by the sleeve and asked. 'What's the story with the girl outside?'

'Who, Precious?'

'What?'

'Precious, that's her name. Precious Smith. Did she give you the look?'

'I think so, what's it all about?'

Terry smiled, it transformed his face and I knew why he was my friend.

'She's looking for love. It's as simple as that. Aren't we all? She gives everyone who comes in the look. But nobody seems to pass the test, you included. Trouble is no-one knows what the test involves. I hope she finds whatever she's looking for one day. She's got a lot to give.'

I looked at Precious as we went out. At least I looked at the top of her smooth dark hair. She didn't bother to look up.

The pub we were making for stood in a quiet, pleasant looking street. It was a typical Victorian gin palace left high and dry next to a sixties council estate. By the looks of it, the pub was in better shape than the flats. Even then, at lunch time, the boozer was quiet, just as Terry had said it would be.

The interior of the huge, polished wood and cut glass saloon bar was sparsley populated. A few builders in paint-stained overalls propped up the counter. Some old dears sucked stout through their dentures. One or two punks stared into oblivion, and a couple of black guys played pool together. Someone was playing 'A Whiter Shade of Pale' on the juke box. But then someone was always playing it in every bar I was ever in. Terry and I went into the lounge where the music wasn't so loud. I bought two pints of lager whilst he inspected some sad looking sandwiches under a plastic cover on the bar top.

I went over to a table as Terry purchased his meal. A tubby old boy dressed in his demob suit was snoozing over a pint two seats away, otherwise we could have been alone. Terry took a pull at his drink and then said, 'It's really good to see you again Nick. Where have you been? Why did you never get in touch?' It was a question I was going to hear a lot over the next few days. I didn't reply. He stared at me. 'You know you haven't changed a bit.' I was flattered, but wasn't so sure. I looked in the mirror every day.

'Nor have you,' I lied. 'You still look as scruffy as ever.' At least that was true. In the light of the pub he looked drawn and ill, and he'd missed some stubble when he'd shaved that morning.

He laughed aloud. 'Just because you used to ponce about in all that natty gent's suiting, you thought you were the business, didn't you? Well you're no better now, look at the state of you.'

'I've been grafting,' I protested. 'Decorating and shit. I didn't expect to be working so soon.'

We were almost back on our old footing, and I was relieved. As we chatted and drank, I discovered that he knew about the shooting I'd been involved in, and he could hardly restrain his laughter as I told him the whole story.

'Go ahead, Terry,' I said. 'Laugh, but it's not so funny when you see your whole life flash before your eyes. Or for that matter when you're limping around on cold mornings, half crippled.' Then I realised what I'd said. He knew as well as I what it was like to be shot. At least I hadn't been left for dead. He didn't laugh much for a while. He didn't think it was so funny either, when I told him about splitting with Laura and my spell in hospital after. I'd say one thing for Terry, he always had a spot for the underdog. I'd seen that as he tried to protect a skinny kid from two eighteen stone coppers in a stinking car park.

After a while, after the preliminaries, when the first lager had been drunk, I finally got down to business.

'What's happening on the manor?' I asked.

'First tell me how it concerns you,' he replied. 'What exactly are you up to?'

I outlined the information that I'd heard from George Bright and John Reid. At the end of the story I pulled the photo of Patsy Bright from the envelope I had brought with me, and showed the likeness to Terry.

He looked at it for a moment and then back at me. Then he read the details on the back. Finally he said. 'The face is vaguely familiar. But I see so many people in the clinic and around and about, that it really doesn't mean a thing. She's too old for me anyway.'

That was another of Terry's problems. He was fatally attracted, and attractive, to young girls. I mean really young. Below the age of consent was his bag, if you'll excuse the expression. I think it was something to do with his stint in the Far East.

'I don't know how you stay in business,' I said. 'Don't the authorities object to you screwing fourteen year olds?'

'They don't know about it' he replied. 'Besides, the whole thing's going to grind to a halt next year now that the GLC is disbanded. There'll be no more grant, no more clinic, no more me.'

I didn't want to listen to his troubles. I wish now that I had.

'Come on Terry,' I said. 'Concentrate, try and help. Why did she send that letter? That's what bothers me, and I don't know why it should. Are you sure no-one's contacted you about her?'

'Of course I'm sure. We get a lot of this kind of thing. Kids on the run etcetera. But I always keep the details and she isn't one I recognise. Perhaps your client doesn't like social workers. That's what most people think I am, you know.'

'Yes,' I said. 'But I don't. So now you know the story, how about some information.'

He took a long pull at his second pint and said, 'Haven't you been reading the papers lately? Or watching TV? The facts they come up with aren't that wrong you know. It's just their attitude that's shit.' I thought it better not to tell him that where I'd been there were no newspapers allowed, and we only watched comedy programmes on TV.

'We,' he continued, 'well society, or whatever you call it, not that I count either one of us in that number, are in trouble. Especially in this sort of shitty area. The fuse has been lit and God knows when the bomb will go off. We've only seen the beginning so far. I'm older than you, and I know what I'm talking about. I've seen it in the States, and I've seen it in the East. Once it starts there's no stopping it. It's my lot, the people of my age who started all this.

'Well now we're in control and trying to run the country, all the garbage is coming home to roost.' He looked at my face. 'I know Nick, you don't think I'm controlling anything. Well I should, instead of poncing about, I should have tried. It's chickens coming home to roost. It's just so damned easy to get drugs these days that everyone's at it.' He tapped Patsy's photograph, lying on the table in front of us. 'What's she into by the way? Whatever it is it'll have a trendy nickname. The media love all those names. There's hit records about drugs. Books, films, and every TV show I see has some reference to them.'

'It's always been the same,' I said.

'But it's never been so easy to get the stuff.'

'What about supplies?' I asked.

'I could get hold of almost anything within the hour, if I wanted to. It's that easy.'

'How much?'

'Cheap.'

'How cheap is cheap?'

'For what?'

'Heroin?'

'Fifty to sixty pounds a gramme,' he replied.

'Coke?'

'Eighty pounds a gramme.'

'Dope?'

'A hundred quid an ounce.'

'Who's bringing it in?'

'Everyone. Blacks, whites, Asians, air hostesses, pilots, oil tanker captains, lorry drivers. The whole world seems to have a few grammes in their back pockets or down their knickers. Or else a Volvo artic. Full of hash.'

'What's to be done?'

'Fuck all my friend. The tide's against us. And the media is our worst enemy.'

Terry had a real thing against the media. I was tempted to ask him why. Perhaps he'd sent a letter to Time Out and they hadn't published it. I didn't have time, he was off again.

'One minute the fucking papers are up in arms about heroin abuse on council estates.' He continued, 'The next, they're coyly suggesting that anyone who's cool is snarfing up half of Bolivia before breakfast. It makes me want to throw up. Every week I read that some fucking pop star or TV hero has kicked the habit. What they're saying is, that if you've got boo coo bread, you can get away with a bit of a monkey. But if you're unemployed, it's a terrible sin. So all that happens is, the kids who are broke steal to pay for drugs. Then the bloody papers scream about a crime wave. Cynical bastards, reporters couldn't care less as long as they're copping twenty grand a year and a BMW on the firm, and their bijou little residence in Clapham is burglar proof. I tell you Nick, sometimes I just despair.'

He looked so angry as he talked that I was reluctant to interrupt. When it sounded as if he'd finished and he was having another hit at his lager, I said, 'I hardly dare mention the police.'

He gave me a scornful look and said. 'Why bother? They're more bent than anyone. The police are a private army of racist thugs. They work for the Tory party breaking strikes and persecuting the working class. It's in their best interests to keep a certain amount of dope on the streets. It helps to anaesthetize the kids who might be real trouble. The cops can use it for bribes, sell it for profit and as a last resort plant it on anyone they want to put away.'

'Beautifully put,' I said.

In the background I heard the Byrds singing 'Mr Tambourine Man'. The boozer was a real oldies heaven. Terry abruptly excused himself in the American way and almost ran to the gents. I sat and waited for him and drank some more lager and heard in my mind's eye something of what T S must have heard almost twenty years before.

I half closed my eyes in the still of the bar and with the sound of the twelve string playing cadences in my ear, I could imagine the choppers thudding down at zero feet above a muddy river bed with just a thin stream trickling down the middle. Swarms of mosquitoes would be hanging above the water, hungry for the sweet blood of the Americans fed on a diet of rare beef and Coca-Cola. I could pick out the sound of sporadic gunfire in bursts echoing around a deserted village. Somewhere in the lush green forest my spaced out friend was lying under a heap of his dead comrades.

Terry came back. He seemed brighter, more alert and almost relaxed.

'You're back on the stuff, aren't you?' I asked with a flash of intuition. He nodded and managed a half hearted grin.

'I always knew you were too sensitive to be a cop,' he said. 'I bet you cried yourself to sleep everytime you busted someone.'

'Don't fudge the issue, T S,' I said. 'I'm not a cop any more, and you shouldn't be doing what you're doing.'

His eyes narrowed. 'OK, so I'm a fucking hypocrite, but don't judge me Nick, not you of all people. I seem to remember hearing some story about vanishing evidence in the form of a quarter of a kilogramme of cocaine going missing from a certain police station's strong room, not so long ago.'

I shut up. He was right.

'But why?' I asked eventually, my fingers greasy on the glass I held.

'I just need that feeling, Nick,' he replied. 'I go dinky doo without it. When your body's lying there, numbed out, and your mind's out amongst the planets. Running free, skittering around amongst the stars. You must know what I mean.'

'Sure I know,' I replied. 'But you always have to come back, and usually you're lying in some strange bed with the sheets all rucked up, and some girl dribbling come onto the bed covers, and looking at you like you're really crazed. You must know what I mean.'

'Yes,' he said with a big grin. 'Great, ain't it?'

Even I had to smile at that. Then I got serious.

'It'll kill you,' I said.

'Bollocks, it will,' he replied. 'It's only a bit of smack. It's good gear.'

'It'll kill you,' I said again.

'That's bullshit Nick. It ain't the smack that kills you, it's what some of these fucking dealers cut it with that's dangerous.'

'You'll never kick it.'

'Kick it, why should I? Who says I want to? Listen Nick, anyone can kick H. It's easy, I've done it loads of times.' He gave me a big grin. 'I mean I can kick it overnight. It's harder to give up barbs, or booze, or cigarettes for God's sake. Smack's easy man. Fucking drug addicts, don't tell me about them. Those suckers make it hard on themselves. They believe their own publicity. Most of them are scared even to try. They've heard too many horror stories about cold turkey. It's about as painful as a dose of flu.' Then it was his turn to get serious. 'But you don't need to get back into anything like that.' I started to protest. 'Hey, I know,' he went on. 'You weren't into horse, but coke's worse, Nick, much worse. That was your thing and it nearly killed you. You've changed, I can tell. I think it's stupid for you to get involved with anything to do with drugs again. Why not just butt out and mind your own business?'

'I've got nothing else to do,' I said. 'I want to find this girl, it shouldn't be beyond my capabilities. I was a copper you know, and a good one at times. Besides I need to get back into the swing of things. I want to start living again.'

'Don't bother, it's hardly worth the effort,' he said.

I knew I'd brought him down again, so I shut up. We finished our drinks in silence. Terry picked at his sandwich, but left most of it.

We walked out of the pub, and parted at the corner of the Stockwell Road with just a brief farewell and a promise to keep in touch. I went back to the car and drove slowly through the afternoon traffic back to my office.

It hadn't changed during my absence. I sat behind the desk for an hour or two thinking about old times. I seemed to be doing an increasing amount of that lately. I bought some fish and chips and shared them with Cat. He'd forgiven me for my behaviour earlier but seemed miserable as he lethargically pushed his food around his bowl.

Eventually we both left. Cat to parts unknown and me to crawl from bar to bar until I tired of the sight and sound of other people's social life and drifted home in the misty blue of the late evening.

8

Saturday morning was bright and sunny, with a light breeze from the south that flirted with the curtains at the open window next to my bed. I lay for a while watching the material billow into my room and dapple the carpet with moving shadows. Then I rolled out of bed to start another day.

I switched on the radio whilst I shaved and dressed. I chose a pair of faded, baggy Liberto jeans, a pink cotton sweater, ancient Nike high tops and pink socks. I felt very modern and colourful.

I decided to breakfast out as my cupboard was bare. I wandered down towards my favourite cafe. On the way I stopped at the newsagents on the corner of the street to pick up a pint of milk and a Daily Telegraph, so that I could look at the crossword as I ate. I glanced at the headlines as I waited for my bacon sandwich and coffee to arrive. Nothing registered.

After I'd eaten I flirted with the waitress as I digested the meal and longed for the comfort of a cigarette. She leant one nylon overalled hip against my table and allowed me to gaze into her shadowy cleavage. I would have asked her out for a drink but the varnish on her finger-nails was cracked and broken, and as she brushed up against me as I paid my bill she smelled strongly of old grease and dried sweat.

As I walked back home I wondered if I was getting too choosy. I let myself into the house and jogged upstairs, favouring my left foot on the steep steps. I unlocked my flat door and entered the empty room. I threw the paper onto the unmade bed and stored the milk in the fridge. Then I dropped into the armchair and contemplated the day ahead. The hours stretched in front of me in an endless stream. I had nothing to do until I could go back to bed again. Outside in the world people were looking forward to a warm Saturday swimming or playing polo, or motor-racing, then on to the opera followed by a light supper at a nightclub. I thought about cutting my toe-nails then getting drunk. I wondered where the action was, and regretted not making a date with my willing waitress.

My life was trickling away like potato water through a sieve, and was about as interesting.

After more minutes staring at the sky through my window, I stood up and began to pace the floor. I went into the kitchen and stared at the empty shelves. I decided to go shopping, I found my car keys and armed with a new sense of purpose and my overloaded Access card, I set off. I drove down to Vauxhall, cutting through the weekend traffic in the Jaguar. I slid to a halt at the entrance to Sainsbury's car park and got a ticket and a big smile from the girl manning the gate. I returned her smile and rolled the car into a parking space just vacated by a Mini-Metro. The supermarket was housed in a massive, low building next to the New Covent Garden Market. I locked the car and walked across to the entrance, dodging the drivers looking for somewhere to park. I found a trolley and pushed it into the air-conditioned chill of the shop.

Ever since I'd been a young student looking forward to making my way in the world, I'd been subject to a number of recurring fantasies. I'd been convinced that one day I would meet the woman of my dreams in a supermarket or a launderette. I can report a definite lack of success at either venue. I must admit to having occasionally bumped trolleys with a young mum struggling with her kids and had a bit of a fling over the frozen peas. But that's as far as it's gone. Once I was infatuated with the lady who did my service wash, but she turned out to be a transvestite saving up for her operation, so that little romance went down the drain with the soap suds. That Saturday proved to be no exception to the rule. I wandered amongst the shelves and cabinets, picking up exotic pickles, replacing them immediately with an embarrassed smile as if to say, would a man like me want hot prawn sauce with his mild cheddar dip? I kept on prospecting and eventually my trolley contained frozen hash browns, half a dozen free range eggs, streaky bacon, baked beans, two cartons of orange juice, two dozen cans of lager, a small loaf and a tub of fake butter. Before I went to the checkout, I went back and found the pet food section and bought Cat half a dozen tins of food. I felt like I was making a gesture of friendship, and it made me feel good.

I stood in line with ten other shoppers and waited patiently while the checkout girl changed the till roll, lost a cash card, flirted with the security man and finally went to tea. When I'd eventually paid my bill and packed my purchases into a brown paper sack, I retrieved the car and headed back to Tulse Hill. I stocked up the fridge and took a walk down to the pub.

On the way I stopped and fed Cat. He seemed pleased to see me as he gobbled down the food. Feeling like a philanthropist, I went into the boozer to swap lies with my bar-room buddies. I had a few pints and got beaten at pool by a crafty old Irishman who tried to get me to bet on his ability to pull off complicated cushion shots. I declined the offer and bought him a pint of Guinness instead.

When the three o'clock bell sounded, I dawdled home again. Patsy Bright had been at the back of my mind all day. I looked at her photograph in the dimness of my room. She stared back with a pouting, enigmatic look. I mentally tossed a coin and lost. I reached for the phone and dialled George Bright's number.

He was at home, just waiting by the telephone, he said. Waiting for news of his lost daughter.

We exchanged strained pleasantries, then I told him I wanted to ask him some further questions and take a look at Patsy's room and belongings.

He agreed that I could go round. He didn't seem to care one way or another. I got the feeling that he had expected me to conjure his daughter out of thin air like a genie from a lamp.

Any action on my part was going to disappoint him I could tell.

I wanted to reassure him, but there were no words in my vocabulary to do so.

I told him I would be at his house within the hour.

I really didn't know if there was going to be any point to my visit, but I went anyway. Perhaps I just wanted to make a date with a phantom. I'd been dancing in the dark too long to stop, it seemed.

9

The address that George Bright had given me for his home was fairly close to my flat in location, but a long way away on the social scale. I discovered that his house was situated at the end of a leafy lane in Dulwich, just off the South Circular Road.

It was part of London that hadn't changed much in years, and probably never would. Few developers' greedy little fingers had left their marks there. The area was firmly buttressed with money. Old money earned during the eighteenth and nineteenth centuries and greedily clung to through slumps and booms, depressions and wars. Mixed with lovely new cash pouring in from the media and the Stock Exchange. After all, it was only a twenty minute run in the old Range Rover from there to the City of London. It was an advantage of course if one could ignore the fact that the drive took one through some of the worst urban blight in western Europe on the way. But once there, all that loot was ready for the taking, inside the glass and concrete monuments to commerce that stood glittering in the sunlight. I'd been reading a lot lately about the foreign banks that had moved into our little island to use it as a clearing house for buying and selling cash. Treating it like an off-shore money rig to pump out profit. The funny thing was that it seemed no-one ever saw what they were dealing. It was just little green figures on the screen of a computer terminal, or neat rows of black figures on a balance sheet. Hell, I was just jealous.

I stopped the car to bathe in the feeling of affluence. It was hard to imagine that only a hundred yards from where I was sitting, thousands of cars an hour were speeding along a major arterial thoroughfare.

The track I drove down was untouched by the local council. I suppose the capitalists thought of it as rural. It was rutted and potholed and had no drainage. It looked as if it would flood every time there was a heavy rainfall. Trees dipped down to the dirt pavements, and together with thick growths of bushes hid the houses set well back off the road.

The people who owned these properties valued their privacy. But even if the council didn't lay tarmac, they weren't stupid. They knew who paid big rates and the street was spotlessly clean. There were no leaking black sacks of garbage on the kerbside, no abandoned cars, and the one man I saw walking his dog was carrying a poop-scoop in his hand.

Finally, I came to a gate-post to which was nailed a board with the name of George's house neatly picked out in clean white letters. I had to get out of the car to open a five-bar gate. I half expected to be greeted by a herd of Friesian cows. I drove through the gate and left it open behind me. The drive stretched ahead, then turned and vanished into a grove of trees. I motored slowly down the roadway. Through the trees I caught sight of a brooding mansion, dark and forbidding like the house of Usher. Once through the trees, the drive opened up into a circular parking area in front of the house.

Close up the building seemed even more sinister. It was a Gothic monstrosity which had orginally been built in the middle of a wood, and trees surrounded it still on all sides. It reminded me of the hospital in which I had spent too many months. It stood three storeys high, and was topped with turrets and curlicues making it appear even taller. It was built from dark red brick, which years of weather had turned almost black. I could almost feel the decades wound tight like watch-springs in the stone-work, ready at a moment's notice to break free and tell their secrets with the smug wisdom of the old. The roof was dark grey slate with a greenish tinge. The windows stared down at me blindly. Two lions made of pale stone flanked the three steps that led up to the massive front door. In front stood a shiny navy blue Mercedes saloon. I parked the Jaguar behind it and got out.

The front of the house was screened by thick banks of rose bushes. I recognised most of the varieties. The flowers were waxy in the late afternoon light, and their fragrance filled my nostrils. I touched first one bloom and then another, disturbing some loose petals that drifted to the ground by my feet.

There seemed to be no sign of life in the house at all. It was almost as if Patsy's leaving had drained all humanity from the building and left a vacuum in it's place. I climbed the stairs and wrestled with the old fashioned bell pull. I heard a faint ringing from within and waited. I half expected Vincent Price to answer the door, but when it creaked open it was only George who appeared, dressed in a black sweatsuit. Naturally it fitted like a glove.

'Good afternoon George,' I said. 'Nice pile you've got here.'

'Hello,' he said vaguely, ignoring my comment.

I stood on the marble step by the front door and scuffed my feet. I felt uncomfortable being there.

I turned and faced the driveway.

'You've got some healthy looking bushes there,' I said, gesturing at the garden.

'You know about roses?' he asked, almost animated for a moment.

'Yes,' I replied. 'At least I used to.'

'It's been a good year,' he said. 'A good year for the roses.'

But nothing much else, I thought.

'Why don't you come in?' George invited at last. 'That's what you're here for.'

I mumbled something in the back of my throat and crossed the threshold at his bidding to find myself standing in a massive, shadowy hallway panelled in dark wood.

In front of me, a staircase carpeted in rich brown wool stretched up to the first floor. George took my arm and led me through double doors into what he referred to as his library. It must have contained at least four books. A full sized snooker table dominated the room and down one wall stretched a professional wet bar with five padded captain's chairs arranged in front of it.

Very ritzy, I thought.

In front of one of the chairs, on top of the bar was a bottle of Remy Martin and a half filled glass of amber liquid.

A massive colour TV with video attachments showed cartoons with the volume turned down.

'A drink?' asked George.

'Maybe later,' I replied. 'Can I see Patsy's room first?'

George cast a sorrowful eye in the direction of his glass and gestured me to leave the room. I allowed him to lead me up the wide staircase. We turned left when the steps reached the first floor and walked down a dark corridor, hung with dark paintings of dark old men in huge dark frames.

I wasn't surprised that Patsy had wanted to leave. I did already and I'd only been there for two minutes.

10

At the end of the gloomy corridor, George stopped in front of a door, hesitated, then opened it and allowed it to swing wide.

After the sombre tones outside it was like walking into another world. The room inside was long, light and spacious. Someone had spent a lot of time and money with their Habitat catalogue getting it to look like it did. The walls were painted white and upon them hung framed posters of Marilyn Monroe and James Dean airbrushed into romantic unreality.

Carelessly tacked up next to them were photos of Madonna and Curiosity Killed The Cat cut out from magazines.

There was a double bed covered with a bright print duvet. On a table under the window was a black and chrome Sony midi-system. Under the table were neat piles of record albums. Along the length of one wall was a built-in wardrobe and dressing table, with full length mirrors on the wardrobe doors. In front of the dressing table was a low stool. In the centre of the room was a leather and metal armchair. The carpet was navy blue and the curtains that hung by the long windows were buttercup yellow. Everything seemed to be in it's place and the whole room was immaculately tidy.

On top of the dressing table was a single wicker basket containing trinkets and badges.

I stood in the room and slowly looked around.

George stood beside me pulling at the seams of his tracksuit with his fingers.

'What do you want to see?' he asked.

'It's OK, George,' I said. 'I'd rather look around on my own if it's alright with you.'

He seemed unsure.

'I won't steal the towels,' I said.

'There's no towels in here,' he replied. 'Patsy's bathroom is next door.'

'Joke, George,' I said, and wished I'd learn to keep my big mouth shut.

'Very well, if that's the way you want it,' he said, and with a sad backward glance at me, left the room.

I started my search with the bed. I checked beneath it. The gap between the frame and the floor was empty. Then I felt under the mattress. Nothing. Finally I flicked the mattress right over. Still nothing.

I went to the wardrobe and opened it. I caught sight of myself in the long mirror as I did so. I looked hunched and ugly.

I pulled open the wardrobe door quickly to lose the reflection. The interior was deep and wide and packed tightly with dresses and coats on hangers. On the left hand side was a section of shelving that held neatly folded shirts and sweaters. That was where the lacquered box must have been hidden.

I took the clothes from the shelves carefully, one by one. There was no sign of anything.

Equally carefully I replaced them. Methodically I went through the garments on the hangers. Where there were pockets, I felt inside them. I came up empty. At the bottom of the wardrobe were piles of children's toys and books. I pawed amongst them, feeling like an intruder. I found a Cindy doll, boxed jigsaws and games. Once again there was nothing extraordinary. I was happy to finally close the door.

I went over to the window, knelt down and went through the record collection. It was pretty much what I'd expected. At the back were yesterday's heroes, like Adam Ant and David Essex. Towards the front were Wham! and more recent flavours of the month, but she was beginning to mix in other, newer bands, some whose names I barely recognised. I checked inside some of the sleeves, but for what I don't know. Finally, I went and sat on the stool in front of the dressing table. I dug through the stuff in the basket on top.

It contained a school prefect's badge and a few cheap silver rings, a champagne cork with a five-pence piece pushed into the bottom and some cocktail stirrers and the little plastic animals that come with them. At the bottom was some loose change. When I'd finished the search I looked up at the mirror in front of me.

I knew that the real secrets, if there were any, would be hidden in the dressing table itself. That's why I'd left it until last. I felt like a voyeur. I'd never got my kicks from delving into people's intimate lives, not like some coppers did. Then I looked more closely at my reflection and the goatish gleam in my eyes, and wasn't so sure.

I opened the drawer in front of me. The inside was packed with make-up. Boxes, tubes, bottles, all colours, all makes, glitter, matte, you name it, it was there.

I lethargically pushed a few items about. I opened a giant box of face powder, and found just face powder. I pushed the drawer shut again. There were four drawers remaining. Two on my left and two on my right.

The top drawer on the right held a hair dryer and a bag of thick plastic rollers. The drawer beneath contained a selection of gloves and belts, a woolly hat and some socks.

In the top drawer on the left were Patsy's night clothes, neatly folded pyjamas and nightdresses. Nothing special, just what any average, middle class, affluent eighteen year old would wear as far as I knew.

When I opened the last drawer, I found what average eighteen year olds don't normally use.

The interior was packed tight with underwear. Not schoolgirl's knickers, but sexy, provocative gear. I pulled out G-strings made out of slippery silk, suspender belts that were no more than froths of lace. Bras with straps no thicker than string and at least a dozen pairs of stockings, all in different colours. Some still in their cellophane wrappings.

And it was all quality stuff. I could tell from the labels attached to the flimsy garments. It was more Bond Street than East Street. I sat there with a hand full of silk and lace and could feel myself almost drooling. Quickly I dropped the underthings back into the drawer and slammed it shut.

And George had told me that Patsy wasn't interested in boys.

I sat for a while longer in that strange room, full of shadows that had nothing to do with the afternoon sun coming through the window. A room that belonged to someone who was half child and half sophisticated woman.

The strangest and somehow worst thing was that there were no photographs, no letters, no diaries, no address book. It could have been a hotel room where the occupant had just taken a stroll down to fetch a newspaper.

Had Patsy got rid of every scrap of paper that bore any importance to her life, or had George, or had none ever existed?

I thought of Judith's room, which was crammed with notes to herself and exercise books full of childish scrawl and all the birthday cards she'd ever had pinned to the walls.

I thought of my own room when I'd been eighteen where you couldn't move for the garbage strewn about.

Patsy's room was like a morgue. Finally I couldn't stand it anymore and left.

There was another door directly to my right. I guessed it was Patsy's bathroom. I entered. It was well appointed if rather small for the house. Just about the size of my whole flat. The room was decorated in pale blue with a navy bathroom suite. All very tasteful and colour co-ordinated.

Dark blue towels hung across a rail. I felt them. They were bone dry, as was the interior of the bath and the sink. I found some blonde hairs stuck to the side of the bath. I held them between my fingers as if somehow I could capture the essence of the girl from the few strands. I touched them with my tongue, but could taste nothing except ancient shampoo.

I opened the bathroom cabinet. It contained a fresh bar of soap, aspirin, Tampax, a dry tooth brush in a glass and a tube of toothpaste. I even opened the cistern and found nothing but dusty water.

I turned off the light and left.

Reluctantly, I walked back down the flight of stairs to the ground floor. I found George sitting in his library like a priest in a strange house waiting for a death to occur.

I felt that he didn't belong in that huge mansion any more, maybe since Patsy had left, he didn't want to belong. In his hand he held a full glass of brandy.

As I walked into the room, he poured me a drink unasked. I took it. I felt as though I deserved it.

'George,' I said, 'didn't Patsy have an address book?'

'Yes, of course,' he replied.

'Where is it?'

'She always carried it in her handbag.'

'No old letters?'

'She wasn't a great one for keeping things. If she got a postcard or something like that, she'd read it, then throw it away.'

'How about her friends? Hasn't anyone called her up or come around to see her?'

'She kept her friends separate from here. She knew I didn't approve of them.'

Now we were getting somewhere.

'Why?' I asked. 'What was wrong with them?'

'Scum, most of them.' He spat, his eyes narrowing. 'I didn't want her to associate with that kind.'

'Do you know any names or addresses?' I asked.

'No.'

'George,' I said slowly. 'You don't know much, do you? You've given me very little to go on. How about her modelling contacts? You approved of them surely? You seem happy for her to do that kind of work. Surely you checked their credentials?

He didn't seem too sure.

'Well, did you?' I asked again.

'I'm a busy man,' he replied lamely.

'What you're saying,' I interrupted before he could continue, 'is that exactly two months ago on the ninth of June, your eighteen year old daughter took a hike. You know she dabbled with drugs. That is all you do know. You don't know where she went, or with whom. You don't know if she had a boyfriend. You don't know any of her other friends. You don't know what she did when she wasn't with you. You don't seem to know anything about her. It's an impossible task for one man to find her. Especially if the police have failed.'

George made no reply to my outburst. He just sat and fiddled with his glass.

'I'll go if you like,' I said eventually.

'No,' he said. 'You're probably right. I've not been the perfect father.'

Which of us can say we have, I thought.

I hesitated before asking my next question.

'Your daughter has an exotic taste in underwear, hasn't she?'

George looked as though he could kill me. I didn't blame him.

'You get everywhere,' he said.

'You didn't tell me not to. I was only looking for hints to Patsy's whereabouts.'

'In her knickers?' he asked sarcastically.

It was my turn to be silent. After a moment, I said, 'In fact her whole wardrobe is on the expensive side.'

'I'm not a poor man,' George retorted. 'Patsy needed clothes. It's vital when you start out in a modelling career. If she wanted anything she had the plastic for the shops I'd opened accounts in. She didn't want for anything.'

'Did she have a lot of cash on her when she left?' I asked.

'I'm not sure, not a great deal. About fifty pounds I expect.'

'That's not bad for a girl of her age.'

'I give her an allowance,' George said stiffly. 'It's hers to do with as she pleases.'

'Does she have a bank account?'

'Of course.'

'Has she used it since she left?'

'I don't know.'

The man was hopeless.

'Did she have a job?'

'She was fortunate enough not to have to. Sometimes she helped me in the office. I can never get a decent secretary. At the moment I'm relying on the answering machine. It's a damned nuisance. Patsy was good at the job.'

'So tell me,' I said. 'What was she really like? As a person, as a daughter?'

For the first time I saw some light in George's eyes.

'She's beautiful,' he said. 'Full of life and looking forward to the future. Here, look.'

He went over to the cabinet upon which the colour TV sat and opened the double doors at the base.

He pulled out a pile of photograph albums and brought them over to the bar. He dropped them in front of me onto the mahogany top. I opened the first book, and realised that George had collected Patsy's life together like an exhibit under glass.

There were baby pictures, then pictures of her as a young child, in what I took to be the garden of the house where I was now sitting. She was pictured with a younger, longer haired version of George, and sometimes with a pretty woman who must have been his late wife.

There were photographs of Patsy in the street, at the zoo, by the seaside, at the fair and at all the other places that children love. Once again, I was taken by her resemblance to my own daughter. I hadn't mentioned Judith to George, as I hadn't wanted to upset him further. Although she wasn't with me, at least I knew where she was. At that moment she was probably sitting, eating her supper in front of the same cartoons that were still being pumped out silently by George's TV. Soon she would be cosily tucked up in her own little bed.

I wondered where Patsy would be sleeping that night. It struck me coldly that she might be sleeping the final sleep that we all go to.

All of a sudden I couldn't look at any more happy snaps.

I reached for my glass again. After I'd taken a long swallow I looked at George and asked, 'What was she wearing when she left?'

He thought for a moment and then replied, 'Jeans and a leather jacket, with a yellow T-shirt. And she was carrying a big black handbag.'

'Big enough for clothes?' I asked.

'No it was a bit of a joke between us. Her bag was always so full of junk that there was certainly no room for clothes.'

'Is there anything missing from her room?'

'No, not as far as I know.'

But would he know anyway? I wondered. If she had charged everything to accounts, she might have had a suitcase hidden outside when she left.

George's mood seemed to have taken a down turn again. We sat there, the pair of us, two men missing our golden daughters who had been snatched away.

We sat looking for comfort in each other, that neither of us could provide. And for comfort in a bottle which is no comfort at all. We were trapped in misery, and as we sat together in silence, the TV set continued to spew out coloured images of happiness which we both ignored.

The minutes stretched out. I could hear the tension in my inner ear, as if fingernails were being scratched along a blackboard inside my head until I felt like screaming.

When the phone rang, it shattered the silence like an axe striking a rotten log.

George walked over to the telephone and answered it.

There wasn't much conversation. George was doing more listening then talking. At last he said, 'I can't talk now. Someone's here. Call me back.' Then he put the receiver down.

He came back over to the bar and said, 'Sorry about that. Business.'

I checked my watch. It was almost six thirty.

'I'd better go,' I said, finishing my drink. 'I've got things to do. I'll get back to you on Monday.'

I told George that I would see myself out, and left him with his possessions. Only his most precious possession was missing. Maybe that had been the problem. Maybe Patsy had got tired of being his little girl. From the contents of her underwear drawer, she was more woman than I'd seen in a good while, if that's how you judge women, and it was one way I suppose.

I climbed wearily into the Jaguar and drove home.

As I drove, I wondered what I'd let myself in for with this job. George Bright obviously wasn't telling the whole truth.

One minute he was proud as Punch of his daughter.

The next, by all accounts, he hardly knew her or what she did.

I couldn't figure it out.

I drank beer all evening with a photo of Patsy Bright in front of me. I toasted her with each new can.

I toyed with the Telegraph crossword, but couldn't concentrate. I spun the dial of my radio and wished I owned a TV set.

I went to bed about eleven and lay awake listening to the cars passing the house until the small hours when I finally fell asleep.

11

Saturday night is the loneliest night of the week, they say. I don't know, every night and day was lonely then. But I think Sunday morning took the prize. The paper boy delivered four papers to me. The Sunday Times, The Observer, The Sunday Mirror and The News of the World.

It was my time for a fix of news, and I took it all in: from Princess Diana's new shoes to President Reagan's cancer operation via tales of debauchery from the home counties that would and did make my hair curl.

I figured I spent a very boring life. No threes ups with the local swingers, no nightclubbing at String-fellows and no winning fifty grand on the bingo. Little did I know what was to come.

After reading the papers I paced my room like a chimp in a cage. I felt trapped in boredom. I looked at the picture of Patsy Bright for the thousandth time. I wanted to see her in the flesh, to know if she was as beautiful as she looked. But at the same time, I sensed that doing so would only bring more trouble into my life. Something I could well do without.

I showered and sat down with a cup of coffee. I reread all the interesting things that were happening in the world, and in the silence of my flat felt as insignificant as a grain of sand on a beach.

I sat for hours staring at the newsprint, and all I got for my troubles were inky fingers and a slight headache.

Time dragged by and I cooked some of the food that I'd bought on the previous day. I washed the meal down with cold beer and listened to back to back chart slop on the radio.

At about four in the afternoon, the phone rang.

It was John Reid telling me that he would be paying me a visit that evening to discuss the Bright case. He was cool and distant on the line and I got the distinct feeling he was coming against his better judgement.

John was as punctual as he'd always been.

He turned up at precisely seven o'clock, leaning on the door bell. I buzzed him up and opened the flat door so as he would know where I was.

'Christ,' he said as he entered the room. 'Those bloody stairs.'

He looked the same as I remembered. Short, barely over the Met's minimum height requirement, but wide and thick in the body and neck. He was dark skinned with lots of five o'clock shadow, even in the morning. He'd lost a lot of hair since I'd last seen him, but he wasn't fighting it. What was left was cut very short, almost cropped. He was wearing a Burberry macintosh over a sharp dark suit. His white Oxford cloth shirt had a button down collar and he wore a discreet dark tie. On his feet were black polished loafers with a little gold chain across the front of each of them.

'You look like the man from the Pru,' I said.

I didn't know how friendly to be. I didn't know if we were in for an old pals reunion or whether he was going to stick one on me.

'Bollocks,' he replied. 'This is known as corporate image. I'm after a bit of promotion so I can get away from all this sleaze.' He gestured through the window.

He looked around the flat. 'What do you call this?' He sneered. 'Bit small, isn't it? You couldn't swing a hamster in here.'

I'd put the deposit on a flat. A recent conversion in an old family house in Tulse Hill. It was described as a studio apartment, which meant I got one attic room with a tiny kitchen and shower/toilet. It all came complete with carpet and curtains, a stove which I rarely used and a miniscule fridge. It was an ideal first time buy, or last time refuge.

I'd added a double bed, an easy chair and a small table, upon which sat a lamp, a radio and a telephone. I kept my socks and underwear in a chest of drawers.

'It's just as well I'm not into tiny furry animals,' I sneered back.

'You always used to be,' he retorted.

I ignored the remark and said, 'Relax, John. Hitch up your gun belt and sit down.'

'Where?' he asked, looking at the only chair.

'That'll do you,' I said. 'I'll sit on the bed. I don't have many visitors.'

'I'm not surprised. But you will. You've been seen, you know.'

'Christ, I've only been back a few days,' I said.

'Come off it. What about that silly ad in the paper? And that bloody heap of yours isn't exactly anonymous, is it? You were clocked going past the nick on Friday lunch time. If you want a low profile, get a Ford Cortina.'

'What, like that lollipop you used to have?'

We both laughed at the memory.

'I'll have you know, that yellow Cortina was local colour,' he replied.

'And now it's corporate image?'

'Right, and a Rover Three-Five.'

'Terrific, fancy a drink?'

'Of course I do, what've you got?'

'Beer,' I replied.

'That'll have to do then, I suppose. You're not much of a host.'

I went to the fridge and fetched him a can of Heineken. He took off his coat and walked over to the wardrobe, which was, temporarily, a chrome garment rail. He tossed his coat over the top and then flicked through my clothes. I felt like asking to see his search warrant.

'Nice threads,' he said.

'I had to buy new,' I said. 'Everything was out of date when I came out of hospital.'

'You spoil yourself,' he said, looking at me long and hard.

'I try,' I replied.

He went back and sat in the easy chair, moving it so that he could peer through the window from time to time.

'Paranoia?' I asked.

'No, good sense. This street'll be a fire zone one day,' he said casually.

'Don't say that,' I retorted. 'I'm nervous about falling property values.'

'Take my word for it,' he said.

The way he looked, I almost believed him.

We sat for a time and drank in silence.

'Tell me about George and Patsy Bright,' I said eventually.

'There's nothing to tell.'

'Don't give me that. She's a missing person. There must be something to tell.'

'If you could only see my case load,' he said.

'Come off it John,' I interrupted. 'Don't give me that old story.'

'All right,' he capitulated. 'I'll tell you what's on the file.'

'Did you bring it?'

'Listen son, if a certain chief inspector knew that I was within a mile of you, I'd say goodbye to any promotion chances I've got left. But if he thought I'd shown you anything on official paper, I'd be directing traffic outside Woollies tomorrow.'

'All right, all right. Get on with it,' I said.

He told me the identical story I'd heard from George the first time I'd met him.

'So that's it,' I said when he was finished. 'You're none the wiser after two months than I am after five days.' He shrugged. 'For instance,' I continued, 'who did she visit that night?'

'No-one knows.'

'Not even you John? I thought you knew everything that went on around here.'

'Piss off,' he said angrily. 'How am I supposed to know, when she wouldn't even tell her father.'

'You're right I suppose, but he's in a right state about it.'

'A state, my arse. I think he's got worried a bit late in the game. It's a guilty conscience if you ask me.'

He was probably right.

'He was prepared to pay me,' I told John. 'In fact he did.'

'Blood money,' said John. 'How much?'

'A hundred quid. Half a day's wages.'

'On those sort of wages you'll be retiring soon.'

'Dream on,' I said.

'Look,' John continued. 'You've done more than your half day's work. Keep the money and tell him there's nothing doing.' He shrugged. 'Big deal.'

'I know John, but what do you think happened?'

Counting on his fingers, he said, 'One, she's pregnant and run off with the father, or gone somewhere to have the baby. She wasn't short of cash. Two, and most likely, she's into drugs heavily and like

I said earlier, she's changed her appearance and gone underground somewhere. Three, she's met a bloke with a bit about him and she's living it up somewhere, which means she'll be back sooner or later.'

'Four,' I interrupted. 'She left to join the gypsies, or run off with the fairies or a travelling circus. How about five, someone's topped her.'

'That's a bit dramatic isn't it? Do you know how many people bugger off everyday in the UK? If they were all murdered, we wouldn't be able to move for stiffs.'

'Have you seen this?' I asked, I went over to the chest of drawers and opened the top one where I had put the black box that George had given me.

I tossed it to John.

'What's this?' he asked.

'Take a look, open it.'

He did so and poked the contents around with his forefinger. 'Where did you get this?' he asked.

'From George Bright,' I replied.

'And where did Mister Bright get it?'

'He found it amongst Patsy's things.'

'He really is a stupid bastard. What was he trying to hide?'

'It's obvious,' I replied. 'He didn't want you to think his one and only daughter was into smoking dope.'

'As if we wouldn't find out. I told you I knew all about it. And then he gives it to a cowboy like you. I give up.'

'What did you find out?'

'I'm not going to tell you everything I know. I've got certain sources, you know that.'

'Please yourself,' I said. I knew John of old, and there was no use pushing him for information. He'd tell me in his own sweet time if he was going to tell me at all.

He threw the open box onto the bed where it landed on its side, spilling the cigarette papers onto the bed cover.

'Some of these wankers think we're stupid.'

'Not stupid, John,' I said. 'Overworked, that's all.'

'Which is more than can be said for you.'

'All right John, don't keep on. I believe you looked, and I believe you're dead right about the drug angle. It's probably just a wild goose chase. But I've got a funny feeling.'

'I remember you once had a funny feeling about a truck load of cigarettes, which meant three of us spending the coldest weekend of the year in the back of a Thames van in a lorry park in Camberwell. Meanwhile, if I may remind you, the firm you had the funny feeling about were hoisting a lorry load of frozen cod from Vauxhall. Free and clear.'

'I remember,' I said. 'I always thought there was something fishy about that case.'

He didn't exactly fall about laughing at the remark, but I could feel the antagonism evaporating.

'Talking of something fishy,' he said, 'have you seen your wife lately?'

'I haven't got a wife, you cheeky bastard. I told you that already.'

'Ex-wife then,' he said. 'Where is she now?'

'In Forest Gate with a dentist. And no fucking jokes about filling cavities, alright.'

'Never, Nick. I was just thinking how I admire women who go for professional men.'

'Very funny,' I said.

'Was it going on before you left?'

'I think so, but it all came to a head when I quit the force.'

There was an awkward silence. Neither of us wanted to be reminded of that particular episode, not when we were slowly mending fences.

'Now you hate her, I suppose.'

'Hate her. No. Anything but.'

'How do you feel about her?'

'Disappointed, I suppose, And angry that the time we spent together was wasted. Precious time for us both.'

'But it wasn't totally wasted, was it? You've got Judith.'

'I haven't got anyone. The bloody dentist's got Judith. I see her one weekend in four.'

'Why did it go so bad?' John asked after a pause.

'The job mainly, but we both changed. We blamed each other of course, but people do change after twelve years. Christ, we were just kids when we got married. Our goals became different. It was more my fault than hers I suppose. I used to leave her on her own for days when I was working, or just raging about. She felt neglected after the baby came. I expected her to cope, and she couldn't, not alone.

'It seemed like I did everything wrong. Every bloody thing. And she never enjoyed anything any more, not with me anyway. It got so that if I had a drink or a joint, or even a bloody cigarette, she'd object. It's funny because I've given up smoking now, but there you go. Anyway, she never said much, just gave me that hurt kind of look, as if I'd beaten her. We finally got to the state where the only way one of us could be happy, was for the other to be miserable. And that's the time to call it quits. But of course we didn't. We just went on pretending that everything would work out all right. The sexual side went totally out of the window. She was insatiable when we first got married. In the end we were screwing once a month if we were lucky. And that was bad luck. Under sufferance, if you know what I mean. The funny thing was, the more she didn't want it, the more I did. At the end she was slopping round like an apprentice bag lady, just to turn me off. Once upon a time she'd have done anything just to get me at it, and it didn't take a lot.' I stopped, slightly embarrassed at being so frank, and went to the kitchen for more beers. The sound of the tabs popping was loud in the silence of the room. John took out a packet of cigarettes and offered me one. I refused and went to get him an ashtray. When we were comfortable again, he asked me,

'So you went to pastures new?'

'Just a bit.'

'Yeah, I remember.'

'But not recently, not for a long time.'

'But you've got the flat, and new clothes and that Jag. Now there's a bird puller if ever I saw one.'

'Not any more mate. It's just transport now. A way of getting from A to B. Laura got the Fiesta and I got the Jag.'

'You must be going soft.'

'I'm not interested, not any more. Laura cured me of that.'

'It sounds like a few harsh words were spoken.'

'Sure. I don't think I ever forgave her for falling out of love with me. But I still needed her and the baby to keep going. I had them in the palm of my hand and I let them slip away. I lost the lot.'

'You still love her, don't you?'

I looked at him. 'Not really,' I said. 'She turned into the coldest cunt I've ever known.'

We sat in silence drinking. Eventually I asked. 'How about you John? How's everything with you these days?'

'Same as ever Nick. Margie keeps the place together. The kids are at the comprehensive now. The bills get bigger every month. I still fuck around with a mystery every now and again. Margie never says anything when I vanish for the odd night. Life goes on, son. Just live it. You think too much. That's always been your trouble. You fucking failed college boys are all the same. You were too sensitive for the job, and that's a fact. You don't like to get in and mix it flesh on bone. You're like a debutante who wants to fuck with her knickers on. No body contact, see. If you'd have stayed on the force you'd've ended up in charge of neighbourhood watch in Kingston or somewhere.'

He lit another cigarette. I wished I still smoked.

'You were always self obsessed,' he went on.

'You sound just like a bleeding psychiatrist,' I retorted.

'Really?'

'Yeah,' I said. 'And I've had some experience of them. But you know all about that don't you?'

'Yes, I heard.'

'I went a bit strange after Laura kicked me out. A nervous breakdown the doctors called it. I pulled a few numbers, broke up the house a bit. I'm not proud of it, but it happened.'

'Are you alright now?'

'Well I'm not going to stick a bread knife into your wig, if that's what you're worried about.'

He gently touched the top of his head with the palm of his hand.

'Still a bit touchy about the old barnet,' I said, and grinned.

He jumped up suddenly and said. 'Listen I've got a bottle of vodka in the car. Blue label Smirnoff.'

I guessed it was his way of saying we were friends again.

'Is one of your massive case load an off-licence job by any chance?' I asked innocently.

'Could be. If a satisfied customer wants to show a token of appreciation, who am I to argue? Got any mixers?'

'As a matter of fact there's a couple of cartons of orange juice in the fridge. I've got to get my vitamin C.'

'Next you'll be telling me you eat up all your veggies too. Still, good enough. I'll go and get the bottle. You polish the glasses.'

He went down to his car and got the vodka. It was our favourite liquor. We'd seen more bottles of it off in our time than I care to remember.

We did not speak about Patsy Bright any more that night. I think we had both temporarily forgotten that she was the reason for us meeting again. We killed the booze instead and listened to Run DMC, 52nd Street and LL Cool J and all the other soul bands being broadcast by the pirate stations on my little FM radio.

We talked about the old days, the people we knew and the things we had done.

I don't remember much of what we said, but I do know at one point John apologised for shooting me. Finally when every drop of alcohol in the place was gone, he drove his car rather unsteadily away in the small hours of the morning.

I stood at the window and watched the red tail lights of his car disappear up the road. When they'd gone it occurred to me through my drunken haze, that if nothing else came of the Bright affair, at least I had regained two friendships during the first few days on the case.

12

When I opened my eyes the next morning, I felt as if someone had hit me right over the head with a club hammer. Meanwhile, something extremely unpleasant seemed to have crawled into my mouth and died. I lay for a while counting my blessings. When I got as far as one, I decided to get up. My throat was sandpaper dry, and a limited megaton nuclear engagement was taking place inside my skull. I fumbled for my watch on the table beside my bed and knocked a glass onto the floor. It rolled under the bed leaving a sticky trail of last night's vodka and orange. I left it where it lay. My watch showed me that it was past nine o'clock. I didn't even know if it was night or morning.

I crawled out of bed and gently parted the curtains. The sun was high. It was a new morning. I was seeing the world through a filter of fine gauze. It was a half litre hangover. The kind I hadn't had for a long time. I hoped that it would be a long time before I had another.

I made a mental note not to drink with any policemen again. They never know when to stop. Well they do. When the alcohol is gone.

As I walked very slowly to the kitchen to put on the kettle, I collected the rubble left over from last night's reunion. I stacked the glasses in the sink and threw everything else into the garbage bin. When I found Patsy Bright's photo lying face down on the floor, I apologised to her aloud and propped the picture against my mirror as I shaved.

I chatted to her as I scraped the stubble from my face and continued the conversation as I drank a cup of tea.

I was inclined to take John's advice and let the case go. I thought I'd phone George Bright and give him a blank. He could have his money back or not, as he pleased. I'd more than put in half a day's work. I couldn't really have cared less. All I cared about was the army of little men marching around inside my head.

I asked Patsy's advice, but she wasn't forthcoming. There was something about her eyes, though, that told me to continue. Why couldn't I get that damned picture out of my mind?

I found some clean clothes and got dressed. The day was dry and rather cool, so I took a jacket when I left the house. I breakfasted at my favourite cafe in the High Street again. I might even have exchanged witty repartee with the waitress with body odour, but I can't remember.

When I unlocked the office door, I felt a little better for having some food inside me; a little, but not much. My skin still felt as if it were peeling off, but that's what strong drink will do. I picked up my mail and slumped into my chair. It seemed as if I was getting lucky again. That morning I could win a trip to Barbados or a free packet of king-size cigarettes.

I consigned the post to the waste paper bin and tried to plan my day.

I wanted to phone George, but first I needed to call a few acquaintances in the legal and financial world to suss out if there was a way I could earn a few shillings and start making an honest living for myself.

I was already on an unofficial retainer from a large law firm based in the city. Of course it was the old pals act again. One of the partners was a guy whom I'd helped on a big case when I first went into plain clothes. He'd lost his star prosecution witness in a long firm case, the illegal profits of which had run into millions. The witness' family had received some pretty heavy threats from the accused, even from their remand cells. So the witness had dropped out of sight.

Then I'd found him. It was as simple as that. If he'd managed to stay hidden, my lawyer friend would have been relegated to fighting car insurance cases in the small claims court, or something similar. As it was, he went from strength to strength.

I was living from week to week after coming out of hospital, when I got in touch with him again. He welcomed me and fronted the lease on the office and a little spending money. He must have been really grateful, as usually getting money out of lawyers is like getting blood out of a conker.

When we'd met to discuss business, I hardly recognised him. Gone was the nervous young man I remembered from Lambeth Crown Court, to be replaced by a plump, sleek upwardly mobile individual, who had the habit of touching the side of his nose and winking when asked a direct question, like someone out of a Dickens novel.

I didn't like him any more, but fate and cashflow problems make strange bedfellows, so I hitched my wagon to his rising star. Then, just as I was about to open my office, he'd vanished off to his villa in the Algarve with his wife and small son, leaving me hanging around like a chicken drumstick in a vegetarian restaurant.

'Don't worry,' he said when I spoke to him just as he was leaving for the airport, 'there'll be plenty of work for you soon. I'll drop you a postcard. If you need any dibs, get in touch with my secretary. She'll take care of you until I get back.' So left at a loose end, I finished painting the office, stuck the ad in the paper, and here I was.

After a couple of hours, I'd made some headway using my benefactor's name as an extra lever as well as my own credentials. I must confess, I left out some of the juicier details of my career in the police force.

There was nothing definite, but with a bit of luck there would be some work trickling through within a week or two.

At a little after midday, feeling a little better with myself, I tried to get hold of George. There was no answer at his home, so I tried the number on his business card which I had stapled to one of Patsy's photographs. After three rings the answerphone cut in. A voice I did not recognise echoed down the line and told me that Bright Leisure was temporarily out on call and pleaded with me to leave a message after the tone. I hung up without speaking as I always feel strange talking to machines. I had enough problems talking to people.

I checked the time. It was exactly twelve thirty. My mouth was bone dry again, so I sauntered over to the pub for a drop of lunch, which I drank straight from the bottle back at my desk.

I pondered as I drank how soon standards slip when you spend most of your time on your own. Cat strolled in as I was finishing my bottle of beer, but I couldn't tempt him to join me.

At one o'clock, the telephone rang. I mentally chalked up another first and answered it half expecting an order for the defunct coal merchant's. The caller was male with a strong West Indian accent. The kind that can easily drop into street patois if the speaker suspects that he is being spied on. He asked for me by name.

'Speaking,' I said.

'You're looking for a girl,' the voice said.

It was a statement, not a question.

'Aren't we all chief,' I replied.

'You're looking for a particular girl.'

A statement again.

'Could be. Who's speaking?'

'No names, my friend. You're looking for Patsy Bright.'

I was suddenly very interested.

'Could be,' I repeated. 'What's it to you?'

He chuckled. 'I've got some information for you.'

'What?'

'It'll cost you man. Cash.'

'How much?' I asked, suddenly wary.

'Fifty quid,' he replied.

'For what?'

'I'll take you to her.'

'When?'

'Right now, if you like.'

I liked.

'Where?' I asked.

'Meet me and I'll show you,' he said.

'Where?'

This monosyllabic conversation was beginning to get me down.

'You got some wheels?'

'Of course I have. Now where?'

'Park outside Brixton Town Hall, opposite the church.'

'OK, but don't jerk me around. I'm not in the mood.'

'It's cool man, don't worry,' he said. 'I wouldn't wind you up. What do you drive?'

I described my car and told him I'd be about half an hour as I had to collect it from my house. He agreed to wait. We both hung up and I pulled out all my cash money. I had exactly sixty notes on me. I counted out fifty quid which I put in my shirt pocket. The rest I filed in my address book under 'C' for cash, which I then locked in one of my drawers.

I walked back to the house and rescued the Jag which I drove slowly into Brixton, still nursing the recurring hangover, which the bottle of beer had done little to alleviate.

I stopped the car by the Town Hall as instructed and waited with the engine running. A tall black guy in a faded T-shirt, jeans and eighty quid trainers pushed himself away from the wall on which he was leaning and ambled over to the car.

He was built like a heavyweight boxer. He had the kind of body that seemed as if it had more muscles than the skin could cope with. They writhed around under the thin cotton material of his clothes as if looking for a way to escape from his frame. He probably worked out for hours with weights everyday. I can never take that kind of shit seriously. Every time I've been to the gym, all that straining and serious building of the body beautiful only drives me to find the local pub. That's why I'll always be skinny and make people boogie to the nearest loose sand when I hit the beach.

I leaned over and slipped the lock on the passenger door. He opened it and folded his long body into the seat next to mine.

'Hi, man,' he said, looking around the interior of the car. 'Nice ride you've got here. You must be loaded.'

'You'd be surprised,' I answered.

'Have you got some wedge for me?'

'COD, son,' I said. 'And how do you know I'm looking for the girl?'

'Word gets round, man. Old face in town checking around makes waves.'

He rippled his fingers and grinned.

'Where is she?' I asked.

'Not far, man. You drive. I'll show you.'

I indicated and pulled the car into the traffic flow. I drove down through the traffic lights by the Town Hall.

'Not too fast,' he said. 'You've got to turn left by the record shop.'

I did as I was told and we drove into the back streets.

'Now hang a right here and stop by the telephone box.'

I knew the area well. I used to walk the beat on these self same streets. They were packed claustrophobically tight with terraces of houses. Mostly in bad states of repair. Here and there some bright young couple would try and gentrify a corner of old Brixton. You could always tell. Sold signs appeared and skips were dumped in the streets outside. It was a bit like trying to tame a mad dog.

Generally though, the houses were split into flats and multi-occupied. If they were left empty for any length of time, squatters moved in and out like squirrels.

'Give me my cash,' demanded the heavyweight.

'Leave it out, pal,' I said.

He hadn't volunteered his name and I hadn't asked for one.

'I want to see the girl and then you get your fifty.'

'She's in there.'

He pointed through the windscreen to the most disreputable looking house on the block.

I turned off the engine and got out of the car. The street was quiet, just the distant rumble of traffic from the main road and from somewhere the bass beat of a reggae record rumbled across the silence.

A chilly wind blew between the houses and filled my eyes with dust. It smelled tired and acrid. I brushed my eyelids with the back of my hand to clear my vision.

'The door's open, man. Just go in,' said the heavyweight leaning on top of my car.

'After you.'

'Sure,' he shrugged.

We walked together across the pavement into the tiny garbage strewn garden of the terraced house.

The front door was closed, but when he pushed it, it swung open. There were three bell pushes by the door, but only one sported a name plate. It was written on a card tucked in to the top bell. In faded ink it read SMITH. That was about par for the course around here when the bailiffs came knocking.

I followed the black man into the hall which was dark and smelled of damp, old cooking and just faintly of urine. I've never liked that smell. It reminded me too much of my time in the force, going round to houses like this after burglars had been in and ripped apart someone's pathetic belongings. Or with a warrant to pull some hopeless villain. I'd managed to forget most of that time and didn't want to remember it now. I suddenly wished I wasn't there. That George Bright hadn't come looking for me. I knew instinctively that the house contained secrets I didn't want to know, things I didn't want to see and people I didn't want to meet.

Only the thought of the look in the eyes of the girl in the photograph kept me there.

I'll admit I was scared.

Suddenly I longed to be back in hospital. Safe and warm and cared for by nurses in their crisp uniforms.

I remembered one in particular, a pretty redhead who hardly spoke to me whilst I was there. When I was discharged, she brought me a book as a leaving present. It was a collection of Elmore Leonard short stories. She knew that he was my favourite author. She kissed me briefly on the lips, then turned and fled back into the hospital corridors. When I plucked up courage to phone her, three weeks later, she'd left and gone to work in Australia of all places.

So much for my effect on the opposite sex. 'Are you coming or not?'

The heavyweight interrupted my reverie. He was standing on the staircase looking down at me. 'I'm coming,' I said.

The floorboards in the house were bare. Our footsteps echoed as I followed him up the stairs. I peered through the gloom. The front door had swung shut behind us, and no-one appeared at any of the doors as we went past.

The house felt cold and abandoned. At the top of the stairs, three short storeys up was a door painted purple with anarchy signs spray painted on it in black. The paint was chipped and scuffed. The door handle was grimy white plastic.

The heavyweight banged at the door with the side of his fist so hard that it rattled on its hinges.

'Anyone at home?' he shouted, then turned the handle and threw the door open.

I was right behind him on the narrow landing as he did so. He turned suddenly and caught me by the upper arm. Half pulling and half pushing, he propelled me past him and into the room.

The first thing I noticed was a terrible smell, much stronger than that of the house itself. I stopped just inside the door. The heavyweight was now behind me and pushed me further into the room with a powerful shove. Then he slammed the door behind him.

The room was bright after the darkness of the stairway and it took a moment or two for my eyes to adjust. When they did, I saw two other men and a girl in the room. Two live men and one very dead girl.

Both men were white. One was bigger even than the heavyweight. But on him the muscle had turned to fat. He was bald on top but he had swept what hair he did have over his scalp. He had grown long sideburns to compensate. He wore a plain white shirt and black flared trousers. I liked him for his cheek. Lionel Blairs indeed!

His big belly strained the buttons of his shirt and bulged over the waist band of his trousers. He was sitting on the ledge of an open window as far away from the dead body as possible. He was holding a handkerchief over his nose.

The other man was smaller, blonde, wearing a baggy grey suit with a black shirt and narrow white leather tie. He was holding a sawn-off shotgun in his hand. It was pointed at me. It was short and stubby, double-barrelled with black insulating tape stuck round the barrels for a firm hold. The stock had been cut down into a pistol grip. All in all it was a very impressive weapon.

Deadly at short range in an enclosed space such as the room we were in, but at long range about as effective as spit-balls.

'How sweet!' I said to the blonde. 'Only one little gun between the three of you, and today's your day to hold it. Do tell boys. Whose turn is it to have the flicknife?'

I must confess that levity was probably not wise under the circumstances, with the shotgun pointed at my belt buckle. But I've always tended to run off at the mouth when danger looms. I think it must be some kind of nervous reaction.

Blondie gestured with the gun. 'Shut your mouth,' he snarled.

I shut my mouth and looked around the ratty room. The terrible fetid odour came from the body of a young girl sitting stiffly in an old armchair by the back wall of the room. She was wearing a dirty white dress, like a shroud. By contrast, her skin had turned dark in death. A shock of dull blonde hair covered her head. Even with her face contorted in the rictus of death, I knew she wasn't Patsy Bright.

'We're glad you're so prompt,' said the blonde. 'It was getting a bit close in here.'

I looked over at Flared Trousers.

'Let's get this over with,' he said through the handkerchief, 'and get the fuck out of here.'

'You've wanted a junkie,' the blonde said. 'Well here's one. We hope you'll be very happy together.'

'I'm looking for someone,' I said. 'But I don't want to get involved in a bring and buy sale. This isn't Patsy Bright and you know it.'

'Don't move, or I'll shoot,' said the blonde.

I looked behind me at the heavyweight who grinned at me, but not too convincingly. Down below in the house I heard a door slam and footsteps start slowly up the stairs.

'You'll hit your mate if you do,' I said.

The blonde moved towards me and stuck the shotgun into my groin.

'I'll blow your fucking balls off if you're not careful.'

I knew he meant it. He was one of those people who just didn't care. The most frightening you can meet. They're polite to women and will bounce little babies on their knees. But come to the crunch and they'll top you without a qualm and then go home and have their dinner as though nothing has happened. As far as they're concerned nothing has.

There are only two kinds of people in the world to them, their own and the rest. If you were one of the rest, woe betide your chances of surviving a ruck.

'Listen, girls,' I said, 'this is fun, but I've got things to do. So why don't you tell me exactly what you want.'

The blonde spoke very softly and clearly as if to a backward child. 'We want you to get your nose out of things that don't concern you. We want you to mind your own business. And we're going to make sure you do. We're going to kill you.'

He emphasised each point by poking me in the groin with the gun. The footsteps on the stairs got closer. Heavyweight leant back against the door.

'What's all this about?' I gestured to the dead girl.

'Well, cunt,' the blonde replied, 'we want to leave you here with her for when the filth arrive. It'll be a touching scene. You and your girlfriend in Hell.'

'You really should cancel your subscription to "Boy's Own Crime

Club"; I said. 'All that florid reading is going to your head.'

He drew his fist back and punched me on the side of the jaw.

I should have known better than to criticise another man's literary taste. My head snapped around and blood filled my mouth. I began to sweat and the smell from the dead body seemed to be getting worse.

With my peripheral vision I saw the drug paraphernalia on the floor by the dead girl. And I noticed for the first time that there was a syringe clasped in her hand.

The footsteps stopped on the landing outside the room. I shook my head to clear the dizziness I felt. I turned towards the heavyweight and as I did so, I sensed the blonde lift the shotgun above his head. I heard the gun displace the air above my head. Suddenly I felt a terrible pain, and then all the lights went out.

It was worse than a dozen hangovers. I felt myself falling into a black ocean from which I was convinced with my last ounce of consciousness that I would never emerge again.

Then I felt nothing.

13

I slowly drifted in and out of a dream.

At first I thought I was lying in bed next to my wife and daughter on one of those happy days we'd had together.

I reached out to keep them safe, but they kept moving further away from me. The bed in my fantasy was hard and unyielding. As I came fully awake, I know I whispered their names.

I found myself sprawled face down on a piece of stinking carpet. What I'd imagined to be the sound of Laura's voice was in fact a man asking if I was alright. I forced open my eyes and found myself staring at a pair of official issue police boots.

I dragged myself, complaining bitterly, back into the real world. 'He's awake, I think,' said the uniformed policeman squatting at my side.

Then to make sure, he caught my right earlobe between two fingers nails and twisted it hard.

That's the kind of thing they teach you in today's police force.

'Alright,' I said through the pain. 'Leave it alone.'

I tried to sit up, but the agony in my head was too much. Not only could I still feel the remains of my hangover, but my jaw was swollen and the blow from the gun barrel had ripped the skin open in a long shallow wound. It had raised a huge bump on the back of my skull.

Finally, some clown had torn off half my ear.

I touched the back of my neck gingerly. Blood had congealed thickly in my hair. I felt a mess. It was not time to meet new people. I tried to speak again but my mouth was dry. It tasted of blood and my tongue was swollen and sticking to the roof of my mouth.

I felt as though I needed a month on a health farm.

The smell in the room was appalling. I moved my head round with difficulty and two police constables swung into my line of vision. One was trying to help me into a sitting position. The other was staring with sick fascination at the body in the chair. He looked as though he felt that it might suddenly jump up and bite him. There was no sign of the other three recent occupants of the room.

I felt the remains of the previous night's vodka and this morning's full English breakfast rise into my throat.

'Fresh air,' I choked. 'I need fresh air.'

'Don't let that bleeder go,' said the copper by the body.

'He won't go far,' said the other.

'I've got to get out of here,' I said, trying to pull myself onto my feet.

The first policeman helped me up and led me out of the room and onto the landing. He held me firmly by the arm and propelled me toward the window. He forced the ill fitting pane up in its frame. I leant out and breathed the fresh air.

Normally it smelled foul, but now it tasted clean and helped to clear my head. I immediately started to feel better.

'Christ!' I said weakly. 'I feel like being sick.'

In the distance I could hear the sound of a siren coming closer.

'Ambulance, Phil,' the officer holding me said, turning towards the open door without loosening his grip on me.

'They can turn that fucking row off. There's no hurry now,' said the other officer from within the room.

'You get in the corner, out of the way. And don't move,' said my policeman to me.

I nodded and let him lead me across the landing again. I slumped down and leant my head against the banisters trying to will some strength back into my body.

The copper towered over me and said, 'Looks like you fucked up here mate.'

I didn't bother to reply. Just asked, 'Got any water?'

He looked into the room containing the dead girl.

'Phil. Get a drop of water, will you?'

'This is not a bloody cafe,' came the reply.

'Do me a favour,' I whined.

'Come on, Phil,' he said again.

In a moment, Phil, as I now knew his name to be, appeared with a mug of water. I grabbed it and greedily drank some even though the cup was none too clean. Normally I'm fussy that way.

I suddenly heard the door of the house burst open and heavy footsteps began to climb the stairs. The sound brought everything back to me. I started to shake. Not so bad that anyone would notice, but bad enough.

'Keep him out of the way, John,' said Phil. 'And you'd better cuff him just to be on the safe side.'

'You're not arresting me, are you?' I asked.

'Cuff the fucker, John,' repeated Phil, then turned to me and said 'Don't be so fucking previous son. There's a dead body in there.'

He gestured into the room. 'What do you think we're going to do? Call you a mini-cab to run you home?'

I drank the last of the water and allowed myself to be hand-cuffed. At least they weren't being rough with me.

The footsteps turned out to belong to two ambulancemen who had come to collect the overdose case.

The ambulancemen stood around waiting for the police doctor to arrive.

He turned up a few minutes after them.

At the same time two detectives and the forensic crew arrived. Both the plainclothes men were unknown to me.

The doctor appeared to be about two hundred years old and took all day to climb the stairs.

Everyone waited with varying degrees of patience. One of the ambulancemen chewed on his nails and the taller of the detectives stared at me as if I was an exhibit in the zoo.

That's one thing you get used to at the scene-of-the-crime, waiting.

The doctor didn't take long to examine the body. A blind man with a good sense of smell could have told him the girl was dead. He mumbled softly to the detectives as he peeled off his rubber gloves. He left as slowly as he had come. Only when I heard the front door slam behind him did it occur to me that I should have had him look at the wound on my head.

I remained cuffed up in the corner of the landing as the ambulancemen went about their grizzly business. They moaned that the body was too stiff to lie on a stretcher and had to be back for a wheelchair, cursing and complaining as they went.

The silver buttons stayed with me whilst the detectives began tagging and bagging the few belongings in the room.

Finally they got round to tagging and bagging me.

They dismissed the uniformed officers with a curt order that they completed their reports immediately, and then introduced themselves as Detective Sergeant Bachman and Detective Constable King.

They came across as a real class act. Something told me they fancied themselves as a pair of snappy dressers.

Bachman was tall, wearing a ratty windcheater over a grubby T-shirt. He favoured elephant cord pants that finished an inch or so above his Adidas sneakers.

King was a tub of lard with a beard. He obviously owned a charge card at C&A. He was all dolled up in an obnoxious light tan leather jacket, a predominantly red shirt and powder blue slacks.

They'd got their sartorial shit together splendidly, looking like a pair of professional darts players out on a spree, but came across as the toughest pair of dudes outside re-runs of 'The Sweeney'.

Bachman hauled me to my feet and stood staring closely into my face as I leaned against the wall.

'Now my friend,' said King, playing the good cop. 'Who are you? What are you? And why did you kill the girl?'

I think with his soft tone that he expected an immediate confession and for me to cry buckets onto the shoulder of his leather jacket.

No such luck.

I painstakingly told the whole story, beginning with the visit from George Bright, through to the heavyweight's phone call and ending when I woke up lying on the carpet. My name seemed to mean little to them.

'Do you expect us to believe that bullshit?' asked Bachman, when I'd finished. 'You topped the girl, and that's that.'

'Jesus!' I said, holding out my cuffed wrists in front of me. 'It's a fair cop. I'll come quietly, guilty as charged. Are you blind? I just got here, and she's been dead at least three days. Didn't the doc tell you?'

'That doesn't mean that you weren't around when she died,' said Bachman. 'And how come you're an expert on how long she's been dead? Unless you were here that is.'

'It's obvious,' I replied. 'Have you got no sense of smell? And if I were here, what did I do? Hit myself on the back of the head and wait for you to arrive? How come you're here anyway? Who called you?'

'A tip from an informant,' said Bachman.

'I'll bet,' I said. 'And when did you get it? Last Thursday?'

Whilst we'd been enjoying the witty backchat together, King had been absent-mindedly going through my pockets.

I thought he'd find my car keys and very little else.

But inevitably, he pulled out an envelope from my hip pocket. 'What have we here?' he asked.

I could hardly wait.

He opened the envelope and tipped a number of little oblong paper packets into his hand. He returned all but one to the envelope which he stashed in his pocket. He carefully unfolded the remaining wrap which contained a small quantity of brownish-white powder. He wet his forefinger with his tongue and dipped it gently into the powder. He tasted the residue and pulled a face.

'Don't tell me,' I said. 'Horlicks.'

'Scag,' he said, and refolded the wrap and tucked in into his pocket with the envelope.

'You naughty boy,' said Bachman. 'You're nicked.'

The rest of my pockets revealed no surprises. Just the car keys as expected.

'Check the shirt pockets,' I said. 'Anything there?'

'Nothing,' said King.

So the heavyweight had lifted his fifty quid!

'You travel light,' said Bachman. 'Just some dope for those precious solitary moments.'

I didn't bother to reply.

Bachman started to get heavy. He pushed me across the banisters until I thought my back would break.

'That hurts a bit,' I said through clenched teeth.

He suddenly slapped me hard on the right side of my face with his open palm.

'I remember you now,' he said, 'you didn't say you were an ex-copper. The blue eyed boy who went bad. I thought I recognised you earlier. Sharman. That's right, and you're up to your old tricks again.'

I declined to mention that my eyes were brown.

'You ever hit me again like that, you'll regret it,' I said.

He hit me again. Harder with his clenched fist. Perhaps he did regret it, but certainly not as much as I did.

'We'll meet again,' I said.

'I'm shaking right down to the tips of my toes,' he replied.

'Bachman,' said King. 'Let's take him to the station. His head needs looking at.'

I tended to agree, but not necessarily in the way he meant.

I must have been crazy to get into that situation. However, King was correct. The force of the fresh blows had made the bleeding start again, both inside my mouth and on the back of my head. I could feel the warm stickiness running down my neck and my mouth filled with blood. I spat a mouthful onto the floorboards, close to Bachman's foot. He scowled at me but said nothing. Suddenly I felt like crying. I wasn't half as tough as I liked to think I was.

King still held my car keys. Bachman looked at them and noticed the fancy key ring.

'Do you drive a flash black Jaguar?' he asked, a big smile spreading across his ugly face.

'Yes,' I replied.

'Not any more, you don't,' he said gleefully. 'You lairy git.'

I didn't know what to expect as they took me downstairs. King holding on to my arm so that I wouldn't fall, cuffed and groggy as I was.

14

When we reached the street, the light was bright from the August sun. I squinted across the pavement to where I'd left the car. If I'd felt like weeping earlier, I came even closer then. Someone had taken a sledgehammer to my pride and joy. The windscreen of the Jaguar had been smashed and the headlights kicked in. It looked as if someone had been dancing on the bonnet, and the paintwork on the roof had been scoured with a screwdriver or something similar.

The two policemen let me peer into the cockpit. The front seats were covered with broken glass and the leather covers had been slashed. My jacket had been screwed up into a ball and tossed onto the back seat. King retrieved it for me and searched the pockets before draping it around my shoulders.

'You could win a prize with that motor,' said Bachman. 'Concourse condition.' I swallowed hard. 'And just look at those tyres,' he continued.

I might have guessed. On the curbside both tyres were down on their rims. I could see the slashes in the white walls. Bachman walked into the road. 'Same this side,' he said. 'Dear, dear, this'll cost you a packet.'

'Fuck you Bachman,' I managed to say.

'It wasn't me mate,' he replied with a smile. 'But if you leave it here for long, there'll be nothing left to cost you anything. Never mind, where you're going, you won't be driving for a long time.'

Bachman led me over to a blue Ford Granada, double parked in the street and pushed me into the back seat. He sat next to me. King got behind the wheel.

As we drove away, the last thing I saw of my beautiful E-Type was the broken glass from the headlights glinting in the sunlight as we turned the corner.

During the journey, Bachman took great delight in telling King the story of my misdemeanours whilst serving on the force. He didn't know the half of them.

When I'd left Brixton nick it had been under bad circumstances, but I never thought that the next time I passed through its door I'd be cuffed to a plainclothes officer.

I was manhandled through to the CID room. Familiar territory.

I was put into an interview room and left in the care of a young uniformed officer. Before King left me, he removed the cuffs from my wrist.

'Greaves,' said King to the young policeman. 'Get the first aid box and look at this man's head. Then get him some tea.'

'I could be concussed,' I said.

'Don't push it, Sharman,' came the reply. 'Think yourself lucky to get anything. We don't like heroin dealers here.'

Talk about giving a dog a bad name.

The uniform fetched the first aid kit and a damp cloth. He cleaned me up a bit, and put two of the biggest plasters he could find on the cut on my head.

'Hell of a bump there, I'm afraid,' he said. 'And that shirt's a write off.'

'It was one of my favourites too,' I replied. 'Did someone mention tea?'

'OK,' he said, and went off to fetch some, locking the door behind himself. When he returned, I told him I could have hung myself with my shoelaces whilst I'd been alone.

'But you wouldn't, would you?' he commented cheerfully. 'Then you'd have missed your tea.'

Coppers! I thought.

I washed the taste of blood out of my mouth with the hot, dark, sweet liquid and relaxed for a bit for the first time since the heavyweight's phone call.

The young bobby offered me a cigarette from his packet of Silk Cut. I desperately wanted one, but refused.

I looked at my watch. It was four ten.

Doesn't time fly when you're having fun?

No-one came to see me. I just sat and ached. I asked the young copper if I could use a telephone. He refused. Finally I just sulked and wished I'd never been born. That would teach them, I thought.

The hours dragged by until just after seven o'clock when the interview room door swung open and in came my favourite person in the whole world. Detective Inspector Daniel Fox. Desperate Dan to his friends and enemies. Personally, I'd always referred to him as Poxxy Fox, but what do you expect?

Fox gestured for the uniformed man to leave the room, then ponderously moved in and sat on the hard wooden seat opposite me. He placed a packet of Dunhill and a gold cigarette lighter carefully before him on the table. How many times had I seen that prelude to an interrogation before?

Fox was well above average height and built like a bull. His temper was notorious. I'd seen him reduce long serving coppers close to tears and what he could do to a small-time villain was legendary. But he had a strange quiet side to his nature. I'd known him to sit in silence with a suspect for hours, saying nothing. Then gently he'd obtain a confession with a few whispered questions. I'd fallen foul of the man often and I knew his opinion of me was that I should never have been allowed into uniform. It was just my luck that he was on duty.

'Good evening, Mister Sharman,' he said. 'Do you remember me?'

As if I could ever forget. 'Yes, Mister Fox,' I replied. I felt like a kid dragged up before the headmaster for giggling in assembly.

'I never thought we'd meet again, you know,' he continued. 'Not after the last time.'

He gazed into the distance over my shoulder as if contemplating the vagaries of the world.

'No, Mister Fox,' I replied.

'But here we are. And once again on opposite sides of the table, as it were.'

I remained silent.

'Now tell me everything that happened this afternoon.'

Once again I reiterated my story.

'You should never have come back to this area, should you?' he mused.

'I've lived here most of my life.'

'But your life is over as far as I'm concerned Mister Sharman. All you've got to look forward to is ten years inside.'

'Mister Fox, if I may interrupt,' I interrupted. 'Ten years is a very long time, and for what?'

'Did the knock on the head bring on amnesia, Mister Sharman? There's the small matter of a dead girl. She died from an overdose of heroin. You were found with the body, and by coincidence a quantity of the same drug.'

It sounded open and shut the way he put it. I shook my head and said. 'Very convenient, wouldn't you agree. Almost too convenient. All it needs is a signed confession. By the way, who was the girl?'

'You mean to say you don't know?' he asked. 'I'm very surprised.'

'It wasn't Patsy Bright, was it?'

'Ah, the Bright girl. One of my junior officers told me earlier that you were interested in her. I'm sure you know which one.'

'I've no idea who you're talking about,' I said innocently.

'We won't pursue the matter for a moment,' he said, making a steeple with his fingers and regarding me gravely over them. 'We located Mister Bright earlier this afternoon, and he has told us that the girl found today is definitely not his daughter who was reported missing in June this year.'

'Who is she then?'

'As far as we can discover from the UB40 found in her room, plus other documents,' he withdrew a notebook from his pocket and donned a pair of national health spectacles, 'her name was Jane Lewis.'

'I knew it wasn't Patsy. Her hair was all wrong,' I said for no particular reason.

He continued as if I hadn't spoken. 'You were supplying her, presumably she was not the only one, with drugs. For some reasons, best known to yourself, you decided to drastically improve the quality of the heroin supplied. The preliminary report tells us that the drug remaining in the syringe was 98% pure.'

'Good shit,' I said.

'The girl is dead, Sharman. She may not be the only one.' The Mister had vanished. 'You were found with the deceased. I feel humour is hardly appropriate under the circumstances.'

'How long was she dead before she was found, Mister Fox?' I kept calling him Mister, old habits die hard.

'A matter of days,' he replied.

'The blood of my shirt is fresh, Mister Fox. As I asked that dildo Bachman. What the hell was I doing camping out in that dump for a couple of days? It's hardly the Inn on the Park, and the room service is appalling. And while I was waiting for the plods to arrive,

I suppose I wrecked my own car so that I couldn't get away even if I wanted to. You've got to be joking.'

'Sharman, why you've done so many things in your life has long been a mystery to me.'

'So now I'm a drug pusher,' I said. 'And at the same time I'm searching for a potential drug victim on behalf of her father. That's a strange juxtaposition wouldn't you say?'

'A clever cover.'

'Oh bollocks, Fox,' I was so pissed off I dropped the Mister too.

'Give me a break will you. I've been out of London until just recently, and I've hardly had time to build up a drug ring since I got back. You can check you know.'

I thought of giving him the name of my solicitor friend, but guessed that funds wouldn't run to phone calls to Portugal. I'd keep him up my sleeve for later.

'I've already done so,' said Fox. 'I don't spend my afternoons chasing the tea trolley, as you may remember. You spent nine months in hospital, mental hospital. Then three months convalescing at your mother's house in Sussex.'

'I was a voluntary patient.'

'Is there any other kind?' he asked sarcastically.

I didn't reply.

'We have analysed the contents of the twenty grammes of powder found in your possession.'

'Twenty grammes,' I interrupted. 'My, but those boys are cutting into their profits.'

He peered at me over his glasses and continued. 'And it is also 98% pure. It is heroin from the same batch that killed Jane Lewis.'

'I'd be amazed if it wasn't,' I said. 'Planting twenty baggies of talcum powder would be as much use as pussy in a gay bar.'

'The inevitable humour, Sharman. Will you never learn?'

'I learnt early on what a fit-up was Mister Fox.' I was expecting the worst so I put the mister back in. I could hardly believe what he eventually said. He stared at me and flicked some lint from the lapel of his suit. 'I think you're probably right. I know you of old, Sharman, and you're much too slippery to get caught like this.'

'Well I'm damned,' I said. 'You believe me then?'

'Up to a point. We'll check your story further of course. I must say it seems very amateurish of them, whoever they are.' He seemed lost in thought for a moment. 'But beware, the next time they may be more professional. Take my advice and get out whilst the going is good.'

'Am I free to leave then?'

'I think we'll let you out on the street again. I'm sorry about your car. You won't function very well travelling by public transport. It hardly goes with your image of yourself. And of course the next time, these individuals might kill you, which will eventually save the courts time and money.'

'You always were a nice bastard, Fox.'

For the first time he showed some emotion. 'Listen scumbag,' he said, raising his voice slightly. 'I'll spell it out for you. I don't want you in my part of the world unless you're in custody. And believe me you could easily be if I pushed it, and down for a long stretch. I don't want you corrupting my officers. I don't want you conducting your pathetic little investigations around here. This is your only chance. I think you're a little man who has always had someone running round after you cleaning up your messes. A little man who's always had a good Samaritan in tow. You had one on the force, and thank God he's gone, just like you.'

Fox was referring to a certain chief super who'd been to school with my father. The old boy had taken my career in hand and helped smooth the way for me on the force. Unfortunately he'd been pulled up one Christmas eve, driving home from a party. He was nearly five times over the legal limit. It would normally have been hushed up by the powers that be. Except that he'd been driving an SPG Range Rover at the time, and had managed to demolish three parked cars, a bus stop, a keep left sign and most of the front of Streatham Sainsbury's before the car came to a halt, wheels up. He took an early retirement before the new year, and from then on my professional future took a nose dive.

Fox continued speaking. 'Well little man,' he said. 'Your time's up. Get away from me and stay away. You disgust me. But remember,' he jabbed a finger at me for emphasis. 'You're out on parole, my parole. If I need you back, if it turns out that you were behind the death of that girl, I'll come looking for you personally. No old friends, no dildos, no plods, me. And you remember what happens to any villain that I get in my sights.'

I remembered and it wasn't a pleasant memory. Fox on the warpath was a sight to see. As for the character analysis, I would never admit it, but it was probably pretty accurate.

'So go now,' he concluded. 'Fuck off.'

After all that I thought it would be pointless asking him if I could use the telephone.

I was ushered out of the station by the back door. I didn't see Fox again, or Bachman, or King, or John Reid. All I did see were a lot of echoing corridors and blank doors. When I hit the paving stones my first concern was for my car.

I found a telephone box that worked, and one solitary ten pence piece in the pocket of my jeans. I phoned my car mechanic friend. There was no answer from his garage, so I tried him at home. A young, eager female voice answered.

'Is Charlie there please?' I asked.

Suddenly she wasn't quite as eager. She must have been waiting for her boyfriend to call. 'I'll see,' she said, and abandoned me. She was gone so long I thought my money would run out. Just my luck,

I thought.

Finally a male voice came on the line. 'Hello,' it said.

'Charlie?'

'Yeah.'

'It's Nick, Nick Sharman.'

I hadn't spoken to Charlie for over two years. I could have been dead for all he knew. There were no enthusiastic greetings, no excitement and thank God, no personal questions. All he said was, 'Hello Nick, how's the motor?'

He always got his priorities right.

'It's about the motor I'm calling. Someone's smashed it up.'

'Are you hurt?'

'Not a crash, vandalised it.'

'Oh Christ, where?'

I told him the street name and he said, 'If it's still there now, it won't be in the morning.'

'Can you help me Charlie?'

'I was just going down the pub.'

'I'll buy you a drink later. Listen, I've got no more tens.'

He thought for a second. 'I've got the low loader outside. I suppose I could get there in twenty minutes or so.'

'I'll owe you one, Charlie,' I said with relief.

'All right,' he said finally. Then the pips went, so I hung up and walked round to view the remains of my beloved automobile.

I had to pull up the collar of my jacket as the blood-soaked neck of my shirt was a pretty unusual sight even in the Brixton Road at that time of night.

As good as his word Charlie arrived not long after I did. He was almost as upset about the state of the car as me. After all, he had put many long hours into restoring it. We managed to manhandle the Jaguar onto the trailer attached to his Ford Transit truck, and he took it off to his garage in Norwood. He declined my offer of a drink and on his way dropped me off at my flat. I was quite relieved, as I was depressed, hurt and skint.

By ten o'clock I was in bed nursing my headache and my pride.

15

The AM rolled over me like a hit and run. I had all the familiar symptoms of a hangover again, except any memory of a good time. I lay on my back trying to remember where I'd been. Some detective, I thought. Then the events of the previous day came flooding back. I moaned at the memory. I couldn't believe it was only Tuesday morning. I had to check. I dragged myself out of bed and hunted for my watch which had a day/date function. After some searching I found it lying in the sink and confirmed the day, date and time which was past nine thirty.

I rinsed my mouth out with cold water in the bathroom and studied the face that stared back at me from the mirror. I looked shitty and felt the same. I gingerly touched the lump on the back of my head and decided to leave the plasters on. I found a torn sweatshirt hanging over the shower rail. It matched my mood exactly. I went back into the living room and pulled fresh jeans from a hanger, then rooted around for clean socks in the chest of drawers.

I made a pot of tea and planned my day over the first cup.

I needed wheels badly, then I had to discover who wanted me out of the way badly enough to hire the black and white minstrel show to fit me up. And why? What was I getting myself into? There were so many questions running around my mind that I could hardly remember my name. I decided to clear my head by taking some positive action. First I rinsed out my dirty cup under the tap, then I pulled on my old leather jacket and went off to see Charlie at his garage.

Fox had been right. I didn't feel much like a super sleuth waiting at the bus stop and then crawling along to my destination, downstairs on a Routemaster wedged between two pensioners and their mid-week shopping.

When I got to the garage, Charlie was working underneath a Ford Escort van. I kicked his foot and he rolled out from underneath the vehicle.

'How's the Jag?' I asked, after he'd pulled himself to his feet and we'd made polite enquiries as to each other's health.

'Bad,' he said, scratching his chin with an oily thumb. 'Very bad. Whoever did it, stitched you up good and proper. What was it all about?'

'I'll tell you another time Charlie,' I replied. 'When I know myself.'

'I'll look forward to it.'

'Is she repairable?'

'Of course. Everything's repairable if you've got the money. Have you?'

'It depends,' I said. 'How much do I need?'

He pondered like all mechanics do. 'Minimum fifteen hundred quid,' he told me.

'Oh Christ,' I said disbelievingly.

'That's straight,' he protested. 'Your motor's in bad shape.'

'Where is it?' I enquired.

'In the back, under canvas.'

I walked through the garage and out into a brick built extension. I recognised the sleek shape of the Jaguar under a tarpaulin. I pulled back the cover and surveyed the wreckage. The E-type was indeed a mess. Worse than I remembered. I tucked her up again and sadly went back to the forecourt. Charlie was leaning against the Escort cleaning his nails with a sliver of metal. He looked at me as I approached.

'Bad,' I said.

'Told you.'

'When can you start?'

'As soon as I've got some money for parts.'

'Alright, I'll get you some,' I told him, although I didn't know where. 'Can I leave her here for now?'

'Of course you can, for as long as you like. I'll take care of her.'

'Thanks,' I looked around for a moment and then asked the big question.

'Any chance of a loaner?'

He considered, then grinned a big gappy-toothed. grin. 'I might have something,' he said. 'But it won't be much.'

'Anything,' I urged. 'I just need wheels.'

He went into the shack that acted as his office and got some keys off a hook on the wall. Then he led me through the garage, past the E-Type and out into a muddy open space at the rear of the building. The area was full of junked cars lying in disarray.

'Try this,' he said.

He pointed towards a huge American muscle car, or the remains of one. It was a Pontiac Trans-Am. It was no particular colour. The bodywork had been sprayed with a matte grey primer, but in some places it had been rubbed down to bare metal blotched evilly with rust.

The bonnet was bright yellow and the boot lid was a dull brown. The car must once have had a vinyl roof, but it had been torn off and all that remained was a slight, black fluffy residue like a badly shaved chin. The front and back wheels were different diameters and widths. The front wheels were white mags and the rear drive wheels were steel and the low profile tyres stuck out from the bodywork at least three inches on both sides. To accomodate the massive wheels at the back, the suspension had been jacked up and huge wishbone springs had been fitted. 'Nice car, Charlie,' I said.

'Don't knock it babe,' he replied. 'It's this or nothing.' Then he added with a wicked smile. 'Of course you could always try Avis.' I pulled a face.

'Listen,' he said. 'You've got eight cylinders here.' He patted the bonnet. 'She may be a bit rough under forty, but she'll smooth out. Then watch her go. I fitted big springs and beefed up the front and rear bodywork with extra steel panels. I thought about Super-Stocking the beast, but I ran out of readies.'

'Cheers, Charlie,' I said. 'It looks like my kind of car.'

I opened the driver's door. The interior stank of damp. Across the front seats lay a jumble of black nylon webbing.

'What the hell's that?' I asked.

'Parachute harness,' replied Charlie proudly. 'You've got a lot of brakes on this little baby, and it'll stop you going through the windscreen. You know how to use it don't you?'

'Yeah, I saw the Dambusters.' I replied as drily as I could.

I pushed the webbing out of the way and sat on the stained upholstery, then tried the ignition with the key Charlie had given to me. The engine turned with a rattle, but didn't catch. I tried again. Again nothing.

'Hold on,' Charlie said, and went round and opened the bonnet. He fiddled around inside the engine compartment.

'Try again,' he said as he emerged.

I tried for the third time. Nothing

'Give her more choke,' he ordered.

I concurred. That time the engine caught with a massive rumble that shook the car. In the rear view mirror I saw clouds of smoke belch from the twin exhausts. The smoke gradually turned from black to blue, then grey, then petered out.

'Let her idle for a minute, then she'll be alright,' said Charlie, grinning again.

'Am I insured to drive this?' I asked.

'If you want to be,' he replied.

I gradually pushed in the choke and the engine note settled to a muted roar.

'Give her a go,' said the ace mechanic. 'You'll soon get used to her.'

I lifted my hand from the wheel in salute, put the car into gear and bounced her through the puddles across the muddy ground, down by the side of the garage and out into the main road.

A bit rough under forty, he'd said. Well I can testify to that. The car sounded like a Sherman tank driving down the Norwood Road. Every time I got stuck in traffic or stopped at the lights, the engine began to splutter, and I had to rev her up hard. The roar from the exhausts echoed between the shop fronts and heads turned to stare at the battered automobile. By the time I manoeuvred into my turning I was hunched down in the seat from embarrassment. I parked in front of the office, where I half expected the windows to be kicked in.

All was quiet and undisturbed, however, even the postman had given me a miss.

My head was still throbbing, so I went over to the pub for a medicinal brandy or two. As I drank I once again tried to piece together the events of the previous few days and once again came up with a complete blank. I decided I needed to speak to George Bright as soon as possible. I went back to the office and dialled his number. He answered immediately.

'George,' I said, when he picked up his receiver.

'Yes, speaking,' came the reply.

'Nick Sharman.'

'Oh,' he said.

For some reason he didn't seem keen to speak to me.

'I need to see you straight away, George. There's been a few developments.'

'I know,' he said. 'I was dragged down to the mortuary to identify a body yesterday.'

'Well, at least it wasn't Patsy,' I said.

'No, thank God.'

'Can you come down and see me at my office?'

'I'm not sure.'

'You were sure enough the last time we spoke. What's occurred?'

'Nothing.' Then he made up his mind. 'I'll get down as soon as I can,' he said.

'Make it fast, George, I'm waiting.'

He hung up without another word.

Something was bothering him, that was for sure. Something more than a visit to the morgue. I didn't have long to wait to ask him what it was.

About ten minutes later, his Mercedes saloon drew up and parked outside my office, behind the Trans-Am. The gleaming paintwork of George's car made mine look even worse. George emerged from behind the driver's wheel. He looked as if he was dressed for the members bar at Dulwich Golf Club. He was wearing a beautiful chunky kit, double breasted cardigan in navy blue wool, a white polo shirt buttoned to the neck and trousers that looked suspiciously like they were tailored by Tavatini in a black and grey Prince of Wales check. On his feet he was wearing shiny black brogues. He looked like a whiz. His outfit made me feel even more like Jack Shit.

George walked slowly through the door of the office and stood looking at me.

'Had a rough night, son?' he asked.

'You could say that George. More like a rough day, though, if the truth be known. It was nice of you to get in touch. I can tell you must have been desperate with worry.'

'I didn't know you'd been arrested,' he said lamely.

'And you weren't interested enough to find out.'

He didn't reply.

'What's got into you George?' I asked.

'It was seeing that girl on the slab.'

I thought he was about to cry again. Too bad.

'Tough experience, George. But like I said, it wasn't Patsy, was it?'

'No. But it could have been, and it might be next time.'

I shrugged.

'It seems as if I've stirred up a hornets nest,' I said. 'Someone doesn't want me looking for your daughter. Now tell me George, who could that someone be?'

'I've no idea.'

'I've only spoken to two people about it,' I continued. 'One wasn't interested, and as for the other, he's a friend of mine who doesn't know you and has no axe to grind. So he would hardly have sicked the heavies onto me. I've just got two questions to ask you. One, why didn't you check around the local drug clinics about Patsy? You knew she was into dope. And two, who have you told that you hired me to look for her?'

'I've already told you,' he said. 'I didn't know how deeply she was into drugs. I expected the police to check out that sort of thing.'

I declined to mention that if he expected the police to look into a drug connection, he should have told them about the box of tricks he'd found in Patsy's wardrobe.

'I've only told a few people about you,' he continued. 'My

employees know. It was obvious something was up. I was forgetting orders, not keeping on top of the job. My foreman came to me, and I told him everything. The other men were very good, very supportive. They took a lot of weight off my shoulders. Besides, they knew Patsy from when she worked there. They're fine lads.'

'Very touching,' I said. 'Anyone else?'

'I think I told some people at my club.'

'Club?'

'The Conservative Club. I drink there.'

I might have known.

'So I'm looking for a right wing fascist army,' I said. 'I don't think so George. The shotgun that geezer stuck on me wasn't for shooting grouse.'

I saw George's eyes widen when I mentioned the gun, but I didn't elaborate. I decided to ignore the Monday Club connection. 'What about your employees?' I asked. 'Can I speak to them?'

'I'd rather you didn't,' he said, looking around the room like a puppy searching for it's favourite bone. 'Listen Sharman, I think I'd rather you didn't look for Patsy any more. It's getting too dangerous. I didn't think you'd raise this kind of stink.'

'You're incredible, do you know that?' I asked. 'You wanted me to search for Patsy because the police were doing nothing. Even though on your own admission you'd suppressed information that might have helped them. And now things are starting to happen, you want me to bow out gracefully. I don't think you know what the hell you do want. It's too late now. I want to see these guys again for myself. They've wrecked my car as well as trying to fit me up. They've done at least fifteen hundred pounds worth of damage and that doesn't include this.' I touched the lump on the back of my head. 'It's personal now.'

George looked even more agitated. 'Look,' he said. 'I'll pay for the car. It's the least I can do. I'll get my accountant to make out a cheque as soon as you submit a bill, plus I'll put in something over the top for your trouble. You know my address. Drop your account in and you'll be paid within twenty four hours. Meanwhile, I don't want you looking for Patsy any more and that's that.'

George was getting petulant, that was all I needed. I knew I was losing him.

'George,' I said, trying to get him back. 'Last week, you were crying for me to take the case on. Today, less than seven days later, you're prepared to pay almost anything I ask for me to drop it. Who's got to you?'

'Nobody.'

'I don't believe you.'

I'd been on the force long enough to know when somebody was lying. He began to protest.

'OK. OK,' I cut him off. 'But what about Patsy? Don't you care any more?'

'Of course I do,' he protested. 'But I'd rather leave it to the police. They've got more manpower.'

'That's exactly what I said to you when you first approached me, and you said fuck them, well now I'm saying fuck you. I want to see the men who work for you. When can I come round?'

'I don't want you to ask them anything,' he interrupted. 'I want you to stop your enquiries as of now. I forbid you to continue. Just send me the bill for your car and I'll see that it's paid. That's all. Now I'm going.'

And he went. I watched him turn and leave the office, slam into his car and turn it around with a screech of tyres. I watched him and could do nothing about it. I wished I'd bitten his leg.

If I'd jacked it in then, as George had ordered me to, got the motor fixed and billed him, how different things would have turned out. How many lives would I have saved by minding my own business?

That thought is never far from me, even now. I must take full responsibility. I was just too clever. I was sure that in the end the great detective would get to the bottom of the mystery and ride off into the sunset with the girl.

I was becoming obsessed with the picture of Patsy. I took it out of the envelope again. I looked at it for a long time.

I knew that the trail picked up back at the house in Brixton where I'd been lured by the heavyweight's phone call. Fox's threats and George's reluctance to continue the investigation aside, I had to go back.

16

I tried to contact Terry Southall at the clinic. I spoke to Precious who told me he was going to be out all day on home visits. I made it clear it was vital that I spoke to him, and to get him to call me if he contacted the office. He had both my numbers, but I gave them to her just in case.

I decided to wait until dark before returning to Brixton, and spent the afternoon at home nursing my sore head and my battered ego with a bottle of gin that I had picked up from the off-licence. I wasn't sure which of the two hurt most, but they were both pretty painful.

I lay on the bed for hours listening to Radio Four buzzing gently in the background. I drank and catnapped and dreamed of dead girls dancing on windblown streets.

When twilight fell I was more than half pissed and ready to take on the world. Armed only with a pen torch and a gutful of gin, once more I drove to Brixton. I decided to park around the corner from the house. Not that anyone would wreck the old Pontiac, they wouldn't bother.

It would be towed away as a dumper before then.

I left the car on the darkest corner I could find. I slunk down the street like a criminal, weaving through the shadows. Most of the buildings on the block were dark, including the one I wanted to visit. I entered the tiny garden, slid onto the porch and tried the front door. It was locked. I fumbled for the bell-pushes and rang each of the three. I couldn't hear a thing from inside. Without any lockpicks on my person, and never having been able to open a Yale with a credit card, I went back to basics and busted the door in. Only one lock held it shut as far as I could tell, and a single hard kick soon dealt with that. Once I was inside I checked the lock. The force of my kick had pushed the screws that held the metal cup secure, out of the rotten wood of the door-frame. I pushed the screws back with my fingers and closed the door behind me.

I searched the house, leaving the lights on as I went. I started at the bottom and worked my way up. No-one was home. It was obvious that the house was being used as a squat when I discovered that the electricity meter had been bypassed with a length of heavy duty cable. Very dangerous, I thought, but not as lethal as being injected with 98% pure heroin.

As I searched, the house seemed to lean inwards upon me. The thin walls closing in as I checked the rooms. The wallpaper that decorated them was damp and faded, and peeling off in parts like skin from a year old corpse. Only two of the rooms seemed to have had recent tenancy. One was where the heavyweight had taken me to visit the deceased occupant. The police had searched it and any clues found were now down at Brixton Police Station. The room was dusty with fingerprint powder. It pearled the dull surfaces like sugar on a doughnut. Even so, I checked around, trying not to leave my prints in the dust and cursing myself for not bringing gloves. As I searched I kept listening for any sounds below. I should have saved the effort, as I came up empty-handed. My head began to throb in the silence.

The room was beginning to get to me. I could feel the dead girl's presence like a persistent itch I couldn't scratch.

The only other room that seemed to be in use was on the ground floor at the back of the house. It contained a double mattress neatly made up into a bed with a single sheet and a couple of frayed blankets. An old stove was in one corner, relatively clean and grease free, with a kettle and saucepan on the hob. There was a record player and some albums lying on the floor. I flicked through the record sleeves. There wasn't much that appealed to my taste. Sex Pistols, Clash, Cramps, Anti-Nowhere League, The Stranglers and a bunch of rockabilly compilations made up the bulk of the thin collection. It's amazing what you can tell about a person from their choice of music.

There was an ancient, battered wardrobe standing next to the bed and inside hung a few items of male clothing. These were mostly basic black and styled circa seventy six. I decided that I'd stumbled into a punk's nest. I decided to wait and see if he returned.

I went back through the house turning off all the lights. By the thin beam of my torch I made my way back to the back room, pulled up an old armchair and settled down.

I sat in the darkness and slowly the interior of the room began to take shape as my eyes became accustomed to the night. Once again I listened to the silence, punctuated only by the slight sounds of the building settling and the tap dripping in the sink. I was impatient for something to happen, yet at the same time content to sit in the comfortable old chair and let time drag itself by. I rubbed my fingers together as I sat and my skin seemed dry and powdery. I felt old and redundant, waiting for someone who was probably never going to arrive.

Abruptly I was aware of a sound that couldn't be attributed to the house. I heard the front door open and quiet footsteps in the hall coming towards the room in which I sat.

I stood up from the chair and moved towards the door. I heard the handle turn and someone pushed it slowly open. I waited until I could see a vague silhouette against the dim light that filtered in from the street to the hallway, then I grabbed for the figure. My hand caught onto the lapel of a leather jacket and I pulled the person wearing it into the room with me.

I heard a muffled cry, half scream, half shout but ignored it. I held onto the jacket with one hand and felt for the light switch with the other. In the harsh light from the unshaded bulb I looked at what I'd caught. He was a spaced out looking gothic boy with long black hair that was mousey at the roots. He wore his studded leather jacket over a loose, faded black shirt and tight denims artfully ripped at the knees. His face was deathly white under the cruel electric light and a bunch of livid red pimples were dotted around his mouth and nostrils. He was young, no more than nineteen or twenty and he smelled bad, like something had gone off in his life and he'd never noticed.

He tried to pull free, but I was too strong and held him tightly. When he realised, he changed his tactics and tried to plant the toe of one of his winklepickers into my groin. I turned away from his kick and caught his left arm with my free hand. I let go of his collar, spun him round and twisted his arm up his back. I held him with his middle finger pushed back against his palm. If he struggled it broke, simple as that. He drew breath to scream, but I grabbed a fistful of greasy hair and tugged his head back hard. The scream died in his throat. He was my prisoner for what he was worth. 'Don't shout, move or even breathe hard or I'll break your bloody finger,' I whispered into his ear.

'Let me go, you fucker,' he hissed.

I pulled his head back further until his already pallid face began to turn grey.

'Don't call me that,' I said quietly, 'or I'll really hurt you.' He was still. I went on, 'I'm going to let you go, but when I do, don't do anything silly. I don't want to cause you any unnecessary suffering, but I will if you force me to. Do you understand?'

He didn't move or speak, so I allowed him his freedom.

He turned and looked at me, rubbing at his neck. I looked back.

'Sit on the bed,' I ordered.

He didn't move, so I pushed him hard in the chest, back towards the bed. I could feel his bones through his shirt. He got the message. He sat down and I remained standing.

'Who the fuck are you? And what do you want?' he demanded, after staring at me for half a minute or so.

'Police,' I said. It was the first thing that came into my mind. It always used to work.

'Bollocks, show us your warrant card,' he demanded. Things seemed to have changed. I raised my fist.

'This is all the warrant card I need,' I said. I think he caught my drift. 'Were you around here yesterday?' I asked.

He said nothing.

'There's only two ways to do this,' I said. 'Either you answer me, or I beat the shit out of you, and then you answer me. Nobody's around. Nobody cares about you. Which one's it going to be? I haven't got all night.'

'You wouldn't dare,' he said bravely. But the expression on his face showed that he didn't entirely believe it.

'Don't be so fucking naive, son,' I said. 'I thought you punks were supposed to be street wise. I don't give a toss what happens here. I just want some answers to a few simple questions. It's easy, tell the truth, I'll go and you'll be alright. It's no big deal.' I roughened my voice and accent as I spoke, it often worked. His face showed he believed the hard talk.

'What then?' he asked.

'That's good,' I said. 'Were you here yesterday?'

'In the night time,' he replied.

'Not before?'

'No.'

'Were there any police here?'

'I waited until they'd gone.'

'What time?'

'About eight.'

'Right, did you know the girl who lived upstairs?'

'Which girl?' he asked innocently.

I moved threateningly towards him.

'You know which girl,' I said between clenched teeth. 'The girl they found dead yesterday.'

'All right. I knew her. So what?'

'What was her name?'

'Don't you know?'

'Don't fuck me about. Just tell me her name. Humour me.'

'Jane,' he said at last.

'Good, when did you last see her?'

'Dunno, last week sometime.'

'Do you know how she died?'

'No.' He didn't seem interested.

'She OD'd,' I said.

He shrugged.

'On skag,' I continued.

He shrugged again. I was beginning to lose my patience. 'Do you indulge?' I enquired.

'What?'

'Do you take heroin?'

'No.'

'What then?'

'Just a little draw.'

'Do you know Patsy Bright?'

'Never heard of her.'

I knew by his face that he was lying.

'Did she ever come here?' I asked.

'Who?'

'Patsy Bright,' I said patiently.

'I told you I never – '

I shut him up by simply hauling him off the bed by the collar of his studded jacket and smacking him around the side of the head with my open palm. The crack of skin on skin rang loudly in the room. The sound reminded me vividly of two previous incidents.

Firstly, walking into the gloom of a filthy basement garage and seeing TS trying to stop two police officers kicking the shit out of a black teenager. Secondly, how I'd felt on the previous afternoon when Bachman had decided to alter the contours of my own face.

I only had one blow in me. I hoped the punk didn't realise that. I still felt like a cheap bastard, beating up on a skinny little boy. As I held him in front of me, watching the skin of his cheek reddening from the force of the smack I noticed his eyes for the first time.

I held him by his jaw and looked into them closely. His pupils were mere pinpricks.

'Just a little draw,' I said. 'You lying little sod. What are you on?'

He twisted his face away.

'Are you on downers?' I asked, pulling his face back towards me and squeezing it hard.

'Might be, what's it to you? You ain't no copper,' he whispered through my grip.

'It's nothing to me, except you lied, and I don't like that.'

I let go of his face and raised my clenched fist. I was getting tired of playing the hard man.

The fight seemed to go out of him all at once.

'Please don't hurt me, please. I'll tell you.' He begged as he cowered back.

'No more lies now, all right.'

'All right,' he agreed.

I pushed him back onto the bed again and pulled the armchair close. I perched on one arm so that I could look straight down at him.

'What's your name?' I asked. I changed to a gentle approach. It was another ploy that worked. That time was no exception.

'Steve,' he replied.

'Terrific, Steve. Do you know Patsy Bright?'

'Yes,' he replied.

'Do you know where she is?'

'No, I haven't seen her for awhile.'

'How long?'

'Six weeks, two months. I can't remember.'

'Where did you see her last?'

'At a Cramps gig at Hammersmith.'

'Was she alone?'

'Yes.'

We could almost have been two friends chatting about a mutual acquaintance, we were so polite.

'Has she ever lived here?'

'Here? In this shit hole. She wouldn't be seen dead living here.'

I didn't bother to point out the irony of that remark.

'Was she into drugs?' I asked.

He looked at me as if I'd asked a particularly stupid question.

'Depends what you mean,' he replied.

'You know what I mean?'

'Are you kidding me?'

I was fed up with him replying to a question with a question.

'I don't kid around. Tell me.'

'She didn't take drugs. Not hard stuff anyway. She wouldn't dirty herself with that shit. She just sold it.'

I couldn't believe what he was saying. 'She was a dealer?' I asked incredulously.

'Sure she was, and a big dealer. She didn't sell little, she sold big.'

'How big?'

'Kilos, that kind of big.'

'Bullshit,' I said. 'I don't believe you.'

'It's true,' Steve was indignant, as if he'd lie, not much.

'All right then, kilos of what?'

'Smack and coke.'

'Where did she get it?' I demanded.

'I don't know.'

'Let's get this straight,' I said. 'You're saying that Patsy Bright was a big time dealer in hard drugs. She's only eighteen for Christ's sake. There must have been someone behind her. Supplying her. Who was it?'

'I've told you, I don't know.' It was probably safer that he didn't.

I thought of Patsy's photograph, and felt betrayed by her angel face.

'How do you know all this?' I continued.

'She didn't keep it a secret. We used to meet at clubs and places. There were a few of us that knocked around together. But a lot of people don't like her. She's weird, spaced out.'

'I thought you said she didn't take drugs,' I interrupted. 'If you're telling me more lies, you'll be sorry.'

He looked genuinely scared. I was beginning to believe him, although God knows I didn't want to.

'She didn't take the hard stuff,' he explained. 'She liked dope though.' He giggled at the thought. 'She said it made her feel sexy. She gave us smack and coke to keep in with us. I told you lots of people didn't like her. Anyway,' he added as an afterthought, 'who said you had to take drugs to be weird?'

'She bought your friendship with hard drugs?' I reiterated. 'I thought you said you didn't take them, Steve. Don't wind me up.'

'I lied,' he said. 'But I'm telling the truth now, honest. I do some now and again, but not as much as some of the others. They loved it, some of them.'

'Did they get hooked?' I asked.

He looked at me through his sleepy eyes and said, 'You do sound like a fucking copper, now I come to think of it. How the fuck do I know?'

Or care, I thought.

He patted his jacket, 'I want a fag, alright?'

I nodded assent and then continued, 'Did she sell dope to your friends when they became junkies?'

'No, she just gave them more. She had loads. She always had loads.'

Whilst we had been talking, Steve had been searching his pockets and finally produced a battered packet of ten Embassy filters and a book of matches. He took out a cigarette and lit it. He even offered me the packet like a perfect little gentleman. I declined his offer.

'Did she supply the girl upstairs?' I asked when his cigarette was burning to his satisfaction.

'I keep telling you I don't know. I haven't seen Patsy for ages, I hadn't seen Jane for days.'

'Before, I mean. In the past.'

'Maybe, who knows.'

'Was Jane one of the friends you used to go about with?'

'No,' he laughed meanly. 'She was just a dirty junkie.'

'Don't you care that she's dead?'

He shrugged. Steve was a natural shrugger.

'Jane got hold of some pure smack from somewhere. Do you

know of any going around?'

I was grasping at straws by then.

'I wish I did. I feel like getting smashed,' he replied.

He was flicking ash carelessly off his cigarette end and it fell onto the bed cover.

'Do you live here alone?' I enquired.

'Sometimes, sometimes not,' he answered.

I could see he was nodding out and was not interested in further conversation.

'You're sure that Patsy never told you who supplied her the drugs or who she sold them to?' I probed again. I had to discover the truth or something that passed for it.

He waggled his forefinger in my direction. He was going with the sleeping pill fast. Or more likely, putting it on. 'She said it was a secret.'

'Did she stay here with you at all?'

'I don't think I was her type.' He giggled again. Giggling and shrugging were big with him.

'What was her type?' I asked, more interested than I should have been.

'How the fuck do I know? It don't bother me. I can always get a tart if I want one.'

'Yeah, I'm sure Steve,' I said. 'You're a prince. I bet the girls flock around you.'

'I'm going to be a rock star,' he said wearily, as if he'd heard the words so many times from his own lips, he no longer believed them himself. 'But some bastard's nicked me bass.'

If it hadn't been so sordid, it would have been funny. He lay back on the mattress and closed his eyes. I took the cigarette end that smouldered between his fingers and stubbed it out in a saucer that lay on the wooden draining board of the sink. The tap still dripped fitfully and the drops drummed down on to the outside of an old tin cup that lay in the sink. I turned the tap hard anti-clockwise to no avail. The washer must have gone. I pushed the cup from under the tap and a cockroach flew blindly to hide in the folds of a dishcloth.

I didn't think there was much more information to be obtained from Steve that night. I left him to his dreams of stardom and easy money and let myself out of the house.

I needed to see George Bright right away. I wanted answers to the questions that talking to Steve had raised. Not for the first time since I had started looking for Patsy Bright, I felt that someone was really taking the piss. And by that, I don't mean a good natured leg-pull down at the local on a Saturday afternoon.

I drove straight back to George's house in Dulwich.

Although I knocked and rang for five minutes or more, there was no answer. I felt drained by what Steve had told me. I hoped that he was lying, but had a suspicion he was telling the truth. It crossed my mind to break into the Bright mansion, but I couldn't think of a good reason why I should. The chances of me stumbling over anything important in a place that size were slim to say the least. Anyway, I'd probably get caught.

So I went back home and sat for a while staring at the picture of Patsy.

She had begun to take on the look of a fallen angel.

At twelve thirty, I went to bed and fell straight asleep.

17

The clanging of the telephone bell woke me in the small hours. I felt as if I'd been asleep for only a moment as I surfaced through confused dreams. It was pitch black in the flat and I fumbled blindly for the light beside my bed. When I found the switch and illuminated the room I picked up my watch from the table. It told me that it was one thirty. I swore out loud as I lifted the receiver from it's cradle. Whoever was ringing was in a call box. I waited for the pips to stop. I recognised the voice at once. 'Nick, is that you?' it asked. 'It's me - T S.'

He sounded slurred and distant, half pissed or stoned, and over-amplified electro-funk music buzzed down the line, which didn't help me to hear him.

'It's a bit late, pal,' I said. 'I've just got to sleep.'

'Sorry about that, but I have to talk to you.'

'Good, I tried to get you earlier.'

'I know,' he said. 'I spoke to Precious. Where have you been? I've been calling you all evening.'

'I've been out socialising,' I said, as the phone crackled loudly in my ear. 'Where the hell are you? I can't hear a thing for all that noise.'

'I'm at the Olive,' he replied.

'You never change, do you?' I asked.

The Olive Branch was a club just off the Brixton Road that catered to a multi-ethnic, multi-sexual, rough trade clientele that was bizarre to say the least.

'Is that dump still open?' I continued.

'Of course it is,' he replied, shrugging off my question.

'Listen, I've got to see you.'

'OK, I'll meet you in the morning.'

'Not in the morning, now.'

'Leave it out,' I said. 'Do you know what time it is?'

'Who the hell cares?' he said. 'I think someone's putting you on.'

'It won't be the first time,' I told him. 'Who in particular now?'

His voice faded on the line, then I heard him faintly again.

'I can't talk from here,' he said through the interference. 'This line is bloody awful. I'll be home in fifteen minutes. Can you come round?'

'I'm in bed.'

'Fuck bed, it could be to our mutual advantage to meet. I've got news about the girl you're looking for, and a slight problem.'

'What news? What problem?' I asked, suddenly wide awake.

'I think I'm being followed.'

'Who by?'

'I'm not sure, it's a salt and pepper team, and it only started after I began asking about your Patsy Bright.'

'Are they there now?'

'No, that's why I'm going to split.'

I could hear the shrieking of female voices in the background.

'Are you on your own?' I asked.

'No.'

'Anyone I know?'

'I shouldn't think so, she's still at school.'

'Well get rid of her,' I said urgently. 'And I'll meet you at your place in twenty minutes or so.'

'No chance, Nick. I want to find out if she's wearing any panties.'

'Don't be a cunt, Terry. It could be dangerous, if these people are who I think they are. Get shot of the scrubber for Christ's sake. She could get hurt.'

'Forget it, she thinks I'm a war hero. I'm telling you boy, this is love. Just get over here. We'll be waiting.'

I tried to protest further, but Terry hung up and left me holding the cold receiver. I lay back in bed cradling the phone onto my chest. Although I was bone tired, I was more than intrigued by what he'd said. And worried that he thought he was being followed. I didn't like the sound of that one bit. It seemed as if someone was determined to fuck up, what on the face of it seemed to be a simple investigation into the whereabouts of a missing girl. If such an investigation could ever be simple.

I felt as if I'd stepped into a den of wolves, when I was only looking for a little puppy dog.

I got out of bed, went into the bathroom and splashed cold water onto my face. The reflection that looked back at me from the mirror over the sink was midnight old and fluorescent pale. I dried my face and pulled it into a semblance of dynamic youth with the tips of my fingers.

I cleaned my teeth to get rid of the taste of my short sleep and went to find some clothes. I pulled on tired jeans and a wrinkled cotton sweater.

I hoped that Terry wasn't throwing a surprise party. I was looking far from my best.

The night was warm, but damp, so I tugged on a raincoat, grabbed my keys and left the house.

The street lights outside were haloed with a fine mist of drizzle. I slid behind the wheel of the Pontiac and turned the key in the ignition. The starter motor whined, but the engine refused to fire.

I slammed the steering wheel with the palm of my hand in frustration. I guessed that the damp had got into the electrics. Charlie would have diagnosed the fault in seconds and had me on my way in a minute. I just sat and cursed the damn car and wished that I had my Jaguar back.

Finally I got out of the Trans-Am and manhandled it out into the street. It rolled gently down the hill, and I managed to bump start it just before I reached the traffic lights at the T-junction with the main road. I allowed the car to idle until the temperature guage began to show a degree of heat. When the needle finally moved out of the blue area on the dial, I drove the car through the streets, slick and black with rain, towards Terry's flat.

The brief drive reminded me of how much I used to love the night. I loved to stand in the shadows and feel the darkness like velvet fingers on my skin.

When I was on the force, I always preferred the nightshift. Prowling the deserted streets under the yellow sodium lights past quiet houses was one of the few good memories I had of that time.

Towards the end it caused problems with Laura, but by then, so did everything. Early on though, before Judith was born, the pair of us revelled together in the darkness. When we were first married, we lived in a little terraced house in Horsham. On my nights off during the summer, we'd take the Jaguar down to Brighton late at night. We'd roll the windows down and Laura would hike her skirt up to let the warm breeze caress her thighs. Somehow I always remember the summers as being warmer in those days.

I loved her so much then, that not touching her actually hurt. We would have to stop somewhere in the dark countryside and make love. She was blonde and cool, but on those nights her skin burned me in our passion. She made me think of a wild animal, tawny eyed, long and lean with a wild streak in her.

She'd come in colours, like a rainbow rising from the sea then plunging down to dash itself on the rocks below. Although I searched and searched, I could never find the pot of gold. Perhaps, because all the time I was holding it in my arms and never knew. Afterwards we'd lie together, barely touching as our sweat dried and listen to the muted sounds of the night. I would look at her by the light of the moon and marvel at what I saw. She was the most beautiful woman I have ever seen, with the kindest heart in the world. To my eternal shame, I crushed it like a dried flower.

On the way back home, I'd drive the car as hard as I could on the narrow country lanes, then without warning turn all the lights off. With Creedence or The Doors blasting out of the stereo we'd race through the night.

Laura would scream at the top of her voice, half in pure terror, half with some kind of sexual pleasure. The black car would roar through the night like a banshee released from the underworld and revelling in it's new found freedom.

When we got home, the adrenalin of the sex and speed still hot in our veins, unable to sleep, we'd sit together and wait for the dawn, smoking joints in the garden, lying on the damp furniture and breathing in the scent of the roses I'd so carefully grown.

I wished that I could have bottled the happiness we felt then and kept it to savour when the shadows in my life grew long and dark, then poured it out like perfume, and tasted its sweetness.

18

I remember checking my watch as I pushed through the glass doors of the block in which Terry's flat was located.

It was two twenty five in the morning as I entered the lobby. Exactly fifty five minutes since he'd called me on the phone. Because of the trouble with the car it had taken me a lot longer than I'd anticipated to get to his place.

I took the weary old lift up to the third floor and walked down the corridor to his flat. I rang the doorbell, but got no reply. The block had been built in the twenties and the front door to the apartment was a solid, old fashioned job, painted dark green. It was secured by two locks, one Yale and the other a Mortice. On the outside was a brass handle, dull and pitted from use. After waiting for a minute or two, I rang again. There was still no answer.

I didn't expect the door to be on the latch, not at that ungodly hour of the night. But when I tried the handle, it turned, and with a push the door slowly opened.

At any other time I might have thought it merely careless of Terry to leave the door unlocked. However, after what had happened to me over the last few days, I was suspicious and wished I was carrying a weapon.

I pushed the door open wide. It moved slowly on it's oiled hinges. The hallway was dark. But the living room door, directly in front of me, was ajar, and a dim light shone inside. From somewhere I could hear music. Just the thin top of recording, no bass, and something else in counterpoint, like a baby crying.

I crept noiselessly across the hall carpet, pushed the living room door fully open and peered into the interior. I was going to call Terry's name, but what I saw in the room silenced me.

The place was much as I remembered it from my previous visit two years previously. It was a mess. Military memorabilia was everywhere. Rifles, pistols, swords and bayonets were mounted on the walls. Above the fireplace was a huge stars and stripes flag, on the wall opposite was a smaller, tattered black flag of the NVA. Books and papers were stacked everywhere. Model military vehicles covered every spare surface. By the side of the door was an army radio equipped with a long whip aeriel. Furniture was sparse. One straight backed chair, a coffee table and a leather chesterfield sofa. There was an old stereo rigged on pale pine shelves along one wall. A console TV was hooked into a video set-up, and on the screen Martin Sheen was busy battling the Viet Cong in glorious technicolor with the sound turned down. The music I could hear was played by the Jimi Hendrix Experience. The sound was coming through headphones via the stereo. The amp must have been turned up to number ten. The headphones lay on the carpet and pumped out their tinny noise into the pile.

The air in the room smelled stale and used. I tried to breathe with the side of my nose. The other sound I could hear, the sound that reminded me of a baby crying was coming from a young girl sitting on the floor leaning against the sofa. She was typical T S material.

As he'd always put it, young and dumb. Except that she kept making that noise, a high keening came from her throat. The sound was soft in the dead air, and Jimi played on through the headphones in the background.

The film had reached the episode where a boatload of soldiers are involved in a night time action against the enemy on a bridge across a river.

The silent screen was full of bright flashes like a firework display and the band was playing 'Electric Ladyland', and the girl was crying. It was too perfect a scene to describe.

She wasn't wearing any stockings, and when I saw Terry, I could tell him that the answer was positive on the panties. They were white and transparent so that I could see the darkness of her pubic hair. They probably hadn't been transparent when she put them on. But they were now, because she was sitting in what I guessed to be a pool of her own urine which had hardly had time to soak into the carpet. I could see all this because her short skirt had hiked up around her waist. I tried to pull it down to cover her modesty, but it was too short, a bare few inches of poor quality leather. I soon realised I was wasting my time. She didn't care about her modesty, or me touching her. She was too far gone on something to see me or anything else. Not right then, not for a while, maybe never.

Her eyes were open, but looking somewhere else. Blue eyes, like two marbles set in a china background.

Her face was young and round and innocent under heavy makeup. Her hair was stiff and spikey with lacquer or gel and smelled like it needed a wash.

I spoke to her gently, asked what the matter was, but got no reply. Just more wailing, soft and far back in her throat.

I switched the TV and stereo off, then left the girl to herself. She'd started rocking gently to and fro by the time I left the room. I left as quietly as I had entered, and checked the bedroom and kitchen. Both rooms were empty and appeared to be undisturbed. That left only the bathroom. I pushed open the door and fumbled for the cord that operated the light. I found it and pulled it gently with my fingers. A bright fluorescent light sprang into life above me. I was momentarily dazzled by the reflection from the shiny white porcelain tiles that covered the four walls of the room. Terry was waiting for me. Just like he said he would. Except that he wasn't going to tell me anything about Patsy Bright that warm, early morning.

Terry had been messily decapitated, and his head mounted on the centre of the closed toilet seat. His mouth had been stuffed with tissue to silence the screams that must have welled up in his throat as he faced whoever had chopped his head from his body. The paper bulged out from between his lips and dangled pinkly to his chin. The stink of death filled my nostrils again, for the second time in two days.

I stood in the doorway at the edge of a viscous pool of blood that stretched from wall to wall. Red splashes had spattered the tiles on one wall. The force of the blow to his neck had sent a shower of blood almost to ceiling height. I was so reluctant to believe the evidence of my own eyes that I looked away as if the vision would somehow disappear. There was no chance, when I looked again the horror became even more apparent. Strings of tendon and skin fanned out across the lid of the toilet seat and watery dribbles of pink liquid ran from his neck across the plastic and trickled down the white porcelain of the bowl to join the scarlet sea on the linoleum covered floor.

Terry's eyes were open too. As I stared into the unblinking depths, my mouth filled with the contents of my stomach. The liquid bubbled thick and foul between my teeth. I turned and spat the vomit into the bathroom sink. I heaved again and again until only bitter bile remained.

I was very neat and tidy. I washed away the stinking mess with clean, cold water. I even sipped a little to clear my mouth before I checked closer. Time seemed to stand still in the flat. My ears filled with the silence as I looked at my old friend's mutilated features. The harsh light reflected off his bald patch, around which the hair stood as if electrically shocked. His skin was blue-white and I could almost count the individual stubble on his chin. I finally dragged my eyes away. I saw that shower curtain around the bath was shut. But I noticed that there were splashes of blood around the edge of the bath tub. I saw a vague, still silhouette through the opaque plastic. Sweat was pouring off me, soaking into my clothes. Avoiding the puddle of blood, I stretched over and pulled the curtain back. I didn't want to look, but I had to. I had to see everything. Terry's headless body was sitting in the bath, with his feet jammed underneath the taps. The enamel was stained with his bodily fluids. His shirt was soaked with the stuff. A saw toothed bayonet lay in the liquid and a sabre protruded from his chest, pinning the photo of Patsy Bright that I had given him at our last meeting to his torso. That final, theatrical touch nearly sent me over the edge. I turned and fled the room. I stood in the hall, leaning against the wall with my heart tearing at the inside of my chest. I almost ran away, but dragged myself together and began to think.

I knew that I musn't be found with the body or even in the vicinity. I wouldn't get away with being tucked up with a corpse for the second time.

I was aware that I was being set up again and that time the law would happily lock me up and throw away the key. It was a real groove. A body, a witness and little old me on the scene. Who'd believe that I'd arrived after the murder. Not too many, I was sure. But the murderers, whoever they were and I had a pretty good idea, had gone too far with the girl. Whether they'd given her a front row seat to the killing or not, she'd overloaded her circuits in the flat that night. She wasn't about to finger me or anyone else. Tough luck boys.

I began to clear up after myself. I went into the kitchen and found a fairly clean tea towel, which I used to wipe all the surfaces I had touched since I entered the place, and quite a few I hadn't. Reluctantly I went back to Terry's headless body and carefully tore Patsy's photo from the blade that held it against the wound in his chest.

That was the closest I came to cracking up. I could hear myself making these peculiar sounds as I peeled the thin card away from his bloody shirt. I think I was apologising to him. I bit down on my lip as hard as I could to stop the whimpering.

By the time I'd wrapped the stained picture into the towel and forced the whole package into my raincoat pocket, blood was dribbling from the side of my mouth. I looked into Terry's face once more, so that my eyes would sear the image of the sight onto my mind and I would always remember the white hot horror of finding him mutilated, then turned and went back to the girl.

I swear that when I went back into that close little living room, after leaving Terry, to wipe my prints from the equipment I'd touched, I was as horny as hell. I looked at the little girl sitting there in a pool of her own piss, still moaning and rocking gently back and forth just where I'd left her. I wanted to screw her into the ground. I'm not proud of the feeling. Maybe amongst death I was looking for life, or maybe that's too noble a concept. Probably I just wanted a quick fuck. I looked at her there with her tiny breasts pouting through the material of her T-shirt, her nipples erect beneath the fabric and felt a surge of desire more intense than I'd had for years.

I'll never know what might have happened next, because then I heard the sirens ripping the night. Soaring and echoing against the walls, and I knew with certainty that they were coming after me. Superb timing, I thought, but no prizes for the racket.

I shimmied the curtain aside and looked down into the street. I saw two squad cars skid to a halt, their sirens dying with one last whoop each. Blue lights flashed, illuminating the dead windows of the houses opposite.

I dropped the curtain and ran back through the room, past the girl and out into the hall. I dived through the front door, then heard from below booted feet on the stairs, and the indicator above the lift door blinked from G to 1. I skidded to a halt on the polished floor of the corridor, then turned again and ran back into Terry's flat, slamming the door behind me. I tore through the hall and into the kitchen, where I pushed the protesting window open and climbed through onto the sill. A narrow, rusty fire escape ran along the back of the building. I climbed out onto the metal which sagged under my weight and flaked paint and rust in equal quantities down into the darkness to patter gently onto the back path. I scrambled along the escape, then heard a noise from below. I pushed myself back against the brickwork, away from the diffused light from the kitchen window and froze. I peered down and could just make out the silhouette of a man in a peaked cup standing below. I moved gently along the escape, trying not to dislodge any further debris. Within a few footsteps I was around the corner of the building and out of sight.

Butted next to Terry's block was another building, old Peabody flats that had stood empty for years. The block was only two storeys high and the flat roof was about twelve feet below me. It was my only escape route. I could hear voices calling behind me. I prayed that the roof would take my weight and jumped down. When I landed, my bad foot sent a stab of pain through my body, so intense that I nearly fainted. I saw colours in my head that don't have names yet, and I bit down hard on my shredded lip to stop myself screaming. I must have made a hell of a row as I landed, but no-one shouted, no windows were flung open and no local burghers cried havoc in the street. After a moment I dragged myself across the flat roof to a gap which had once housed a door, now long gone for firewood.

I limped down what seemed like interminable flights of stairs until I hit civilization in the shape of an exit onto a gravelled path which led me onto an anonymous back street. I walked around searching for the Trans Am.

By this time I was completely disorientated through a combination of what I'd seen in the flat, climbing around outside buildings and the pain in my foot, so I took some time to find it. Especially as I had to keep one eye out for marauding squad cars. I was glad I'd taken the precaution of tucking the Pontiac out of the way. Then I realised I hadn't shut T S's eyes. As I limped along the pavements to the car, keeping as close as possible to the shadows of the buildings, through the sultry air, I remembered that I hadn't shut his eyes. I'd left him staring sightlessly into eternity. As long as I live I'll wish I'd taken time to shut Terry's eyes. My luck held. I didn't see a soul as I made my escape. I just heard more sirens and saw more blue lights flashing in the distance.

The car started immediately and I drove straight home, favouring my left foot on the clutch pedal.

All at once I didn't like the night time at all. When I got back to the peace of my own flat, I retrieved the bundle from my pocket. I knew all about the laws of evidence, and hi-jacking that particular piece from the scene of T S's murder was very serious indeed. I wrapped the whole caboodle in a black plastic rubbish sack and stuffed it into the back of the tiny freezer compartment of my fridge. Not very original, but it would have to do.

19

I sat up for the rest of the night waiting for the law to arrive. They'd come close to finding me at the scene of the crime in Terry's flat. It would have been a sweet collar if I'd been pulled standing over his body. I wondered who'd called the Old Bill in. Once again it didn't take a lot of imagination to guess.

I looked through the window and watched the dawn break through the drizzle. I mourned T S in my own way and washed his memory down with the remains of the gin I'd started the previous day.

I tried to work out a motive for his murder. He must have asked the wrong person about Patsy Bright. I couldn't think what could be behind so violent a crime. I could still see his corpse, and his dead eyes boring into mine. I promised myself that one day soon I would avenge this murder.

I should have shaved but I didn't want to look at myself too closely in the mirror, I didn't think I would've liked what I saw. I made endless cups of tea between the hits on the booze. The street outside became busy as people went to work, peaking at about eight thirty, then quieting down again as the rush passed.

I'd like to say I envied their normality, but to be honest, I didn't. I knew most of them led lives of quiet desperation. I'd seen too many babies battered to death by normal mothers, and wives dismembered by normal husbands. I could feel the depression building inside me as I gazed through the window, and wondered how good the cure for my breakdown had been.

My nerves were humming with stress and I guessed I'd better get busy before I cracked up again.

I felt grubby and itchy, but couldn't be bothered to change my clothes, so I simply grabbed my raincoat and hit the bricks.

I walked down to my office and let myself in. There was one solitary letter waiting for me. It carried no stamp, and must have been hand delivered. I opened it and read the typed message, printed on plain white, bond paper.

Sharman Mind Your Own Business
Remember Your Daughter

It was unsigned of course. What did I expect?

At least the writer hadn't put 'A friend' at the end. That would have been too melodramatic.

If I thought I was stressed before the note arrived, after I read it, I knew what pressure was really all about.

The screws were being tightened down.

At that point I began to get really pissed off. Who did these people think I was? They seemed to think that they could follow me from place to place, kill my friends, and now threaten my family. And get clean away with it. However, there was one thing they were forgetting.

The only person that still mattered to me was my child. If they dared mess with her, they would see some serious shit go down.

I was sweating under my light raincoat. I shucked it off and checked my watch. Ten ten. I reached for the phone and dialled my ex-wife's new number from memory.

'Hello,' she said, after a few rings.

'Laura, it's me,' I said. There was a pause.

'What do you want?' she asked.

She was as warm as ever. I didn't quite know what to say.

'Come on, Nick. What do you want?' she repeated.

'I don't quite know how to put this,' I said.

'Put what? Spit it out.'

Spoken like a true lady, as always.

'Is there somewhere you can go for a few days?' I asked.

'I am somewhere,' she replied.

'No, I mean somewhere else.'

'Why?' she demanded. I could tell she was losing her patience already.

I seemed always to have that effect on her.

'I've had a letter about Judith.'

'Who from? What kind of letter? What are you talking about?' I could hear the old tone creeping into her voice, part fear, part anger.

'I'm afraid it's a threat to her.'

'What do you mean it's a threat? She's only eight years old for God's sake. How can anyone threaten an eight-year-old child? What have you got us into now? Have you told the police?'

She said the word 'police' as if it hurt her mouth.

'Not yet, I've only just got the damn thing.'

'What does it say?'

'It's not specific.'

'Oh, it's not specific,' she interrupted. 'What a shame. Not specific, then how do you know it's a threat?'

'Laura,' I said, 'just listen, will you. It doesn't say anything in particular will happen. It doesn't say anything really. But I think I know who sent it, and these guys are serious. I want you and Judith out of the way where I don't have to worry about you.'

'What guys?' she demanded. 'You mean you know these people.'

'Not socially. We don't drink together. We're not arsehole buddies, if that's what you mean.'

I didn't want to be unpleasant, but since the breakdown of our marriage she always managed to bring out the worst in me. When I tried to be cool, and in control of a situation that was fast running away from me, she refused to let me be, or maybe it was simply that I wouldn't let myself be.

There was silence at her end of the line. Then in the background I heard Judith's voice.

'Can I speak to Judith, please?' I asked.

'No you can't,' Laura replied. 'Haven't you caused her enough grief?'

I could hear the tears in Laura's voice.

'Laura,' I said, 'do I have to beg to speak to my own daughter?'

She was silent, then said, 'Alright, Nick. You win as always, but I'm going to fetch Louis.'

Win as always, it never ceased to amaze me how wrong her conceptions of my little life could be.

The phone crashed down, then I heard the mumble of female voices and the receiver was picked up again.

'Hello daddy,' my daughter's voice said.

'Hello sweetheart. How's my best girl?'

'I'm fine daddy, but mummy's crying.'

'I know darling. I'm afraid I might have frightened her.'

'Why did you do that?' Judith asked in a puzzled voice.

'I didn't mean to, don't worry. She'll be alright in a minute.'

'Promise?' she asked.

'I promise.'

I would try to keep the promise, but there are no guarantees in this life. Still, try and explain that to an eight-year-old.

'When am I going to see you?' she asked.

Everything was fine. Her mummy was going to be alright. Daddy had given his word. I hoped Laura would be placated as easily.

'I don't know. I think you're going away for a while.'

'On holiday?'

'Yes, a little holiday.'

'Oh good. Are you coming?'

I couldn't believe she'd asked that. What a little lunatic. As if the four of us could pop off together for a cosy weekend. I loved her so much. For the first time in days, I smiled, then laughed out loud. No-one would ever be allowed to hurt her as long as I had breath in my body.

'What's the matter daddy?' she asked. 'Why are you laughing?'

'It doesn't matter Judy. But I don't think I'll be coming along. You'll have a good time with mummy and Louis.'

'Daddy?' All of a sudden she was whispering. That meant secrets were in the air.

'What?'

'Mummy's gone to fetch Louis. Can I ask you something?'

'Of course, what is it?'

'Can I like Louis?' she asked.

'What do you mean?' I asked back.

'Can I like him? Will you mind?'

Another kind heart, I thought. How long will it be before yours is broken too?

'Of course I don't mind,' I said. I swear I felt a catch in the back of my throat as I said it. 'You should like him, I know he likes you.' I refused to say 'loves'.

'Does mummy really like him?'

'Oh yes, she does a lot.'

I wondered why the admission hurt so much.

'But you'll always be my real daddy.'

'I know darling, and you'll always be my best baby.'

Until, I thought, you're eighteen with dope in your wardrobe and you've taken it on your toes.

'I'm not a baby,' she said indignantly. 'You mustn't call me that. Mummy said so.'

'I just can't forget what you looked like when I first saw you,' I explained. 'You were so tiny, I forget you've grown up.'

She took pity on me.

'Alright daddy,' she said conspiratorially, 'you can call me anything you want.'

'Thank you darling,' I said. 'Is mummy back yet?'

'They're just coming now.'

'Put her on please, and enjoy your holiday.'

'Alright, goodbye now,' she said. 'I love you.'

Then she was gone. I said, 'I love you too.' To the empty air.

Laura came back onto the line. 'Louis is here,' she said.

'Listen Laura,' I said, 'I appreciate that he's tops when it comes to dental hygiene, but I wonder if he's ready for this sort of thing. Couldn't you just take a few days, you and Judith. Somewhere where no-one knows you. A bit of holiday?'

'Don't patronise me Nick. Louis goes where I go. Do you think I could keep a thing like this from him?'

She was crying again. Her sobs faded for a moment and then Louis came onto the line.

'What exactly is going on, Sharman?' he demanded.

'Hello Louis,' I said eventually, and repeated the facts as I'd told them to Laura.

He thought for a while, but thankfully not too long.

'As a matter of fact,' he said, 'we can get away for a while. But this whole thing is unforgivable, Sharman, and I hold you fully responsible. Can't you keep your messy business out of our lives? I can tell you that it doesn't please me to turn tail and run on your say so.'

'This is not the bloody Alamo,' I said wearily. 'Just go where you're not known, and make sure you're not followed.'

'I'm going to call the police first.'

'I'd rather you didn't.'

'Yes, I'm sure. But this is a civilised country and I demand protection for my family.'

'They're not your family. They're mine,' I said.

I think I would have said a great deal more if he hadn't hung up on me.

I looked at the dead receiver in my hand, and thought of Terry's murder.

I could tell Louis a thing or two about being civilised.

But at least my wife's new husband had listened, and was going to do something about it.

Next I telephoned John Reid.

I tracked him down at his home. I explained the situation yet again, being careful to say nothing about Terry Southall. John agreed that a few days away for my family was the correct solution to the unimplied threats in the letter I had received. He asked for Louis' address so that he could liase with the local law on my behalf.

'Just make sure they're not followed,' I said finally.

'OK, I'll contact their local station as soon as I put the phone down.'

'At least Louis got the message and didn't panic,' I said thankfully.

'He sounds like a super chap, does old Louis,' said John.

'But as for you, you had to keep on didn't you? You had to mess with things that don't concern you.'

'That's just my way,' I replied.

'And look where it's got you. Up to your kid's armpits in hot water.'

'Sure, John, I think I get the picture.'

We were both silent for a moment.

'By the way,' he said, 'I'm glad you didn't mention my name when you spoke to Fox the other night.'

'Don't you mean when he spoke to me?' I asked. 'Anyway, I think he knew we'd seen each other.'

'That's too bad. It's none of his fucking business. I'm just glad you didn't tell him.'

'I'm a super chap too'.

'Yeah, if you weren't you'd be on your own now. Listen, check back with me later. I'll get straight onto this letter thing for you now. And don't worry, Laura and Judith will be alright. I guarantee it.'

'Cheers, John,' I said and put the phone down. It was then, as I sat alone in my office, afraid for my child's life, that I decided to get a gun.

20

I needed a weapon, and there was just one place I could think of where one might be available. Only it was a little too early in the day to make an appearance at that particular venue, seeing as the proprietor was famous in his neck of the woods for never showing his face until the streets were aired, as it were. So I went and collected the Pontiac and made my way to Clapham to have a few quiet beers in a little pub I know there. I had a lot to think about. I knew I wasn't being particularly smart. As a private investigator, I'd probably make a reasonable window cleaner, and earn more. I was hardly the Philip Marlowe of the inner city. I probably wouldn't be able to find the mean streets, let alone go down them.

Everyone had told me to get off the case, and everybody was probably right. But it just seemed too pat. I felt as if every move I made was pre-ordained. I was being manipulated at every turn, and I couldn't see where the manipulation was coming from. I felt like Pavlov's dog without a biscuit for my troubles.

Patsy Bright must have made some pretty heavy friends, or enemies; which, I didn't know. But I was determined to break the chain. Because only by doing so could I solve the mystery in which I was involved. I sat and drank, and came up with theories, and had another drink, and discarded them. Finally the bell for last orders interrupted my tangled thoughts. I finished my last drink and left the pub. I got into the car and drove to Clapham Junction. I parked the heap on a yellow line close to the market and walked through the crowds to Emerald's Club.

Now, a little about Emerald's. It's not the kind of establishment that you'd take your old mum to visit, unless of course your old mum is a raving piss artist. It's a rough little drinking club down at the end of a seedy alley close to the Junction station. There's only one reason to go there, and that's to get an alcoholic drink outside licensing hours. Apart from, that is, to fence a little bent gear, get laid by one of Emerald's young ladies, connect for some dope, plan a little villainy in private, or, as in my case, to purchase a gun without the formality of the license required by the law of this fair country of ours. It is not a nice place, believe me.

I made for the alleyway where the club was situated and walked down towards the blind end. The blank front of the crooked old building gave no indication that there was a jolly little afternoon drinking club within. An open door led to a flight of stairs that disappeared down into the basement. Once at the bottom there was another door. I could just make out the steady beat of music through it. Emerald's was open for business. Leaning against the second door was a huge black man dressed in a maroon track suit. His muscular arms and legs stretched the fabric almost to splitting point. He sported a modified afro and a gold earring. I showed him my most fetching smile.

'Good afternoon,' I said cheerfully.

'What the fuck do you want?' he demanded. Which was hardly the warm welcome I'd expected.

'I want to see Emerald,' I replied.

'Who?'

'Emerald,' I repeated.

'Never heard of him.'

'I think you have, and I think he's in there,' I said. Emerald had been holding court in his bar between three in the afternoon and eleven at night for the last twenty years to my certain knowledge. Although he would occasionally pop out for some nefarious business during that time, I didn't think he'd ever missed an opening or closing. The black man poked my chest with a forefinger the size of a small cucumber. I noticed that his fingernails were bitten down to the quicks.

'If I say I've never heard of him, I've never heard of him. You'd better believe me white boy. Now get the fuck away from here. We don't want you around.'

'Listen,' I said, still smiling. 'All I want you to do is to go inside and tell Emerald that Nick Sharman is here. Nick Sharman, got it? If he doesn't want to see me, fair enough. I'll turn right round and leave. But I do need to see him urgently, and I'm not going until he knows I'm here.'

'And if I don't?'

I looked at the huge man. His arms were as thick as my legs. I knew I had less chance of forcing my way past him that I had drinking soup with a fork. I was just fed up being pushed around. I wanted to push back a bit.

'There'll be a row,' I said. 'And the last thing I really want right now is a row, especially with you. But I promise you, if there is one you'll regret it. I'm not leaving unless Emerald says so.' The black man stared at me. I stared back. I thought he was going to smack me right in the mouth. There was nothing I could have done about it if he did, except fall over.

'What do you want with him?' he eventually asked.

'That's my business, but he'll want to see me,' I said, I hoped the bouncer was convinced, because I wasn't. He kept staring, then shrugged and turned and knocked heavily on the door. After a moment it was opened by another, equally large black man. That one had dreadlocks to his waist and wore a green, orange and black sweatsuit. Behind him I could clearly hear Ramsey Lewis belting out of the juke-box.

'Tell Emerald that Mick Sharman wants to see him,' the first bouncer said to the second.

'Nick,' I said.

The door was slammed shut on us and I heard a bolt click. The first black man pushed past me and looked up the stairs.

'This isn't a raid,' I said. He ignored me. The bolt clicked again on the other side of the door and it slowly opened. The second bouncer beckoned me to enter, and I passed into the inner room.

Emerald's club consisted of one huge cellar, which smelled in equal parts of clamp, cheap perfume and the odour of fish and chicken being cooked in the kitchen behind the bar.

The bar itself was L-shaped and made of polished mahogany. It ran for three quarters of the wall opposite the door which I entered. In the centre of the room was a pool table covered in blue baize. Against the right hand wall sat a massive Wurlitzer juke-box. It used to contain one of the finest sets of singles in London. There had been many a long afternoon spent feeding coins into its slot and listening to Otis and Aretha and their soul brothers and sisters wailing their hearts out. Along the left hand wall was a bank of fruit machines, the old fashioned kind with hundred pound payouts. None of the new electronic trash, where you need a degree in advanced electronics to win three nicker. These were one armed bandits, battered and chipped with use. Where there was room on the floor, a few lino topped tables and wobbly wooden chairs were clustered to form an eating area.

In the gap formed by the right angle of the bar, stood the other seats in the place. Two tall wooden bar stools with thick, red plush covers. The one nearest to me was empty, on the other perched the gross form of my old friend Samuel Watkins, aka Emerald, aka Em the Gem. In front of him, on the bar stood a white, push button telephone. Next to the telephone was a folded newspaper.

As it was early in the afternoon, there were few customers in the place. A man sat trying to eat fried chicken and smile at the same time and two Rastas were playing pool for their giro cheques, watched by a third one leaning against the juke-box and minding the stakes.

The second bouncer who had allowed me to enter, tossed his dreads like a debutante and closed the door behind me. The pool match stopped and the chicken eater paused with his mouth agape to check me out.

I walked over to where Emerald was sitting. He was a huge man. Quite how big, I'd forgotten, or else he'd been eating too many of the cook's fish dumplings since we'd last met. When Emerald stood, he was a shade over six foot tall and must have weighed close to twenty stone. His bulk was shoe-horned into the tightest, baddest, most stylish suit this side of the Motown Revue, 1964. It was a single breasted, grey, shot silk affair. The jacket was button free and very short with two tiny hacking vents at the back. The trousers were suffocatingly cut and were short enough to show an inch or two of black sock. His feet, which were incredibly small for such a big man, were laced into tiny, patent leather, pointed toed shoes. His shirt was violet with a tab collar with which he wore a narrow dark grey tie. On the little finger of his left hand was a gold ring that contained the biggest green stone I'd ever seen. Hence his nick-name.

'Still sharp, Em,' I said as I reached the bar.

He spun on his seat and opened his arms as if to embrace me. 'My man Nick,' he said. 'How are you?'

'Suffering, Em, suffering,' I replied.

'So you've come to Emerald's for some solace. A wise move my friend.' His face took on a serious expression. 'I've heard that bad things have happened to you Nicky. Why have you stayed away so long? I thought that friends stuck together in times of tribulation.'

Emerald's mother was a Baptist. She'd brought her boy up strictly by the good book. When he was drunk, Emerald could quote great chunks of the scripture verbatim. His speciality was the Book of Revelations. In another life he would have been a preacher, and a good one at that. 'Into every life a little rain must fall,' I said. 'And I'm fucking drowning.'

He laughed a good deep laugh.

'How's your little Judith?" he enquired. He'd had a soft spot for my little girl, since, when she'd been no more than a toddler I'd bought her up to see Father Christmas at a West End Store. On the way home I'd stopped off at the club for a well deserved drink, being trampled on by hordes of weeny-boppers not being my idea of a fun afternoon.

She'd totally taken over the place. The language from the punters would have graced a Sunday school outing. The girls had fussed over her like a princess and Emerald had sent out for enough toys and sweets to sink the Titanic. At first Judith had been wary of the big black man. Then he'd shown her the ring he wore on his finger. I've never seen him take it off before or since, but he gave it to the child to hold. She was fascinated by the way the stone reflected a thousand lights into her eyes. Within thirty minutes she was curled up asleep in Emerald's lap grasping the ring in her tiny fist. Before we left I had to prize it from her. Of course Laura had gone crazy that I'd taken Judith into 'a den of thieves' as my dear wife described the club. But when I remembered how my little girl had looked snuggled up against the big man's jacket, I knew I could trust her with him any time.

'She's not so little now,' I answered. 'And she's fine.' I didn't want to go into details for a while.

'It's good to see you, Nick. But I can tell you are very troubled,' Emerald said.

'You're right Em,' I replied. 'I've got a few problems.'

'You know I'll help if I can, but first let me get you a drink. I find a drink in my hand always helps with mine, and believe me, I've got plenty too.'

I looked over at the dread-locked bouncer who was leaning, arms crossed by the door.

'I see you've bought in some muscle to help you solve them,' I said. 'You used to be more discreet in the old days.'

'I need obvious muscle these troubled times. Things have changed around here since we last met. Now, what about that drink?'

'What've you got?' I asked.

'Same old stuff.' Emerald's had never been noted for its long wine list. I opted for a light rum and Coke. Emerald gestured to the girl behind the bar, who was hovering just out of earshot. No-one liked to be accused of eavesdropping on the boss of Emerald's.

'White rum and Coke for my friend, and the same for me,' Emerald called. She brought us two large drinks then moved back to the far end of the bar and began polishing glasses whilst watching the pool game that had recommenced. I walked over to the juke-box and picked out a few good tunes to keep the noise level up, so that Em and I could talk in private. I chose some Four Tops, Thelma Houston and a selection of Blue Note 45's that Emerald had picked up somewhere. The opening bars of 'The Preacher' helped to lower my stress level a little. Then I went back to join the big man.

'Nice stuff, Em,' I said. 'Been going round the jumbles again?'

'French imports,' he replied. 'Expensive, but worth every penny.'

The sound of Jimmy Smith's Hammond swirled through the club.

'Still the old mod, aren't you?' It was as much a statement as a question.

'Always, my friend, always,' he replied with a giant grin.

We sat for a while in silence, as old friends can, sipping our drinks and listening to the jazz. I leaned over and picked up the paper lying on the bar. It was the early edition of that day's 'Standard'. It was folded back to the racing pages. I re-folded it so that I could see the front page. T S's murder was headline news. **'HEADLESS BODY HORROR'** read the banner headlines. I carefully placed my hands face down on the bar to still the shakes. I scanned the story. The hard information was sparse.

Apparently an anonymous call had been made to Scotland Yard. It must have been just after I arrived. The nameless girl was in hospital suffering from shock. The police were waiting to interview her. One unidentified man had fled the scene on foot. That must have been me. Terry's past had been dredged up briefly. Fashion designer, fashion photographer, war correspondent, a smattering about his capture, then the fact that he was a GLC funded drugs counsellor. Finally the reporter started guessing. 'Drug murder.' 'Ritual slaying.' Because the killing had taken place in Brixton all sorts of innuendo was allowed. I ignored it, I knew better. Only the last sentence worried me. It read:

'Police are anxious to contact Precious Smith, who worked at the drug centre with Southall. It is understood she may have relevant information about the murder.'

I guessed Precious had done a quick runner. She hadn't struck me as someone who'd welcome police enquiries. Stay away Presh, I thought, and if they do catch up with you, forget I ever existed.

I folded the paper again and tossed it across the bar. When I looked up Emerald was staring hard at me.

'Don't ask, Em,' I said.

'I won't,' he replied. 'But I thought I recognised the name.'

'Put it out of your mind.'

'He's been here, yeah? With you?'

'Forget it.'

'Bad news.'

'You said it.'

We sat in silence again, but a subtly different silence. The bar was beginning to fill up as the afternoon progressed. I sat and watched as the crowd grew and drank and gossiped and checked out the only white man in the place. Finally Emerald broke the silence again. 'Nicky, my boy,' he said, 'you've been absent for a long time. Now you've come in all uptight and trying to be cool and hide it.'

I flashed him a warning glance. 'OK, OK,' he admonished, putting a giant hand on mine to placate me. 'I'm not saying anything about that.' He tapped the paper. 'It's just that I've missed you since you became a stranger, and I don't think this visit is for old times' sake.'

'It's not entirely,' I replied. 'But even if it was, you make it very hard to get in here these days. Your man at the door said you didn't exist.'

Gales of laughter shook Em's huge frame.

'I know man,' he said. 'We don't get many honkeys,' he put a long inflection on the last word, 'down here now. You're too much trouble. Too many fights, and the girls said there was a lot of bad mouthing going on. And you change the subject too quick for us poor darkies.'

I ignored the last comment and said, 'Still girls, eh Em?'

'But naturally,' he replied. 'The old place wouldn't be the same without them. Stay awhile and meet the new faces.' He paused. 'And get re-acquainted with the old.'

'Anyone in particular?' I asked.

'Don't bullshit me Nick. You know who I mean.'

'I've no time for that today Emerald.'

He was silent again, then he said, 'I can't help unless I know what the trouble is. Don't you trust me any more?'

'Of course I do,' I replied, then reluctantly told him something of my story. I briefly mentioned T S, and was a bit more detailed about the letter concerning Judith. When I had finished the edited highlights he sat and regarded me gravely.

'You have got big troubles,' he said quietly. 'But what can I do about them?'

'Get me a gun.'

'Hey man, who are you kidding? Don't give me that gun shit.' He laughed with his mouth, but his eyes were cold.

'I'm deadly serious,' I said in a low voice.

'Guns aren't my style no more. I told you things have changed.'

'For the worst, Emerald. There's at least one blood in here right now, tooled up,.' Emerald rolled his eyes. 'Don't kid a kidder,' I continued. 'I know your form my friend, remember? One of the main reasons you've stayed open so long is because the CID know exactly who to keep an eye on.'

'But not no more,' Emerald interrupted. 'I told you I'm clean.'

'About as clean as a used Durex. Now are you going to get me a shooter or not?'

Emerald changed his tack and got offended all of a sudden. 'You hurt me Nick,' he said. 'Coming in here and talking about offing people before you've finished your first drink. It's not friendly.'

'Who said anything about offing people?' I asked. I could get offended too.

'You don't have to. The look on your face when you read that paper was enough. And even if it hadn't been, what the hell do you want a gun for? Swatting flies? They must be growing bluebottles as big as horses round your way.'

I took his point. 'It's for self defence,' I said.

'Not even for that, not any more,' he said. 'But listen, don't go away mad. I've got some calls to make, then we'll get drunk like in the old days.'

'The old days have gone, Emerald, haven't you heard. Now times are hard. Old friends should stick together, so don't brush me off.'

He leaned over and gently tapped me on the chest. His ring sparkled in the lights. 'You've got no juice now Nick,' he said. 'Not being the law and all. We're still friends, but only as long as you stay cool. So just lighten up and everything will be fine.'

I dug my fingers into his upper arm. Under the fat was hard muscle. I squeezed as hard as I could. I saw just a little pain behind his dark eyes.

'Em,' I said. 'Don't make me tell tales. I may have no juice now, but I know some of your juicy secrets.'

'Yesterday's papers,' he scoffed, and shrugged my hand off.

'We can always find out can't we?' I asked. 'Why don't you let me make some calls? I think I can remember the number of Lavender Hill nick.'

'Don't threaten me Sharman, not in my own place, or you'll be carried out on a plank.'

'Just don't fuck me about Em. In the last couple of days, I've been spat on, shat on, lied to and beaten. Now someone is threatening my daughter.' I paused as I realised it wasn't the black man's fault that I was being got at, and I shouldn't take it out on him. 'Christ Em.' I said. 'What the hell's going on?' We're old friends who've been apart for too long and we're threatening each other. It's my fault, I'm sorry. This thing is driving me crazy.'

I smiled a tight smile and put my hand on his arm, but gently that time.

Dreadlocks suddenly appeared beside me. 'Is everything cool Boss?' he asked, giving me a vicious look.

'Everything's mellow D,' replied Em. 'Just a little disagreement. Get back to work Josh, and if I hear about anyone carrying a shooter in here again, you'll be down the Job Centre double quick. You and that goon outside. I employ you for security, not to look at your pretty faces.'

Josh slunk away with his tail between his legs, meanwhile Em turned back to me and said, 'I understand your predicament. Friends are friends and you did right to come to me. Just relax and have another drink.'

After we'd been served Em sat and looked through me for a while. I sat and watched the clientele enjoying themselves. The place was pretty packed by then. I recognised one or two of the drinkers, but most were strangers to me. Two of Em's girls came over to say hello. They flirted with me for a minute or so, then Em dismissed them with a flick of his fat hand.

'Got any cash, Nick?' he asked.

'I'm about as poor as a lost dog,' I replied.

'What do you want then? The loan of a shooter?'

'Whatever it takes, I'll get,' I told him.

He thought for a moment, then decided.

'I can't call from here,' he said, 'because walls have ears, and some phones have ears too. Have you got a number that I can contact you on later tonight?'

I gave him my home number written on the back of one of my cards.

'Be there when I call, or all bets are off.'

I told him I'd be there all evening and left the club. On the way out I saw Em's two girls again. They waved and giggled at me. I waved and giggled back.

I took a takeaway Chicken Madras back to the flat. I thought about Cat. I hoped he was making out alright as I hadn't had a chance to feed him lately. I hardly tasted the food and left most of it to congeal in the foil container.

I tried Laura's number, but there was no reply. I prayed that she and Judith, and Louis too for that matter, were safe. John Reid had gone to ground too. I spoke to his wife, but she had no idea of his whereabouts. I didn't tell her who was calling. I had no need of instant nostalgia. Finally I checked with George Bright. I had no luck there either.

21

I paced the floor and kept peering through the curtains. I felt frustrated and angry. Finally, just before nine, as it was getting dark, the phone rang. It was Emerald.

'Hello, Nicky,' he said. 'Are you alright?'

'Just fine Emerald. What's the story?'

'I've got a little something for you. Are you going to be home for a while?'

I told him I was staying put. I didn't tell him, however, that Old Bill might drop around with a few questions about a certain body found in a bathroom in Brixton. Why spoil what might turn out to be a pleasant evening?

'What's your address there?' he asked.

I told him.

'Is there space for me to drive in?' he enquired.

I took the phone over to the window and looked down onto the square of tarmac that we, the proud owners of the plaster-board separated dwelling units, euphemistically referred to as the drive.

Only one of the other occupants of the house owned a car. It was parked neatly on the front. There was ample room for another vehicle to sit next to it.

'It looks fine,' I said, and explained the layout of the house.

'Right,' said Emerald. 'I'll be there in about half an hour. I'll drive straight in. Keep an eye out for me.'

'What do you drive these days?' I asked. I'd have bet money on it being a white BMW.

'A BMW,' he replied.

'What colour?'

'Black.'

Close, I thought, but no cigar.

'Seven series?' I asked.

'How did you know?'

'It's my job.'

He chuckled down the phone. 'Just keep an eye out,' he said, and hung up.

It was more like an hour before he arrived, and fully dark. I saw the big, black car crawl up the street, then stop and reverse into the driveway. I ran downstairs and let myself out of the front door. Emerald had switched off the engine and the lights of the car. It sat in front of me as shiny and black as a giant cockroach. The night was silent except for the ticking from the engine as it cooled in the still air. For a swift moment I was grabbed by panic. I was perfectly placed for a trap. I bent and looked through the rear window. Emerald's silver grey suit softly gleamed in the glow from the street lamps. The rest of the car seemed to be empty, so I relaxed. I hated being so paranoid, but it came with the territory.

I moved to the driver's side of the car. The window slid silently down on its electric runners. Emerald stuck his big, smiley face through the gap.

'Hi Nicky,' he said. 'Sorry I'm a bit late.'

'No problem, Em, what have you got for me?'

'Be patient, man,' he said as he opened the door and eased his great bulk out of the car. I noticed that the courtesy light had been switched off. I was glad that the big man was on my side. He gestured for me to go to the back of the car. He unlocked the boot and gently raised the lid. A dim light lit the interior, but as the car was facing into the street we were shielded from the gaze of anyone passing by. I looked back at the house. It was all quiet. Everyone was busy with News at Ten. I peered over Emerald's shoulder into the boot. It was empty except for a bulky black garbage sack. The twin of the one hidden in my freezer containing the picture I had peeled from Terry's body earlier that day. I suppressed a shudder at the thought.

'Check it out,' said Em, barely able to contain his high spirits.

I opened the top of the sack, and peeled the plastic back. It contained a real goodie. In the faint yellow glow from the boot light I saw the pistol grip of a shotgun. I pulled the weapon out and realised I was holding a Franchi Spas 12 bore, with a folding stock. It was no longer than two feet, and with its bulbous cartridge feed slung under the short barrel was a very tasty shooter.

'For fuck's sake, Em,' I said. 'This is heavy duty.'

'Sweet, ain't it?' he replied.

I pushed the gun back into the sack.

'I'll check it out later, in private,' I said.

'That ain't all,' he said. I rooted further into the bag and discovered three heavy cardboard boxes.

'Check that one,' said Emerald, and pointed at the largest of the three. I opened the box and discovered a short barrelled revolver. It had a black rubber grip and the metal parts were slick with oil. 'Colt Cobra,' said Em proudly. 'Chambered for .38 calibre. It's brand new, never been fired.'

'You're a marvel, my friend,' I breathed. 'What's in the other boxes?'

'Shells for the shotgun, and fifty rounds for the Colt.'

'How much?' I asked.

'Have them on me Nicky,' he said, then grabbed my arm until the muscles cramped. 'But no more fucking favours, understand. We're still friends, but we're all square now. And if you ever tell anyone where these weapons came from,' he drew his finger across his throat, 'you're dead meat.'

'I can dig it, old buddy,' I said as I picked up the sack from the floor of the boot.

'Families are sacred, my man,' said Emerald. 'And any son-of-a-bitch who involves them in business deserves all he gets. Come and tell me what happened when it's all over, if I don't see it on TV first.' He giggled, slammed the boot lid, sashayed around to the driver's door and got into the car. He looked back out of the window when he had the engine fired up.

'Teresa came in after you left. She was sorry she missed you. She told me to tell you to keep safe and come back and see her soon. She said she's never forgotten you.'

The window hummed shut and he drove off the forecourt, turned into the street, and with a faint squeal of tyres, away into the night. I took the sack upstairs, reassured by it's weight and spent the rest of the night cleaning and dry-firing the guns and thinking about Teresa.

Her name was a real blast from the past. Teresa Monette was a coffee coloured beauty who worked out of Emerald's club. She was tall, nearly as tall as me in her spike-heeled shoes. Her eyes were the biggest I've ever seen. They swam in the whites like black olives in twin bowls of milk. Her hair was a kinky mass that exploded from her scalp and cascaded down her back like a waterfall of pure jet. Her face and figure were enough to make the most hardened sinner repent and reach for his Bible.

I first met her when I was spending an afternoon drowning

my sorrows at the club. We liked each other immediately, and she ignored her potential customers to keep me company over a bottle of gin. I was intrigued that such an obviously intelligent woman was making her living selling her body. When I approached the subject she scornfully told me to mind my own business. Quite right too. I never mentioned the subject again. We spent hours that day talking about books, music and cooking. At the latter I was to discover she was an expert. I made it my business, over the subsequent months to keep a protective eye on her. Not that she really needed it. Emerald and his boys were her minders. She walked proudly through the nether-world that she inhabited. The girls who formed Emerald's team were safer walking the streets of South London than most straight women. I'm not endorsing the system, but if one of the girls was hassled, they didn't go running to the law. Emerald took care of business and there were no suspended sentences from his little firm. More than one John who'd turned a bit nasty had been dumped outside St. Tommy's with a multiple fracture.

It's even rumoured, and who am I to disbelieve a tasty rumour, that when a certain stretch of derelict dockland is turned into the British Disneyland and the contractors dredge the quiet, still waters, they'll find more than one or two cars sunk there with all the windows open and corpses roped securely to the steering wheels.

Teresa turned out to be the proverbial tart with a heart, and believe me there's not many of them about, no matter what you see on TV. Or perhaps she just turned out to be a good friend. I must admit that when things got really desperate between Laura and me, there were times when I took comfort between Teresa's slim thighs. Often I fell asleep with my head supported on her breasts, my drunken tears wetting her soft, dark skin.

But that was before I went strange and started living like a monk. I knew that the sight of us holding hands across a table, over the sizzle-grilled prawns in some quiet Chinese restaurant caused many a raised eyebrow and a cynical laugh amongst other members of the force. But I couldn't have cared less. When I'd started getting into drugs, Teresa had tried to help me. It was ironic, a total reversal of the expected roles. The whore trying to straighten out the copper. It was a hopeless task. The last time I'd seen her was just before I resigned. She came to visit me after I'd been shot. She bought me a bunch of white roses. She wanted to get into bed with me, and I wanted her to. The sister in charge of the ward had interrupted us, and regretfully we'd pulled apart from each other. Sister had hovered around with a disapproving look on her face until Teresa left. We hadn't met since. I was glad that she remembered me. I hoped that if I could get out of my present situation, Teresa and I could meet again.

22

So I was armed, but just with guns, not knowledge. I felt as if I'd been lost in a fast shuffle and been made to look like a complete fool. Two years off the streets had reduced my suss quotient to zero. I slept late on Thursday morning, or at least I lay in bed late and stared up at the fine cracks in the ceiling above me. When I was a kid in my little room at home, I'd imagined that they were the frontiers of vast continents that I would someday conquer. That morning they seemed to be maps of roads that led nowhere fast.

I eventually dragged myself out of bed and showered and shaved. Whilst I was in the shower I shampooed my hair and removed the sticking plasters from the cut on my head. There was still a sizeable lump, but the wound was scabbing over and seemed to be healing satisfactorily.

The morning was misty, but I could see the sun trying to break through, and the weatherman on the radio told me to expect an August day of uninterrupted sunshine. With that in mind I decided to give blue jeans the elbows for once. I pulled on a rather natty pair of Armani strides in a muted blue check and teamed them with a pale blue, long sleeved chambray workshirt. I found my navy espadrilles under the bed and wore them sans socks. I admired my bad self in the mirror and felt prepared for whatever the day might bring. Of course I was wrong, but why spoil a perfect record.

I tried phoning Laura, but there was no reply. I actually felt hungry for a change and cooked myself a pan of scrambled eggs. I boogied around the tiny kitchen and sang along with the radio as I prepared the food. For some reason I was feeling good, although God alone knew why. I should have been depressed, but I didn't fight the mood, just rolled with the flow.

I sat at the little breakfast bar that separated the kitchen from the living room and ate my food and drank three cups of tea. At eleven the telephone rang. It was Laura. She sounded distant in both senses of the word.

'Are you alright?' I asked with relief at the sound of her voice.

'Yes, but no thanks to you,' she replied.

'Leave it out Laura, please,' I said exasperatedly. 'I'll get dizzy from ducking the ricochets.'

She was silent, and I listened to the crackling on the line.

'Yes Nick, we're all OK.' She heavily underlined the 'all'.

'Where are you?' I asked.

'In a hotel,' she replied.

'Where?'

'Does it matter?'

'Not really. If you don't want to tell me, don't. Just as long as you're alright. How's Judith?'

'She's fine. She thinks she's on a mystery tour, and in a way I suppose she's right.'

'And Louis?' I enquired.

'This is not a social call Nick. I just phoned to settle your mind.

Your friend asked me to.'

'Who? John?'

'Yes,' she replied.

'Good, I'm glad he was useful. I spoke to him yesterday,' I said.

'He was unusually helpful for a policeman,' she commented. Once again I could tell the word hurt her. She'd never forgiven my job for coming between us, as she always put it. I would have thought by then, with all the free dental care, she'd be grateful.

'Did Louis get in touch with the local police?' I asked.

'Yes, they weren't very pleased with you apparently. Hasn't anyone been to see you?'

'No, John said he'd liase for me. That probably ruffled a few feathers. I've had enough of Old Bill.'

'So have I, believe me.'

'So everything's alright. You're sure no-one followed you?'

'I'm sure. We borrowed a car from one of Louis' friends. We all met up at some motorway services and switched cars in the petrol station. Then we went back down the motorway and changed over to B-roads. I think Louis quite enjoyed it.'

'This isn't Starsky and Hutch, Laura,' I warned. 'This is serious.'

'I know Nick, we're taking it seriously.' I could almost feel warmth in her voice. Just like in the old days, before things went sour. Then she remembered herself. 'I've got to go. Louis is waiting,' she said.

'Be careful now, and keep in touch. Give my love to Judy,' I managed to say before she hung up without another word. Perhaps she'd heard the warmth too, and decided to put me back in my usual cold place. Still, what had I expected? A declaration of undying love? They'd gone out of the window when I joined the CID.

As soon as I put the phone down it rang again. My, but I was popular that morning. It was John Reid on the line. 'Good morning

Nick,' he said. 'I see you're keeping bankers' hours these days. Has good old George Bright come up with another sub?'

'George fired me two days ago,' I replied.

'Oh really, what a wise man. So business is slow?'

'Business is out of the window, John. It's down to me now. George Bright doesn't figure in it any more. He was history the minute I got that note about Judith.'

'That's what I'm calling about,' said John, in an official tone. 'The shit's really hit the air conditioners about that. I tried to keep it as quiet as possible, but Louis the Lip was on the blower to his local nick the minute he finished talking to you yesterday. Fox got wind of it, and believe me he's doing his pieces up here. It's a good job you don't fall under Brixton jurisdiction, or you'd have been back for another little natter last night. Rubber hose job, I wouldn't be surprised. As it is Streatham CID aren't your biggest fans.'

He was dead right. It was just as well the local law hadn't called round for a little chat. They might have bumped into Em and me with handfuls of illegal arms and ammunition. That would have given Fox food for thought.

'Bollocks to them,' I said. 'What was I supposed to do? Go and tell the Station Sergeant? Get in the queue with all the wallies reporting their missing dogs? Or that someone's nicked the milk off the front step?'

'That's beside the point,' John continued. 'I've put myself on the line for you again. Christ alone knows why. And as yet, nobody's seen this famous threatening letter. I supposed it does exist?'

'What do you think?' I asked disgustedly. 'That I invented the sodding thing, then got Louis to take the girls off for a trip in the country for fun? You must think I'm really mental. Of course it exists. It's here now.'

'I want it,' said John, as if I hadn't spoken. 'I've been told to handle it myself. And that's over the head of the DI at Streatham. He's not well pleased. There's been a lot of talk about special treatment for an ex-copper who left the force under ... how can I put it? Rather dodgy circumstances.'

'I don't care how you put it John, just as long as Judith is safe.'

'I hope the press don't get hold of this,' he remarked.

'Fuck them too.'

'Alright, big man,' he interrupted. 'We all know how tough you are. Just do me a favour and shut up. Now I want to see you with the letter.'

'Where?' I asked. I'd rarely been able to impress John.

'Right, do you remember when we used to go drinking in Waterloo?'

'Yes.'

'Remember the pub we used in the market?'

'Yeah, the Spanish whatsname?'

'That's right, The Spanish Patriot.'

'Of course I remember it.'

'Good, meet me there in an hour, and don't forget the letter.'

'That's a bit of a rough old pub, isn't it?'

'Who are you then? Little Boy Blue? It's not rough now. The brewery have done it up.'

'It's not a continental style brasserie pub, is it?' I asked suspiciously.

'You're never happy are you? Of course it's not. That's hardly my style is it? It's fine, believe me. Be there in an hour.'

'Alright,' I said, then he hung up on me too. I wondered why no-one said goodbye any more.

I pottered around for a while, washing up my breakfast things and making the bed. After half an hour of domestic chores, I got ready to leave the house. I put the letter in the inside pocket of a white, double breasted jacket, and as an afterthought, slipped the Colt Cobra into one of the side pockets. I hoped it wouldn't pull the material or leave any nasty, oily stains.

I felt in an even better mood knowing Laura and Judith were safe. I drove slowly and carefully to Waterloo, over Denmark Hill and down the Walworth Road. East Street Market was as busy as usual and I amused myself by looking at the South London girls in their summer dresses.

There were some real beauties about that morning. The sun had brought them out like exotic flowers. They were taking advantage of the glorious day by showing off their new schmutter. I felt a twinge of guilt about feeling so good. I'd seen an old friend mutilated not forty eight hours previously, but I could forget about him and enjoy the weather. That's just human nature. I'm not going to apologise for it. Nothing I could do would bring him back so I continued eyeing up the women on the street. My libido was back with a vengeance.

I got to Waterloo within the hour and drove down to Lower Marsh Market to meet John. The pub we used to drink in had always been a bit under the arm, but now it had been tarted up and turned into a 'Victorian Parlour', whatever the hell that was.

I parked neatly between two vans unloading goods onto the stalls.

Because the market sold mainly clothes and electrical items, it didn't really get started until lunch-time when the office workers came out to play, so there was still some space at the kerbside. I grabbed my jacket from the back seat and got out of the car. As I was locking up, a little guy in glasses sidled up to me.

'You can't park that there,' he said, with a disparaging look at the state of the the Pontiac. 'There's somebody coming in to unload in a minute.'

'There's room,' I pointed out politely.

'No mate, he always parks there.'

'Tough,' I made as if to walk away.

'Yes mate, tough on you. He won't like it.'

'Who is he then? King Kong?' I asked. The little man didn't crack his face.

'Worse,' he said.

I knew what he was after. 'Listen, son,' I said, and reached into my jacket pocket for a quid to tip him to take care of the car. I knew the markets and it was worth parting with a coin for no hassle. As I fumbled in one pocket, the Colt dropped neatly out of the other and landed with a clatter on the pavement between us. We both stared at the gun on the ground for a heartbeat of time. Luckily there was no-one passing, and luckier still, because the Pontiac was left hand drive I'd exited on the pavement side and the bodywork of the car shielded the sight of the gun from the shoppers on the other side of the road. The little guy looked at the gun, then me, then the gun again. I thought he was going to salute.

'Don't worry sir,' he said. 'You park here, I'll take personal care of your car. It'll be my pleasure.'

I nearly laughed out loud. I didn't know who looked the bigger twat, him or me.

'Just make sure you do,' I said, and bent down and scooped the pistol up, then tucked it into the waistband of my trousers. I put on my jacket and buttoned it to hide the gun from view. 'Or I'll come looking for you.'

'No problem, Guv,' he said. 'Trust me, leave it here for as long as you like.' Then he turned and almost ran across the street. I would have to be more careful in future. The bloody gun could have gone off. I might even have shot myself in the other foot.

I strolled into the boozer. Things certainly had changed there. What had once been spit and sawdust, had been converted to oak and velour. I saw John straight away, sitting at the bar on a stool and reading the morning paper.

'Hello John,' I said. He looked up from his copy of The Sun. 'Still reading the quality press, I see.'

John looked me up and down. 'Christ Nick, what are you wearing? You look like a bloody waiter in that jacket.' He stared at my feet.

'Can't you wear your socks, who do you think you are? Boy George?'

'Very satirical John,' I replied.

'What do you want to drink?' he asked.

I opted for a lager top, and waited for the landlady to pull the pint. I could see what attraction the place held for John. The woman serving the beer was big and brunette. She must have stood nearly six foot tall in her heels. She possessed a voluptuous figure, well strapped in, but I could imagine what she looked like when she loosened her corsets.

'Brenda,' said John. 'This is Nick Sharman, he used to be on the force.'

'Charmed,' said Brenda, with a big, red lipped smile. When she opened her mouth to speak, I noticed that her teeth were stained pink with lipstick.

'Hello,' I said. 'This place has changed since I was last here. What happened to Dot and Tom?' I was referring to the couple who had run the pub when I used to visit it regularly.

'They took a place by the sea,' replied big Brenda. 'A nice little retirement cottage in Bournemouth.'

She put my pint in front of me and John paid her. I took a sip of the sweet, cold mixture. Brenda would have continued chatting I'm sure, but John growled 'Business,' and led me over to a quiet table close to the door of the pub.

'I can see what the attraction is here, John,' I said. 'I bet old Brenda puts it about a bit.'

'I wouldn't know,' replied John severely.

'Oh yeah, I believe you. I bet you've had afters here a few times, and some main course too. What does she look like naked?' I asked with a grin. 'I reckon she's white all over. Is that her natural hair colour? She looks like she might be ginger to me.'

'Shut up Nick, will you? I haven't got all day. Where's this letter?' I reached into my pocket and pulled out the typewritten note. John took it from me, carefully by the edge of the envelope. A real pro.

'I suppose you've put your dirty paw prints all over it?' he asked.

'Yeah, I suppose I have. At the time I didn't know it was evidence. I'm not psychic and I can't read through envelopes.'

John ignored my attempts at insolence, read the note carefully several times, then folded it neatly and put it into a plastic bag which he took from his pocket.

'Have you heard from Laura?' he asked.

'Yes,' I replied. 'She called this morning, just before you did.'

'Did she tell you where she was?'

'No, she wouldn't say.'

'Good.'

'I suppose that was your idea?'

He said nothing.

'Do you know?' I enquired.

'Yes.'

'Great, they always say the husband is the last to know.'

'You're not her husband, Louis is.'

'Really John, thanks for the newsflash,' I said petulantly.

'Don't get uptight with me Nick, just because you're still in love with your ex-wife.'

I began to protest, but he cut me off with a sharp gesture of his hand. 'There's no point arguing. I don't care one way or the other,' he continued. 'Anyway, you're wasting your time. I told her to tell no-one where she was, and that includes you. Especially on the phone. He suddenly changed the subject. 'Who do you think wrote the letter?' he asked.

'It's obvious,' I replied. 'The bastards I met in Brixton. The ones that gave me this.' I put my hand to the back of my head. 'Any news on them by the way?'

'Not a lot,' John replied. 'The whole place was covered in prints.

Nothing we could use. It was just a crash pad and shooting gallery for every junkie in the area. You should have seen the state of the mattress in that girl's room.' He made a face full of disgust at the human condition.

'I went back,' I said.

'Did you now?' He looked at me through slitted eyes. 'You're a fucking glutton for punishment, aren't you?'

I went on, ignoring the look. 'I met a bloke called Steve, who lived downstairs, on the ground floor at the back. He told me that Patsy Bright was into heavy dealing.'

'Of what?' John looked interested suddenly.

'Serious stuff,' I continued. 'Skag and Charlie, mainly.'

'Was he stoned when he told you?'

'Yes.'

'There you go then. You're so gullible, you'll believe anything you want to believe. I went back too, yesterday, and the place was empty. Whoever you spoke to has done a runner. I suppose you frightened him off. Get a bit physical did you? That's about your speed. Beating up on wigged out junkies.'

'Fuck me John,' I said. 'I can't do anything right, can I?'

'Not a lot,' he replied. 'Just get innocent people into trouble.'

'There are no innocent people left,' I said darkly. I could feel a shadow over my previous good mood.

'Where did you read that?' he asked sarcastically.

I didn't bother to reply. We sat and drank and John lit a cigarette. After a minute had dragged its feet by, he spoke again. 'I want you to lie low for a while. Leave all this to me and the force. You're becoming very unpopular again. I'm not joking. There's a lot of talk about giving you a taste of porridge. Memories are long down at the nick, and tempers are short. If it wasn't for the fact that I feel responsible for you, I'd let you sink. Now for the last time, stay out of sight, and mind your own business. Your family is safe and you're off the Bright case. Can't you just vanish for a week or so? Go and visit your Mum or someone.'

'Perhaps you're right, John,' I said wearily. But I knew I was in until the bitter end.

'Just do it,' he said, and finished his drink with one swallow. 'I'm off now, but I'll be in touch. It would be best all round if I can't find you.'

'OK John,' I said. 'Take it easy.'

He stood and left the bar with a wave to big Brenda, who simpered back across the pumps.

As he went I realised I was beginning to wonder about him. He hadn't said one word about T S's murder. Not one word.

23

I finished my drink slowly, thinking about what John had said to me. Eventually, I too left the pub. I received a brief nod from Brenda as I went. Obviously I wasn't her type. I went out into the hot street. The temperature was still rising, but I felt none of my previous good humour. The market was in full swing and more trucks had arrived to unload. The little man was standing by the Pontiac, directing traffic around it.

'Perfect,' I whispered into his ear.

'Oh, hello Guv,' he said with a start. 'There you go, no one's blocking you in, see.'

'Thanks,' I said. 'Do you want a drink?'

'No, no. It's my pleasure.'

'What happened to the geezer who usually parks here, then?' I asked.

'He's alright, he's over there, well happy with himself. I put him straight,' the little man said, gesturing vaguely in no particular direction.

'See how easy it was,' I remarked. 'I'll look out for you again.'

His face went slightly green and he swallowed. 'Anytime, Guv, you just find me and I'll take care of your motor. Robbo's the name.'

'Alright, Robbo,' I said, and bared my teeth in an approximation of a smile. I unlocked the Pontiac and climbed behind the wheel. I buckled myself into the seat harness, then started the car and it roared into life with the usual gush of black smoke from the exhausts. I put her into gear and drove slowly through the crowds.

Now before we go any further, let me explain a little of the geography of the Lower Marsh to those of you who've never done a bit of shopping down there. It's a fairly long, narrow thoroughfare that runs east to west between the back entrance of Waterloo Station and Westminster Bridge Road. It is split almost evenly into two one-way sections going in opposite directions. You can enter the street by car from either the Waterloo or the Westminster end, but it's impossible to leave the Marsh from either end legally. The only way out is down little Frazier Street, an extremely narrow little road, which acts as a filter from the market into Bayliss Road that runs roughly parallel with the Lower Marsh. Confused? Don't worry about it, so are most of the drivers who get caught up in the system. It's a bit like squeezing a cream doughnut from both ends at the same time. Everything shoots out of the middle.

I was driving from the Waterloo end of the street. I had to stop at a white line, then hang a left away from the market. Any cars coming from the Westminster end would be facing me. I noticed one in particular. A bright red Ford Capri with a power bulge on its bonnet was parked on the corner of the Marsh and Frazier Street. Two men were sitting in the front seats. With a shock I recognised them as the two white men from the Brixton squat. The blonde and flared trousers. The latter was in the driver's seat. They must have followed me from home. Whilst I was doodling through the traffic, trying to look up bimbos' skirts, they'd been tailing me to see what I was up to. That was really going too far.

As I slowed to make my left turn, the fat man started the engine of the Capri. I pulled into Frazier Street and the Capri followed me. I drove slowly down the street which was only one car wide because of all the market cars parked by the right hand kerb. I kept one eye on the interior rear-view mirror and saw the blonde poke one arm and his head out of the passenger window of the red car. He was holding something in his hand. Suddenly the mirror on the Pontiac's right wing exploded with a crash of broken glass and twisted metal. The bastard had shot at me. So much for John's advice to lie low. Yes son, I thought, tell me about it.

I floored the accelerator of the Trans Am and felt her fish tail, then the wide drive wheels gripped the road and she took off like a rocket. I smashed the gear stick into second and swung left into Bayliss Road, heading east with a screech of rubber. The Capri was right behind me. I headed down towards the Old Vic and when I saw that the lights were green at the junction with Waterloo Road, I pushed the fast pedal even further to the floor. Charlie had warned me about the sluggish behaviour of the big car below forty miles per hour, but the car accelerated like a greyhound. I shot across the lights into the Cut. I snicked the gear lever into third and felt a satisfying response from the big engine. The Capri was close behind but losing ground. It was just like driving a squad car in the old days. I started to recite the road conditions out loud, as I had done when I'd been taking a police driving course.

'Lights coming up,' I said. 'Red.'

I decelerated and banged the gear stick into second again. The car slowed without the benefit of brakes. With the sort of BHP that baby had, I didn't need to use them. The Capri came up fast behind me. I spun the power assisted steering wheel hard to the left to make a turn into the Hatfields to avoid stopping at the lights. I hit a puddle of water and spray covered the windscreen. Without thinking I pushed the wiper button to clear my view.

There was a Telecom van approaching me and blocking the road, so I powered up onto the pavement and screeched around it. I took a chance that no-one was coming around the blind bend under the railway bridge towards me, so I just hit the horn and prayed. Charlie had fitted one that played the first five bars of 'Dixie'. What a wanker. Some twerp in a Datsun Cherry tried to pull out of Joan Street in front of me. I touched the horn again and saw his terrified face as he juddered to a halt, halfway across the road. The Hatfields was clear for half a mile in front of me. I accelerated through the gears and realised that I was fast approaching Stamford Street, which meant a continuous stream of traffic, unless someone was using the zebra which crossed the road just to the east of the junction towards which I was heading.

I could only see moving traffic in front of me. The Capri was tight on my tail again, and the blonde leaned out of the window and fired once more. I saw a puff of smoke and flame from the barrel of the gun in the mirror. Nothing seemed to hit the Pontiac, but I huddled down in my padded seat nevertheless. I wished for a miracle and slammed down on the brake pedal. The tyres caught, slid, then caught again. I could smell burning rubber in the car. I skidded to halt, broadside, at the end of the Hatfields, took a quick look to my right and saw a petrol tanker grinding towards the junction. It was just yards away when I banged the car into first and pulled into the tanker's path. I shimmied into Stamford Street and heard the blare of the tanker's klaxon, but I was away and accelerating. A quick glance into the inside mirror showed me just the grille of the tanker and the angry face of the driver through his windscreen. Suddenly the Capri shot past him and dropped in behind me again. Oh shit, I thought, but that fat bastard is a good stoppo. I saw traffic stalled at the roundabout ahead, so I spun the wheel to the right and swerved into Coin Street, scattering a trio of young women crossing the street. The rear end of the Pontiac broke away, but I righted it with a tweak of the wheel. The damned Capri followed me as if it was on rails. I turned left into Upper Ground by the National Theatre then left again and up the incline to approach the roundabout at the southern end of Waterloo Bridge. The Colt was digging into my stomach, so I pulled it from my belt and threw it onto the passenger seat. For once I longed to see the familiar white shape of a Rover squad car, but there's never a policeman about when you want one. There was a bang from the rear end of the Trans Am and I checked my mirror again. Blondie's aim was improving. I knew I had to do something, and fast. I remembered Charlie telling me about the strengthened panels he'd put into the Pontiac to go stock-car racing. I skidded through the traffic on the roundabout, narrowly missing a single decker red bus, and roared onto Waterloo Bridge.

There was a taxi in the outside lane doing about twenty miles an hour, so I overtook it on the inside, then changed lanes to aim the Trans Am at the entrance of the Strand underpass. The Capri was about two car-lengths behind me. The opening of the tunnel was clear, and I must have been doing close to ninety as I hit the downward gradient. I lost control of the car for a split second as I entered the tunnel, and felt the nearside tyre touch the kerb. I swore from fear and pulled the wheel to my right and kept my foot on the accelerator. I could see the walls rushing past. The Capri was with me all the way. If Blondie could get a shot off at me now, it would be perfect for him. I was a sitting target. He stuck the top half of his body out of the car window and fired. I saw a chunk of wall in front of me explode into splinters. At that split second I hit the brakes hard. A terrible screaming sound from the protesting tyres echoed around the interior of the tunnel as the rubber bit into the metalled surface. I cringed at the thought of a blowout. At the same time as I braked I used the engine power to slow me further. I dropped into first and allowed the clutch to spring out. The car rocked and slid, and decelerated so fast that the belt harness dug into my chest painfully. The fat man's reflexes were too slow. The Capri hit the back end of the Pontiac with a deafening crash. Blondie was thrown neatly out of the car onto the road. Steam enveloped the two cars and filled the underpass. Still in first gear I accelerated, and began to pull away. With a screech of protesting metal, something pulled off one of the cars and clattered to the ground. The Capri was stalled in the tunnel with it's radiator split. Blondie staggered to his feet and raised his pistol, but he was too late. I was around the bend and up into Kingsway before he could fire. I drove sedately into Covent Garden and lost myself in the back streets before checking the damage to my car. I parked in front of a shop selling such vital items as pink leather Filofax and transparent plastic wrist watches. Personally I'd take the back of an envelope and a genuine Rolex any day. I sat in the car in the heat and watched myself shake. Eventually I got out and checked the back of the Trans Am. One rear light cluster had gone, leaving only bare bulbs on view. I must have pulled the Capri's bumper off in the crash because mine was still attached to the bodywork. Dented, but firmly bolted on. The primer paint was scratched and the metal had suffered some damage, but no big deal. I blessed Charlie and his garage. I found one bullet hole punched into the rear panel. I'd been lucky, if it had entered on the other side, it would have hit the petrol tank and I'd have been medium rare. I leant weakly against the car and wished for a cigarette. In the distance I heard the sound of police sirens and hoped that my would-be assassins were going to have their collars felt. Fat chance, I guessed. I drove home by a circuitous route and retired to my room to play with my gun collection. I couldn't think of anything else to do.

24

The front door bell of my flat rang at about eight that evening. I was sitting on the bed in the semi-darkness, staring at the wall in front of me, holding the Colt Cobra loosely in my right hand. I jumped slightly at the sound, then slid off the bed and went over to the window. The street outside was quiet in the gathering nightfall, and the orange lamps shone faintly against the pale evening sky.

There were no strange cars parked outside and I couldn't see anyone by the door, so I thought I'd better take a squint. I padded silently down the stairs on my bare feet, gun in hand. I didn't turn on the hall light to avoid making myself a target for any potential shootist who might be lurking at the front of the house. Being paranoid was a state I was adjusting to fast. I carefully opened the front door a crack and peered out. There was a woman standing in the shadow of the porch with her back to me, looking out into the street. As she heard the door open she swung round on her heels. I could hardly see her in the gloom.

'Nick?' she asked hesitantly.

I screwed up my eyes against the evening.

'Teresa, is that you?' I asked. She stood facing me, then put her hands on her hips in that old familiar way, and I knew that it was, for certain.

'God, it is,' I said disbelievingly.

'Can't you recognise a girl in the dark?' she asked. 'Or do I have to smile so's my teeth shine?'

'I don't believe it, what are you doing here?' I asked, in that dumb way that you do, when someone you used to sleep with, and has now become a stranger again, turns up.

'I've come to see an old friend, what else?' Her voice had cooled by a degree or two. She was as sensitive as ever to the nuance in my voice. I stepped back and opened the door wide.

'I've been thinking about you,' I said. 'I saw Em. It's just such a surprise that you're here.'

'Pleasant?'

'What do you think? Come in,' I allowed her to enter, then couldn't resist a quick look up and down the street. It was completely deserted. As I stood on the drive I realised that I still had the Colt in my hand and hastily pushed it into the hip pocket of my trousers. I followed Teresa into the house and put on the hall light using the switch by the front door. I looked at her in the yellow glow from the bulb. She was exactly as I remembered her. Beautiful, perhaps even more so than when I'd last seen her at the hospital, almost two years before.

'You look good,' I said.

'You don't,' she replied, studying my face closely. 'You look ill, aren't you sleeping?'

'Not a lot. Did Emerald give you my address?'

'Who else? And don't change the subject. Are you sick, or what?'

'Or what, mainly. Anyway are you a doctor now?'

'You know better than most what I am, what's the matter with you?'

'Nothing.'

'Some nothing, do you always greet visitors with a gun in your hand?'

I smiled in a half embarrassed way. Teresa never missed a trick.

'Keep your voice down,' I said. 'Let's not tell the whole world. Go upstairs, my flat's right at the top.'

I followed her up the three flights of stairs, and all the way I watched her bottom as it twitched under her tight leather skirt. It looked good, like water to a man dying of thirst.

I drew the curtains at my windows before I switched on the lights. She stood in the centre of the floor and looked around.

'Is this all there is? It's not very big is it?' she asked, with rather more accuracy than I liked.

'Everybody says that,' I replied.

'Entertain a lot, do you?'

'Yeah, I had a dinner party for eighteen last night, silver service, you've just missed the clean-up crew.'

'Don't be sarcastic, Nick. It doesn't suit you.'

'Sorry, sit down.'

'Where?' she asked, looking around. Everyone did that too.

'Bed or chair,' I replied.

She sat on the edge of the bed and swung her long legs up, showing more than a little thigh, and lay back against the pillow propped on the headboard where I'd been sitting in the darkness.

'This suits me,' she said. I almost laughed.

'Trust you to choose the bed,' I said. 'You don't change, do you?'

She pulled an innocent face and asked, 'Don't I?'

'You've probably got worse.'

'Thank you,' she said, looking guilelessly through her long eyelashes. All in all she was about as innocent as a back alley tabby.

'Don't be coy with me Tess, I know you better, remember. Do you want a drink?'

'Sure, what've you got?'

'Beer, beer or vodka.'

'Vodka, on the rocks please.'

'Sophisticated lady.'

'Don't take the piss,' she said, but with a smile to soften the words. 'If I remember rightly, I was the only one allowed to.'

She pouted prettily and I went to get the ice out of the freezer. As I hunkered down I saw the ugly plastic bag stuffed behind the ice-cube tray. I ignored it and put the chill I felt down to handling the cubes. I was glad to slam the fridge door. I threw a handful of ice into each of two tall, thick bottomed glasses and added a good slug of colourless liquid from the vodka bottle.

'No lemon, I'm afraid,' I said.

'I'm sure I'll survive,' she replied.

I handed her one of the glasses and holding mine I sat down on the armchair and rested my foot on the bed next to her.

'How's your leg?' she asked.

'Fine, most of the time. It aches a bit in the cold.'

'Have you seen the guy who shot you?'

'Yes, a couple of times. Today as a matter of fact.' I didn't go into any details.

'Friends again?'

'I think so,' I replied. I'd been wondering about that myself as I sat alone earlier.

'Good,' she seemed pleased, although I didn't know why, as she'd never been particularly keen on John Reid. In the past she'd often used a particularly rude West Indian slang expression to describe him.

'Do you still dance?'

I was surprised at the question.

'Are you kidding?' I asked. 'I haven't been dancing since I got shot. I'm not exactly in condition, besides I'm too old.'

'Never, you used to be great.' What a diamond the girl was.

'Thanks, Tess, coming from you that's a real compliment.' And it was, when she got on the dance floor she set the sucker on fire.

'Don't you remember the old motto?' she asked.

'Sure I do, can't dance, can't fuck.'

We shouted it out in unison and then both burst out laughing, though I must confess mine was rather hollow laughter.

'What did Emerald tell you?' I asked, changing the subject quickly.

'Nothing much, he was very close. He said you might be in some sort of trouble.'

'And then he gave you my address, so you could walk right into it. How thoughtful.'

She moved slightly towards me. 'Don't blame him Nick, I practically had to beat it out of him.'

'What with? Your suspender belt?' I enquired.

'Very funny,' she said. 'What is the matter? Please tell me.'

I knew she was worried about me, and I was grateful. But she was just another hostage to fortune, and right then I didn't need any more of them.

'It's nothing I can't handle,' I said, tough cookie that I was. At any moment I might beat her up, or stamp my foot on the carpet in a fit of pique.

'Sure,' she said. 'I'm impressed.'

'Did you drive over?' I asked. Changing the subject again.

'I still don't,' she replied. 'I caught a cab. It dropped me off on the corner.'

'I'm glad I was in.'

'I called some friends who live close by. If you'd have been out, I'd've paid them a visit.'

'I feel like a bus stop,' I said, with more venom in my voice than I'd intended.

'Stop it Nick,' she said. 'What's got into you?'

'Nothing Tess, I'm sorry, I'm just a little tense.'

I remembered the pistol in my pocket and went over and put it into the top drawer of my dresser, where it nestled amongst my clean socks. I left the drawer open. Under the circumstances it was probably not a discreet thing to do. Teresa watched me with wide, frightened eyes.

'That sort of tense can be unhealthy,' she said.

'You're talking like the TV again, Teresa,' I replied.

'And you're acting like the TV. Who the hell do you think you are?' I looked over at her from where I was standing by the dresser.

'You tell me, you seem to know everything,' I said.

'Well I'm sorry, pardon me for living I'm sure. I think I'd better go.' So saying, she banged her glass down on the bedside table, splashing two drops of liquid onto the polished wood where they caught the light and reflected twin bright spangles at me. Then she swept off the bed and stood glaring at me. I walked over and carefully put my glass next to hers. All of a sudden I desperately wanted her to stay. 'Don't go,' I begged. 'I didn't mean to be unpleasant. It's just that there are things happening that I don't understand. You being here just complicates matters.'

She moved as if to pass me. I grabbed her wrist and pulled her close to my body. She tried to pull away, but I held her tightly. I told you I was tough. Jesus, sometimes I scared myself.

'Tess,' I whispered, close to her ear. 'I apologise, honestly. I'm sorry I'm acting like a cunt. Remember me, it's Nick, your old buddy.' After a moment she relaxed and leant up against me. I could smell the perfume in her hair, and the sharp scent of the skin beneath it. I let go of her wrist and moved back away from her. She sat down on the bed again and picked up her glass. As she drank I took a long look at her.

Her hair was as long and thick and dark as ever. Her face reminded me of a black angel. Perfect skin, brown eyes that could shine like stars or glitter in anger, high cheekbones and luscious lips coated in deep red lipstick. She was wearing a thick white cotton sweater, her leather skirt came to just above the knee, exposing black fishnets and black suede shoes with thin, high heels. The shoes were just beginning to go shiny at the ends of their pointed toes.

'Are you in civvies tonight?' I asked.

'That's right, no work today.'

We sat and smiled the sort of silly smiles at each other that started the mutual remembering that was necessary to make our old friendship fresh again. As I looked at her, I saw her begin to twitch inside her clothes. I was almost embarrassed as I watched her subtly begin to turn herself on.

'Oh Tess,' I said. 'What the fuck's all this about? Did Emerald send you round as a welcome home present?'

She never turned a hair. 'It was a mutual idea,' she replied.

'What a fucking pair,' I said. 'You're unbelievable.' I jumped up from my seat and went over and sat next to her on the bed cover.

'Why didn't you just call me up?' I asked. 'You must have known I'd want to see you.'

'I was scared. It's been a long time.'

'Are you crazy? I was dying to see you again. But you didn't have to come gift wrapped.'

'I'm sorry,' she said.

'Don't be, I'm glad you're here.'

'But you said I complicate things.'

'I did, and you do. I'm a bit mixed up. I don't know what I do want.'

'You used to. Me.'

She leaned over and kissed me. The kiss tasted of warm beaches and blue skies. I felt my blood running hot and thick, like lava through my veins. As she kissed me I began to smile.

She pulled back and regarded me closely. 'What's the matter?' she asked.

'I'm just smiling, you don't mind do you? It doesn't happen very often lately.'

'Am I that funny?'

'Shut up,' I said, and we kissed again.

As we kissed she touched the back of my head. I flinched at the contact. She pulled me around and studied my wound.

'What happened?' she asked.

'Someone tried to ventilate my brain.'

'Why are you always trying to be so tough? It looks as if whoever it was nearly succeeded.'

'You should see the other guy.'

'There you go again.'

'OK Tess, you win. I could never fool you anyway. I got hit on the head by someone who was trying to frame me on a manslaughter charge. There are some threats flying about concerning Judith. That's why I've got the gun. Now I don't want any of these characters finding out about you, that I care for you, or they might try something on. That's why you shouldn't be here.'

She sat and stared at me for a while. 'I'll go in a minute,' she said. Then she leaned over and kissed me again. This time I was ready for her and kissed her back. Her mouth was wet and warm and fitted mine perfectly. We kissed long and hard. Although I was beginning to enjoy all the attention I was getting, there was just one small problem, one tiny ghost in the machine. I pulled back.

'Do you want to know something?' I asked.

'What?'

'I haven't slept with a woman since the last time I slept with you.'

'You're kidding,' she said incredulously.

'It's true.'

'But that was two years ago, maybe more.'

'I know.'

'Are you gay now?'

'I don't think so,' I said. 'I haven't tried it.'

'Why not?'

'I haven't met any men I fancy.'

'Not that, stupid. Why haven't you slept with a woman in all that time?'

'Jesus, Teresa,' I said. 'I didn't sign a contract that said I have to act like a bunny rabbit.'

'A rabbit's one thing,' she said. 'But total celibacy is another. I just don't understand. You used to like it, hell you used to like it a lot, and you were good at it,' she added.

My natural modesty forbade anything more than a simper on my part, but it was nice to know I was appreciated.

'I was ill,' I said. 'Up here.' I tapped my forehead. 'I took a long time to get over it. And then I never met anyone I wanted, or who wanted me. There were too many women in my past for me to go looking. Too many memories.'

'Was the illness serious?' she asked.

'Everyone I tell about it wants to know if I was certified. Well I wasn't. I had a breakdown. It happens, and one of the results of it was that I don't feel any particular sexual desire any more, especially when I'm under stress, which is exactly what I'm under right now.' I thought about it for a minute, I felt confused about my feelings for Patsy and the girl I'd found at Terry's flat. The thought of her was too heavy and I pushed her out of my mind quickly. 'Well I didn't,' I continued. 'Then I did again, but in a strange way.' I noticed the look on Teresa's face. 'Don't worry,' I said. 'It wasn't too weird.' As if being turned on by a photograph or a catatonic girl wasn't weird enough. 'I guess I was well on the way to being cured, or whatever you'd call it, then something happened today that knocked me back again.'

'What?'

'Somebody tried to shoot me.'

'Christ, Nick,' Teresa said. 'What's happening in your life?'

'It's better that you don't know.'

She seemed to take my word for it.

'So I can't turn you on?' she asked.

'Yesterday, you could have,' I replied. 'But now, I don't know. Maybe you can, but maybe it's not worth your time and effort to try.'

'You don't seem to care,' she said.

'Of course I care, but I had to learn to stop worrying about it. That only makes it worse. The doctors said that when I was better, I'd know.'

Teresa thought about it for a while, then said. 'Don't worry about it Nick. In my line of business I meet loads of blokes who can't get it up.'

'Gee thanks, Tess,' I said. 'I feel heaps better now.'

'Well you know what they say, don't you?'

'What?'

'Fuck you if you can't take a joke.'

With that she stood up and began to undress. Oh, God I thought, men would pay to see this, correction, men do pay to see this. And here I am getting a free show and I knew I'd do nothing about it. I wanted to, but what with my breakdown, that still loomed so large in my life. And the two dead bodies I'd seen that week, and then the attempt on my life, and the threats to Judith. I knew I couldn't handle it. I couldn't concentrate. I was just too aware that under the bed I was sitting on, was a loaded, pump action shot-gun with the safety catch off, and I was listening too hard for visitors to call.

Visitors from either side of the law. It was a glamorous life alright, but a tough one to live.

Teresa pulled off her sweater; she wasn't wearing a bra. Her brown breasts were firm and upright, with the deep purple nipples standing erect. Next she unzipped her skirt and allowed it to slip to the floor, then kicked it into a heap by the wall. Her shoes landed next to it one by one. She was wearing tights which she peeled off in a second. She stood before me dressed only in black silk bikini briefs. She removed them in one fluid motion and came and lay next to me and took me in her arms.

Somewhere at the back of my brain, or wherever these things happen, rusty locks were beginning to turn, and bolts that held the doors of emotions that hadn't been used for a long time were trying to open. I felt like a teenager who was seeing a naked woman for the first time.

'Lie back,' she ordered. 'Let's get re-acquainted.'

In the light from the bedside lamp I looked down the length of her. I wondered, not for the first time, how anyone could describe her as black. She was a thousand different colours and shades of colour. Her hair was inky, but her body was tinted from coffee to bitter chocolate colour, yet the palms of her hands and the soles of her feet were pale yellow, seamed with brown. Her tongue was a deep pink and between her legs, where her hair was like mink, she was the colour of strawberry sorbet. I started to kiss her mouth, then her neck and down to her breasts. I took her nipples in my mouth, one by one and chewed on them gently with my tongue and teeth. I felt her start to respond. I kissed her underneath her armpits and felt the stubble where she had shaved rasp against the inside of my mouth. The taste of her was bitter and salt, and mixed with the chemicals from the deodorant that she used.

'You taste good,' I whispered.

'You mean I taste like a nigger bitch.'

'Correct.'

'You bastard.'

'But I love the taste of nigger bitches like you.'

She relaxed and I began to nuzzle inside the crook of her arm and she started to moan softly. I turned her face downwards on the bed. I felt like the great lover. The great lover who couldn't come up with the goods. Not for ever, though, I knew. Things were starting to happen to me that hadn't happened for a long time. And at last with a real live woman.

I began to rub her buttocks and she slowly opened her legs. I rolled her back to face me and she moved under my hands passively. Her pubic hair was tight and curly and looked as if it had been soaked in oil. I moved down and began to kiss her stomach. Then I slid my head down until it was between her legs. My tongue flicked out to touch her clitoris and I felt her hands on my back urging me to kiss her harder. I took no notice. I rolled off the bed and began to kiss and bite her legs. She moved onto her side and I started to kiss the backs of her knees. I remembered how much she loved that. I went even further down her body until I was kissing her feet. I sucked at her toes and bit down hard on her painted toe-nails until she screamed in protest. 'Come back up,' she said. So I did. I kissed her lips again and she stuck her tongue straight into my mouth so I could suck on it. I put my hand down into her wet pubic hair and found her clitoris with my fingers. I began to tease and play with it, softly at first, then more roughly until I heard the breath catch in her throat.

'Harder,' she begged. 'Harder Nick.'

I pushed down my fingers as hard as I could, and began to whisper in her ear all the things I wanted her to do, and all the things I was going to do to her. Her breath was ripping in and out by then, and I knew she was on the brink of orgasm.

'Come on baby,' I pleaded. 'Come on.'

She screamed a tiny silent scream, then threw herself against me.

I could smell the woman on her, and her face and neck had become visibly darker as the blood rushed to the surface of her skin. We held each other tightly, and slowly her breathing returned to normal.

'You remembered,' she whispered.

'Yes.'

'How do you feel?' she asked shyly.

'You know,' I replied. 'Maybe you are a doctor, after all. Or at least a district nurse. If we work on this thing together, I think that a complete cure could come about in time.'

'But nothing now?' she sounded disappointed.

'On the contrary,' I replied. 'There was a lot happening, but it's too soon Tess. And besides you've got to go. If we get started it could last all night.' I corrected myself with a grin. 'Well 'til at least a quarter past ten.'

She grinned back. 'You ambitious boy?' she asked mockingly.

I didn't want to get started on all that. 'Seriously, Tess,' I said, 'I couldn't handle it if you were hurt, and the longer you're with me, the more likely it is to happen.'

'I've got Emerald to take care of me.'

'Right, and thank God you have. Give him a message from me. Tell him that he's got to take special care of you. He'll know what I mean.'

'OK,' she said.

She lay naked on the bed with her legs open. When I didn't respond she pulled the cover over herself. I got some more drinks and went back to the armchair. We sat in silence together, sipping at our vodkas.

Finally she broke the silence. 'Pass my handbag, will you Nick?' she asked. When she'd entered the room she'd dropped the bag just inside the door. It wasn't particularly big, but I knew what it would contain from experience. Enough cosmetics to make up a theatre group, a thick paperback book and at least one change of clothes. I went and fetched it for her. It weighed a ton. She reached into it and after hunting about for a bit, she produced a joint. It was a single skinner, short and fat and rolled in yellow paper.

'Do you mind?' she asked politely.

'Not in the least,' I replied equally politely. We learned all the drug graces at finishing school.

'Have you got a light?'

I fetched her a match from the kitchen and she lit the cigarette. After a long drag she offered it to me.

'No thanks,' I declined.

'Christ, you've changed.'

'I know, I've even given up regular cigarettes.'

Her voice was strained from keeping the smoke in her lungs. 'So you've cleaned up your act, eh Nicky boy?'

'Well sort of.'

'I'm glad,' she commented. 'When I first came in, I thought you were still dipping into Charlie's bag.'

'Lack of sleep has the same effect,' I said.

I could smell the grass in the warm atmosphere of the room. It mixed with the muskiness of Teresa's sex and reminded me of many things from the past.

'Good?' I asked.

'The best.'

'What is it?'

'Colombian.'

I was impressed.

'Oh well,' I said. 'As long as it's not South African.'

She smiled a languorous smile as the dope hit. I even got a buzz from the residue in the air. I was tempted to take her to bed for the night, but I couldn't.

'Where are you going? Do you need a lift?' I asked.

'No, I'm fine. I'll go and visit my friends. I'll stay the night there. That means I'll be sleeping just two streets away. Does that do anything for you?'

'Yes,' I replied, and it did. It made me afraid for her. Although I didn't tell her so.

'I'll walk you round,' I said.

'Don't bother,' she retorted. 'I'll sneak out by myself, I'm used to that.'

'Don't belittle yourself Teresa. You're worth more than that.'

'I know exactly what I'm worth, to the penny.'

I never could win an argument with her.

'At least tell me where you're living,' I said.

'OK.'

'Write it out here.' I gave her my notebook and a pen. She scribbled something on a blank page. I took the notebook back and put it in my pocket.

'Come by any time,' she said 'You're always welcome.'

'How often do you go to Emerald's these days?' I enquired.

'Every day, every day at five, I'm there for something to eat.'

'If this thing I'm involved with works out alright, one day at five I'll be there too. Just watch the door.'

'And if it doesn't work out?' she asked with a frown.

I felt like saying that if it didn't, she could have a drink for me one day at five and then forget she ever met me. But I didn't.

'It will,' I replied.

Perhaps she didn't believe me, because she jumped up suddenly, and I knew that if I looked closely I'd see her tears. So I didn't look. It would have been too easy to beg her to stay. She got dressed with her back turned towards me, then said, 'Take care of yourself, promise me. I'll watch the door every day. Just don't leave it too long,

I'm getting tired of waiting for you.' She turned briefly and looked at me. I saw a future in her look and almost said the words we both wanted to hear. Something stopped me and she left without another word. I watched her from the window. She didn't look back. Nothing moved in the street. No-one followed her, and no cars pulled away as she crossed and vanished into the suit of the night.

The last I knew of her was the clicking, clacking of her high heeled shoes on the pavement. But that too soon died into the darkness. I lay back on the bed and smelled her perfume on the pillow until I fell asleep fully clothed.

25

At some time in the night I must have undressed myself and got under the bed covers. I remember it was a night of disturbed, restless sleep, haunted by dreams of Laura, Teresa, Patsy Bright and all the other characters I'd encountered over the previous week.

I rose early and got dressed to kill. I chose tight, faded jeans, baseball boots, an Oxford cloth button down collar shirt and one of those loud, checked, baggy cotton jackets that were so popular that summer. For my main accessory I chose the Colt Cobra I tucked into the waistband of my jeans, at the back, well hidden by the drape of my jacket. I put an extra dozen bullets into my trouser pocket, where they nestled lumpily against my groin. Reluctantly I had to leave the shotgun. I hid it in the crawlspace in the roof of the house with the 12-gauge shells and the rest of the ammunition for the .38. I'd decided to go on the offensive at last. That Friday was going to be my day. The day to finish the Bright case once and for all. I drove the Trans-Am down to the office and parked it right outside. I was determined to get hold of George Bright and talk to the men who worked for him. I was sure that one or more of them had information that I could use.

There was no sign of Cat, I guessed he'd deserted me for pastures new and a more regular food supply.

It was still early, not quite nine and there was no answer at George's warehouse when I called. I decided to make a personal visit. I went back out to the Pontiac and climbed behind the wheel. I sat staring at the controls for a long time. Finally I started the engine; it caught first time. I put the car into gear and pulled away from the kerb. I drove to Herne Hill with George Bright's business card on the seat next to me.

The warehouse was situated close to the railway station and I parked the car tight up to a wall surrounding the goods yard. I could hear the noise of the trains from where I sat. George's building stood alone in the centre of a block waiting for redevelopment. It was built like a fort, in grey stone which had been repaired and enlarged with concrete slabs. The long, narrow windows looking out onto the road were streaked with grime and I could see moss growing up the walls where water had leaked from the guttering on the roof. On the left of the main building was an archway that led from the street into a courtyard surrounded on three sides by a high, brick wall. A heavy duty wire grilled gate had been set into the archway, and it was fastened by a large, brass padlock hooked through a length of chain. I saw through the grille that the courtyard itself was a muddy quagmire, dissected by a cobbled drive. The whole place was as quiet as a church. Facing the street, opposite to where I had parked was a huge metal door, set into the stone. Upon it was mounted a wooden plaque with the words BRIGHT LEISURE picked out in chrome lettering. The chrome was as discoloured as the rest of the building. There was a battered entryphone mounted by the side of the door. I left the car and walked over to the warehouse. I pressed the button on the machine and waited. A distorted voice asked me my business. It could have been anyone speaking.

'Nick Sharman to see George Bright,' I said into the plastic mouthpiece. There was no reply. I pushed the door, it was securely locked. After a few seconds a buzzer sounded and I pushed the door again. That time it opened and I stepped through into George's little empire.

Inside the door was a reception area. The room was painted beige and the floor was covered with dark green carpet. Photographs of juke boxes and pin-tables decorated the walls. They all looked like relics from the late fifties. There were three closed doors leading out of the room. Between two of the doors, on the wall opposite me, stood a dark brown leather chesterfield. In front of the sofa was a low, glass topped coffee table with several trade magazines scattered on top. Directly in front of me, blocking access to the room was a light coloured wooden desk supporting a telephone and a typewriter. Behind the desk was a typist's chair. That was where Patsy must have sat when she worked for her father. I pictured her sitting there. Apart from the furniture, the room was empty.

The middle door of the three opened and George Bright came into the room. He was wearing a grey, single breasted, three piece suit, a grey shirt and a grey tie. I checked his shoes, thank God they weren't grey too. He was wearing black Gucci casuals. I must admit that George's wardrobe was top class. I stood and waited and felt like a scruff. George half ran, half walked towards me. One look at his face told me that I was about as welcome as a bacon sandwich in a kosher snack bar.

'What do you want here Sharman?' he shouted. 'I thought I told you I didn't need you any more.'

Now I knew how a used Kleenex feels.

'And I told you it was personal,' I said. 'Well it's even more personal now.'

I told George about the letter that had been left for me at the office. When I'd finished his face was shocked and his hands were trembling. 'I don't know what to say.' He wasn't shouting now. His voice was hoarse and deep. I didn't blame him, I didn't know what to say either.

'Don't say anything George,' I said. 'Just introduce me to these blokes that work for you. You told them that you'd hired me and strange things started happening.'

'What about the people you told?' George interrupted.

'They're both above suspicion,' I retorted. 'One was the detective sergeant that you reported Patsy's disappearance to, and as for the others,' I hesitated. I could hardly tell George about Terry's decapitated body, that was even now decomposing in the police mortuary. 'He doesn't figure any more.' I finished half heartedly.

George didn't seem to notice.

'I am going to see your men George, I'm not asking you I'm telling you.' He looked at me pleadingly. 'By the way,' I continued, 'you've never told me, how many of them are there?'

'Two, just two,' he replied. 'On a permanent basis. I use other lads casually as I need them. Cash in hand, you know.' I knew.

The old black economy rearing its head.

'What are their names?'

'That's really none of your business,' he blustered.

'Just tell me George,' I insisted.

'Lynch and Grant,' he capitulated.

'Describe them.'

'What do you mean?'

'What I say, describe them.'

He thought for a while.

'Lynch is tall and dark with a beard and Grant is getting on a bit, he's got grey hair, but he's well built too, about six foot tall.' The descriptions meant nothing to me.

'Where are they?'

'I've told you I don't want you talking to them. I simply mentioned your name. Besides you don't seem to understand. I don't want you to do anything more about Patsy. I've told you that enough times already.' He seemed to be getting more and more agitated with every moment that passed.

'Stop fucking me about George,' I said through clenched teeth. 'I don't care what you want. It's what I want that matters now, and I want to see your staff, and if I don't get to see them -' I didn't finish the sentence. I think I would have hit him if I had. 'Where the hell are they?' I asked finally.

I think George sensed my mood.

'They're out delivering some machines. They won't be back until late this afternoon.'

'Have you got a list of their calls?' I asked. 'I'll catch them up.'

'They left early this morning. The drops were in Leicester. You'll never catch them now, come back later.'

'Let me see their manifest,' I demanded. I know bullshit when it's waved under my nose, and what George was giving me was 100% proof.

'We don't work like that. I just give them receipts to be signed and the addresses to go to. They know most of the calls anyway. This is just a small firm.'

'Have you got a list of your customers?'

'Of course.'

'Show me where they've gone and I'll call ahead.'

I didn't think he liked the idea, but he said, 'Come on then, the book's in my office, downstairs.'

I followed George out of the same door as he'd used to enter the reception room, which led straight into a windowless storage area. We walked through and down a flight of stairs to the basement.

George led me down a bare corridor and through a door at the end. I found myself standing in a tiny office. It smelled of old chips and sweaty feet. George obviously put most of his profits into his own house and car, and onto his back. The walls were painted white and stained with nicotine. Close to the ceiling in one corner was a small, permanently sealed window glazed with dirty opaque glass. In the centre of the room stood an old, scarred desk with some papers and a telephone sitting on it. Behind the desk was an executive swivel chair, upholstered in some vague, grey, tweedy material. Next to the chair, hard up against the wall was an old fashioned metal safe. The only other furniture in the room was a battered filing cabinet made from dark green tin. On it stood an electric kettle, an assortment of chipped cups and mugs, and tea and coffee-making paraphernalia. The floor was covered with an off-cut of carpet, worn and ragged at the edges.

'So this is the hub of your little universe,' I said. 'I'm impressed. It's just like home,' I continued, letting an edge of contemptuousness enter my voice. George ignored it and went behind his desk and sat down. But then he's never seen my home. As there were no other seats to be had, I perched on the edge of the desk. He opened a deep drawer and produced a bottle of brandy and two misty glasses. 'It's a bit early for you, isn't it George?' I queried.

'Have a quick one while I look up that phone number for you,' he said.

'You mean you don't know it?'

He looked at me as if I was stupid. 'Not off-hand. I've got lots of customers up there. It's here in the book.'

He drew a battered ledger from another drawer, opened it and flicked through the pages. He was either very clever or telling the truth. I poured a good measure of brandy into each glass as he searched. 'Right,' he said, pulled the phone in front of him and started to dial.

'Let me do that,' I said.

He passed me the book and pointed to the name of a club in Leicester. I dialled the number and listened to the ringing tone. After three rings the inevitable answerphone cut in.

'Very good George,' I said. 'It's another fucking machine.'

'That's the way it goes,' he replied, glancing at his watch. 'No-one ever answers in clubs at this hour. They'll be shut, and some barmen or other will be sitting, sampling the booze and waiting for the delivery. I do my business during licensing hours. What did you expect?'

I couldn't work out if he was taking the rise out of me or not. I slammed the phone down on the mechanical voice and got to my feet. 'Write the number down for me,' I ordered. He copied it out onto a scrap of paper as I finished my brandy. 'I'll try again later. If I can't get through, I'll come back here. You'd better tell your people to hang on for me, or else things could get ugly.' I didn't quite know what I meant by that, perhaps I'd wear a gorilla mask.

'Fine,' said George, quite unfazed. 'I'll do that.'

I followed him to the front door. We paused briefly to say goodbye. George was on the step above me. It made him taller than me. I didn't like that. George smirked slightly as he began to close the door. I thought I'd get a quick one in below the snakeskin belt he was wearing. 'I spoke to one of Patsy's friends the other night,' I said. George blanched until his face was the same colour as his suit. He said nothing.

'I tracked him down to where he used to share digs with Jane Lewis. You remember her don't you? You saw her body in cold storage on Monday afternoon.'

'I remember,' said George.

'He seems like a nice boy,' I continued. 'The way he tells it, it was just two kids trying to make their way in the world together, sharing a squat in picaresque old Brixton Town. Just them and every other doper around. And who was supplying the goodies? Why sweet little Patsy Bright. That's who.'

I made as if to leave.

'What?' spluttered George, his hands working themselves into fists. I turned back. 'He told me Patsy was a dealer, a very big dealer in very hard drugs.'

I thought George was going to faint or hit me, or both. 'Have you told this preposterous story to anyone else?' he demanded.

'I might have mentioned it.'

'Now see here Sharman,' he said, and hustled close to me. Too close. His breath was full of brandy and anger, or was it fear? 'You make that allegation to anyone else and I'll see you in court. Patricia was a good girl.' He paused. 'Is a good girl,' he went on, correcting his tense. 'And I won't have you blackening her name.'

He raised his hands still clenched into fists. They were the size of small cauliflowers. I realised that George must have once been quite a heavy geezer. I wondered if he'd run with any of the famous South London gangs of the fifties.

He unclenched one fist and put his hand on my shoulder. It weighed heavily. His face had gone from grey to livid red. I thought he must have read my mind when he said. 'Don't underestimate me Sharman. I might not be all that now, but once . . .' He left the sentence unfinished as if I was going to be impressed. I felt sorrow more than anger. I couldn't be bothered by more threats. I'd been threatened by the cream.

'Lay off George,' I said, shrugging his hand off. 'It's too late. You'll have to do more than serve papers to stop me.'

'I'll - ' he said. I never found out what.

'No you won't,' I interrupted. I turned and walked back to the car. George remained on the steps of the warehouse and watched me go.

I glanced back as I unlocked the car. He looked like an old man all of a sudden. I wondered when that would happen to me, when some jack the lad would ignore my threats and just walk off in disgust, too confident that I was bluffing to even worry about turning his back. I got into the car and drove off. George's figure shrunk in my rear view mirror until it disappeared completely as I turned the corner.

I drove straight back to Tulse Hill, dumped the car outside the pub and checked the office. No mail, no nothing. Another storm was grumbling in the sky somewhere to the east.

I was at a loose end again. I went to the pub and drowned a few sorrows. Not enough, there wasn't a bottle big enough. I left the office door open and hung around outside the pub in the sunshine with the rest of the unemployed. The hours stretched and I wondered where my ex-wife and daughter were. I wondered where Patsy Bright was. I wondered about the meaning of life and lots more. I felt about as useful as a tailor in a nudist camp.

I kicked my heels through the lunchtime, watching the other drinkers come and go. I was becoming a fixture. I didn't drink too much, spacing out the bottles of beer like milestones on a long, straight road to nowhere. Around three I heard the telephone on my desk ringing. I ran across the road and scooped up the receiver. It was John Reid. There were no preliminaries. He got right to the point. 'What the fuck have you been doing?' he demanded.

'Drinking beer,' I replied,

'Not today, yesterday.'

'Drinking beer,' I said.

'Get serious Nick, you prat. I told you to keep your head down didn't I?'

'You mentioned something like that.'

'Then who was it chasing through Waterloo yesterday, endangering the public and shooting, for God's sake? Where the fuck do you think you are. New York?'

'I wasn't shooting, and I wasn't doing much chasing.'

'So it was you,' he said.

'Listen John,' I cut in. 'No sooner had I left you than those bastards who've beaten me up, tried to frame me for all sorts and threatened my own daughter, start using me for target practice. I wasn't about to stick around and reason with them.'

'Can't you stay out of trouble for five minutes?'

'It doesn't look like it. Did you get them by the way?'

'No, but we got the remains of their motor. Talking of motors there's an anti-terrorist squad looking for that stupid thing you're driving, right now.'

'It's parked here,' I said.

'I should tell them that.'

'Why don't you?' I asked.

'The same reason I haven't told them anything. They don't know it was you or you'd be banged up by now.'

'What reason?'

'Old time's sake, I guess,' he replied.

I didn't say a word.

'And Nick.'

'Yes.'

'I heard it on the grape-vine that there's a contract out on you.'

'Are you kidding me?' I asked.

'No, you've upset some heavy people, being busy.'

'I haven't done anything.'

'Look, I can't talk now. I'm snowed under. I get the feeling that people are finding me little jobs to keep me away from you. There's nothing I can do now. So take my advice and drop out of sight tonight. Get right away from the manor. I'll call you tomorrow morning and we'll get together and sort this out once and for all. Can I trust you to do that?'

'I've got to see George Bright this afternoon,' I said.

'Stay away from him,' said John exasperatedly. 'He's bad news. You'll get yourself killed if you're not careful.'

'Like Terry?' I asked.

'Who?'

'Terry Southall,' I said.

There was a long pause.

'Of course, you knew him didn't you?'

'Come on John, you know I did.'

'I'm sorry Nick, it never occurred to me.'

'Who did it?'

'We don't know. At least I don't think we do. It's not my case, but I'll have a word and give you the full SP tomorrow morning.'

'What time?' I asked.

He thought for a moment. 'Tennish,' he said.

'I'll be here. Have you heard from Laura?'

'Yes, she's been in touch.'

'Not with me she hasn't.'

'I told her not to. Anyway you're not exactly flavour of the month.'

'So what's new?' I asked. 'Is everything all right with them.'

'Of course it is. Don't worry, they're well out of harm's way. Just keep a low profile tonight. There's a few cowboys who'll be cruising around looking for you after dark.'

'Who's put out the contract, do you know?'

'Tomorrow, Nick. I'll find out everything by tomorrow.'

'Do they know where I live?'

'It's no secret, is it?'

'I guess not.'

'Then get out of town Nick,' he said. 'Come back tomorrow and I'll call you.'

'I'll be here.'

He said goodbye and hung up. I pushed the button down on the phone and when I got a tone, dialled Bright Leisure. No answer, no answerphone. That slippery bastard was giving me the runaround.

I thought that a quick trip to Herne Hill wouldn't be too dangerous so I locked up and drove down to George's warehouse.

The whole place was as tight as a drum. I tried to call him at home from a callbox that worked, or nearly. There was a notice stuck to the mirror in the box that said that the telephone was only in service for emergency calls. I got the operator and after pleading with her for what seemed like hours she connected me with George's number. No answer there either. George Bright had gone to ground. Now it was my turn.

26

I wasn't going home. I had a strange feeling down my spine that I'd have visitors if I did. But my choices of where to spend the night were strictly limited. I just didn't know anyone anymore, not anyone I could trust. I looked in my notebook where Teresa had written her address. She'd said I'd be welcome any time, and now was any time as far as I was concerned. I decided to pay her a visit, unannounced. She'd probably be out, but what the hell. The only thing was, I didn't want anyone else to tag along. I climbed back into the Trans-Am, switched on the ignition and waited for the engine's note to sink from a howl to a subdued rumble. I slipped the car into gear and drove away from the kerb. I swung the car into the flow of traffic and headed towards Streatham. I drove across the lowlands of the South Circular, going north, but turned off at Clapham and dropped down Lavender Hill towards the junction. I constantly checked in my mirror as I drove, but couldn't make out if I was being followed. I nicked a space on a single yellow line at the back of Arding & Hobbs and went through one of the rear doors into the store. I loitered about just inside, but didn't see anyone who looked suss, just a few shoppers coming and going. One or two gave me funny looks but I just shrugged and grinned inanely back as if I was waiting for the wife to turn up loaded with Marks & Sparks carriers. After a few minutes I began to wander through the shop, taking it slow and easy like any innocent punter looking for a new pair of strides or a top up in the after shave stakes. I passed by one of the front doors leading out to St John's Road and checked the cab rank on the corner. There were a couple of black cabs waiting for the commuter travellers from the station. I let my eyes rove around the shop. Everything looked clean. I pulled a tenner from my back pocket and palmed it. I pushed through the glass doors and dodging a 37 pulling up at the bus stop legged it across the street. I quickened my pace, gauging the green lights and dived through the traffic towards the central reservation where the cabs were parked. I pulled open the back door of the first in the rank and collapsed into the back seat. The driver dropped his paper and half turned.

'Drive,' I said.

'Where to, mister?' he asked.

'Just drive,' I said, leaning forward and pushing the tenner through the partition into his hand. 'I'll tell you where.' He crashed the gears as we pulled abruptly into the traffic. 'Straight on,' I said.

'What's up then?' he asked out of the corner of his mouth as we headed back up the hill.

'Wife trouble,' I replied.

'Oh yeah?'

'Yeah, someone elses.'

'Gotcha,' he said with right good humour and cut up a brewery truck. I turned and checked the cars behind us. All seemed OK.

'Left here,' I said. He swung the taxi through an amber and down towards the river. No-one followed. 'Take a tour,' I instructed. 'Up to Vauxhall, then back to Stockwell, and if you jump a few red lights I won't mind.'

'It'll cost.' I could tell he was getting into it.

'No problem,' I told him. 'The cockle's just a sweetener.'

'You got it,' he said.

'And if you don't mind,' I went on.

'What?'

'No conversation, I need to think.'

'No probs, mate, I'll be as quiet as the grave.'

The cab sped down Queenstown Road, round the roundabout and snaked up to Vauxhall Cross. The driver pushed it through some back doubles, down a couple of mews I didn't even know existed and, after a brief stop under a railway bridge by a building site hidden behind an overflowing skip, drove serenely down as far as Stockwell Tube. He was good, I'll give him that, and he knew it. I gave him another tenner when he dropped me off in Larkhall Lane. 'If her husband was after you we've lost him now,' he said with a grin as he pocketed the cash.

'Cheers,' I said.

'Take care,' he replied as he drove away. 'And be good.'

I stood for a time in the empty street then turned and pushed into the deserted public bar of the pub behind me. I ordered a lager and wedged myself on the battered vinyl of a corner seat and watched the door. No one came in until I'd almost finished my second drink, and then it was just a pensioner with a stick and a seedy old dog on a piece of string instead of a lead. I relaxed a bit after that and had another drink and a listen to the jukebox. Yeah, 'A Whiter Shade of Pale' was on that one too, but I didn't select it. The address Tess had given me was two or three streets down from where I was sitting but I waited until a group of likely lads came piling into the pub before leaving. I walked down the lonely streets under a dark and treacherous sky. It looked and felt as if another storm was in the air. I didn't know if it was that or me that made the air feel so tense and static. The street lights clicked prematurely on as I passed, forging a lighted path for me through the murk.

27

I knocked on her door around nine thirty, quarter to ten. There was a soft light behind the deckled glass, but no sound. I knocked again and leant back against the brickwork of the porch. I heard the soft pad of feet before I saw a diffuse shape appear. She opened the door on a safety chain. 'Hello Tess,' I said.

'Nick, so soon,' she said as a greeting.

'Yeah, bad penny time. Can I come in?'

'Of course, it's liberty hall at my place, or had you forgotten?'

She fiddled with the chain and pulled the door open. I didn't answer, just slid through the doorway and pushed it gently closed behind me. I turned and refastened the chain. We stood and looked at each other in the hallway. 'What's up?' she asked.

'The usual,' I said.

'Are you armed?'

'No, I'm just pleased to see you.'

'Funny,' she said, without cracking the least sign of a smile.

'Yes, I'm armed.'

'Well I don't want to see it.'

'Good enough.'

She led me through the flat, into the living room where a portable colour TV was buzzing quietly in the corner. I didn't see what was on, the faces on the screen were blurred as if covered with a fine gauze.

'Are you hungry?' she asked.

'Could be, what have you got?'

'Eggs, bacon.'

'And a fried plantain?'

'Why not?'

'I love your fried plantain.'

'There's a joke in there somewhere.' For the first time she touched me. She rested her hand on my arm. Her nails were long and scarlet.

'Come on then,' she said. 'But get rid of the gun.' I walked over to a chest of drawers, opened the top drawer and laid the Cobra gently on a pile of papers inside, then followed her into the kitchen. It was large and white and looked into an overgrown back garden. All the windows were open to allow some air in from the sultry night.

Somewhere far away, across the river, I guessed, there was a brief flash of sheet lightning that lit up the leaves on the trees and turned them electric green for a second. Teresa shivered in the heat.

'I hate storms,' she said.

'I love them,' I replied.

'I remember.'

She went over and opened the fridge and pulled out eggs and a packet of bacon. She loaded the meat onto the mesh of the pan under the grill and turned on the gas. She took a big plantain out of the wicker basket on the dresser, peeled it and sliced it lengthwise. All of a sudden, the heat and the scent of the fruit took me back to another flat in another part of town during another forgotten summer.

Teresa and I had just started seeing each other seriously. My wife was on another planet, and with the help of certain illegal substances, so was I.

One weekend I stayed up with Teresa. I gave Laura a cock-and-bull story about a seminar at Bramshill. I don't know if she believed me and cared less. She was probably glad to see the back of me for forty eight hours.

Tess and I stayed in for the whole weekend. We ate take-outs when we ate at all and fucked each other's brains out. The weather was tropical. The sky was cloudless for weeks and the city boiled like a cheap kettle. We wore the minimum of clothing for the two days which didn't help, and I watched the drops of sweat roll down Teresa's back from her hairline until they soaked into the band of her panties. I'd cleared the glass topped table in her living room and it was streaked and smeared with coke dust. We smoked dope, snorted coke, screwed, sucked up strong, cold mixtures of vodka and juice, picked at pizzas and Chinese and screwed again. She'd bought in a hand of bananas and put them on a window sill in a glass bowl. When she'd bought them they'd been green, but I could almost see them ripen in the sunlight that poured through the window. The room filled with the perfume of the yellowing fruit and the Thai stick we were rolling and smoking and the smell of stale sex and stale bodies. In the late evening when the sun finally dropped down to the horizon and the tower blocks turned black and golden we'd sit on the bed by the window, dazed and wiped out from the sex and booze and drugs and listen to the trains rattling across town until it grew full dark and we fell asleep in each other's arms.

'A penny from them,' said Teresa and I was back with her.

'Thinking about that place of yours in Battersea, remember?'

She smiled. 'Yes, good days.'

'Good enough for me,' I said.

She drained the bacon and scooped two eggs and the fried banana onto a plate. 'Ketchup?' she asked.

'Just a bit.'

'You always say that.'

'Not much alters, does it?' I asked.

'Doesn't it?'

I shrugged. 'I dunno,' I said through a mouthful of egg.

She sat and watched me as I ate. She fiddled with her hair and a seam on the skirt of her dress. The food was good. She fetched me a bottle of Bud from the cooler and I swallowed a mouthful from the neck. It tasted cool and rich as it washed the last of the food down my throat. At last she asked the inevitable question. 'Why did you come?'

'I'm on the run,' I said only half jokingly.

'Serious?'

'I don't know for sure, but I think so. Anyway don't worry, I haven't brought any little friends along.'

'Do you want to stay the night?'

'Can I?'

'Of course. You wouldn't have come if you'd thought differently would you?'

I ignored the question. 'Not going out?' I asked instead.

'Not tonight, I'm sort of on holiday.'

'Costa Del Stockwell?'

'Something like that.'

I sat and finished the beer. 'You're sure no-one's followed you?' she asked when I'd put the bottle in the garbage pail.

'Not a chance.'

She relaxed a little and lit a Marlboro from the red and white pack on the sideboard. She didn't inhale the first drag, just allowed the smoke to drift between her lips in a grey-white, bite-sized swirl. I looked at it greedily and she spat it towards me. 'Want one?' she asked. I nodded but stopped her as she pushed the packet towards me.

'But I won't,' I said.

'Please yourself, you always do.'

'Am I doing something wrong?' I asked.

'Just the usual.'

'What?'

'Using people, using me!'

'Tess, I'm not, I swear.'

'I knew you'd come when I could be of some use.'

'I'll go then.'

'Where?'

'God knows,' I said. 'I'll walk the streets.'

'You fucking drama queen. "I'll walk the streets." ' she mimicked pretty well too. 'You know I wouldn't kick you out.'

'I know,' I said.

'There, you see.'

'Jesus Tess,' I said. 'What's got into you?'

'I'm sorry, I've had a rough week.'

'Why?'

'It's no good any more.'

'What?'

'What I do.'

'I didn't think goodness ever came into it,' I replied, rather tactlessly.

She flashed me a dirty look. 'Don't get funny, Nick,' she said. 'It's a living. What the fuck do you do that's so special?' There was really no answer to that one. 'I hate being pawed around by those dirty bastards.'

'So quit.'

'And do what?'

'Whatever.'

'Well tell me Nick, you're so smart. What should I do? What little career do you suggest I should get into?'

I said nothing.

'There you see, no bright ideas. Well I did quit for a while, and what do you think I did?'

I said nothing.

'Well I wasn't on the check-out at Sainsbury's. I worked in a peep show, what do you think of that?'

I said nothing.

'A sleazy little peep show in Wardour Stret. Do you know what that means?' I shook my head, it beat saying nothing, but I didn't quite get her point. Did she mean morally or philosophically? Or did she mean the nuts and bolts of the thing? I soon found out. 'It means I showed off my pussy to a bunch of scumbags for half a quid a throw. Do you know how that feels?' She was full of questions that night. I shook my head again. I was beginning to feel like a metronome.

'Of course you don't,' her voice rose, full of tightly suppressed fury. 'I had to open my cunt to someone I didn't know, someone I couldn't see, someone I hadn't even been introduced to. Do you know what that does to a person?'

My head shook again.

She came up so close I could feel her spit on my face. 'It's disgusting!' she shouted. 'Fucking disgusting. You wouldn't show your precious cock off for a few quid would you?'

I was still shaking my head.

'It makes you less of a human being.' She was close to tears. 'And once a month you have to take unpaid sick leave. It brings the profit margins down. It's not fair. Not many punters get off on a bit of string sticking out of your crack. 'Cos that's all it is, a half nicker crack, a fifty pence gash and a bit of cunt hair.' She stopped then, I was glad. My head was shaking so fast by then that I thought my brains would start trickling out of my ears. 'So I went back on the game.'

'I'm sorry,' I said weakly.

'What the fuck do you know? Nothing as usual, right.'

'What can I say Tess, you're not interested. You won't listen. I know it's tough out there, especially for a woman on her own.'

'Spare me that shit will you, next you'll say especially a black woman. Well don't. That would really piss me off.'

'Even more than you are now?' I asked.

'Yes, if you must know,' she replied.

I looked at her.

'Don't you look at me like that, Nick,' she said coldly. 'Who the fuck do you think you are anyway? You fucking liberal white bastard. If you talk to a nigger, you think you're a real open hearted guy. If you fuck a nigger, you think you're something special. Mister superstud. Then you probably go and brag about it to your friends. If you've got any of course, which I doubt. Bollocks, Nick. Don't patronise every black you see. If you see a black tie his own shoelace you make a fuss. You jump up and down and clap your hands, like it's a big deal. Why don't you just leave us all the hell alone?'

I was confused. She was as changeable as the weather. 'I must be missing something here,' I said. 'Just tell me exactly what's brought this on.'

'Don't you know?'

'No.'

'It's because I thought I was long over you, and then I heard you were back and I just had to see, and of course I wasn't.' I must have looked as amazed as I felt. 'It's because I love you, you stupid bastard,' she said, and literally collapsed into my arms.

28

She dropped like a stone and I had to catch her or she'd have hit the deck. I almost slipped a disc as her weight fell onto me. I held her close and kissed her mouth and whispered that I loved her too, and you know what? I really did. 'You are pleased to see me,' she said, when we came up for air. 'I thought you couldn't get it up.'

'I told you I was armed,' I said into her neck.

'Then you must have two guns.'

'Perhaps I have.'

'Well this one I do want to see.'

'Be my guest.'

She went straight down on me, sliding down my body, then was battling with my belt and Mister Levi's silver buttons, when I lost it.

The TV was still yapping away to itself in the corner. I was looking straight at the screen. Some kind of late night local news was on, and there, all of a sudden, replacing the smug face of the presenter was a picture of Terry, taken years ago when he still had hair. Then a photo of the girl I'd seen in his flat appeared. I couldn't hear what was being said, and the next thing on was coverage of cricket at the Oval. The brief glimpse was enough. It all came back like a movie running ten or twenty times too fast. And the movie went back, back from Tess's flat to Terry's flat, back to the squat, then to the hospital and the hospital before that, and being shot and everything until mercifully the film broke and left me with nothing, not even a hard-on. That was when I lost it.

The worst thing was that I couldn't tell Teresa. She would really have freaked out. She thought it was her fault and I didn't say anything to the contrary. I could tell she was furious. She looked up at me. 'Fucking typical!' she spat. 'Some nights you can't even give it away.'

'No Tess,' I said, but it wasn't any good. She pushed herself to her feet and tugged the simple black dress she was wearing over her head. Underneath she was dressed only in brief white panties. 'You fucking wimp,' she said in disgust, and went and threw herself onto the long white sofa in front of the TV. 'Well if you can't do it, I'll do it myself.' She pushed her fingers into her crotch and began to play with herself. 'What's the matter Nick?' she asked breathlessly. 'Can't you handle a real woman any more? Or is it that I do it for money? Is that what you really can't handle? Don't you trust me sweetheart? Is it because I'm unfaithful every night?' She changed her tack. 'Why don't you punish me then? Go on Nick, show you're a man for Christ's sake.' She was sweating and breathing hard. I was really pissed off and getting horny again at the sight of her, and angry at her and the world.

'Come on Nick,' she went on. 'Punish me, you fucking nonce.' I walked over and looked down at her. 'Come on Nick.' She was nearly screaming by then. I could feel my finger nails cutting the palms of my hands, my fists were clenched so tightly.

'Wanker,' she said and came.

I could have killed her then. She sat up and grinned at me and I slapped her so hard that she bounced off the sofa and onto the floor.

She caught her balance and without missing a beat came up with a right hook that loosened one of my wisdom teeth. God she was strong. The blow took me totally by surprise and knocked me onto the back of the sofa which toppled over and deposited me on the floor up against the skirting board. She was on me like a demon. She dived over the sofa, slashing at my face with the nails on her right hand, which I just managed to catch and keep the skin on my cheek in one piece. I held her tightly, but she was so strong and slippery that I almost lost her. Suddenly she relaxed. I saw the drops of saliva on her chin. We looked into each other's eyes and I put my fingers up and gently wiped the drops off. I was waiting for her to attack me again when her eyes filled with tears like winter lakes and she went totally limp in my arms. 'Some punch you got there babe,' I said through a fat mouth.

'Better than yours, Nicky boy. You punch like a girl.'

And there was me thinking I was tough. What a put down.

If I felt that I could have killed her before, the feeling was stronger then, but in a different way. So I rolled her onto her back and performed a little murder on her body right there on the Axminster, whilst she committed a ritual suicide underneath me. Then she took over the dominant role and I died under her ministrations. At last we dragged ourselves into the bedroom and collapsed onto the bed. We were slithering all over the sheets, kissing and nipping at each other like a pair of puppies. She went down on me again, spearing me with her tongue and hardening me up again. Finally we joined together for the last time and made tired and mellow love. Mouth to mouth, chest to chest and groin to groin. She was soaking. So wet that I thought I was going to be squeezed out of her cunt like an oversized orange pip. 'No way baby,' she whispered. 'You don't get away that easy.' She crossed her legs over my back and linked them together at the ankles and pulled me tighter into her. We came together in a heated rush, then rolled apart and lay exhausted and panting in the sticky night air. We held hands and turned over and smiled at each other. 'I do love you,' she said.

'Me too, you,' I said back.

'Don't fuck me up Nicky,' she said through a yawn.

'I'll try not to,' I replied as I reached for her. That was about as much as I could promise anyone. To try not to fuck them up. Some commitment.

We lay snuggled up in each others arms for a bit, not saying much. Finally she fell asleep. I lay back and relaxed, looking at the ceiling in the soft yellow light of the bedside lamp.

That was when they came through the door and the bedroom window. Three of them, no-one I recognised, dressed in khaki and navy and camouflage gear, all armed with semi-automatic weapons and handguns. I pulled myself up to a sitting position as they stood in a menacing triangle with their ugly weapons trained on the bed. Three thoughts went helter-skelter through my mind. I'd been followed, however clever I'd tried to be. They'd been watching Tess and me all evening, and my fucking pistol was in a drawer in the other room.

The smallest of the three covered me with an AK47 whilst the biggest walked over to the bed, carefully staying out of the line of fire. He looked down at me. 'Nice show, soldier,' he said. 'We thought the scwarze was going to swallow your dick.' Then he popped me on the side of the head with the gun he held in his right hand. That time I definitely lost the wisdom tooth.

I woke up at the sound of my own scream. My heart was beating like a drum machine on self destruct. I was tangled up in a single sheet that was slick with sweat. Just a dream. I went and rescued my gun anyhow. I put it down by the side of the bed where Tess wouldn't see it if she woke up, then gathered her into my arms and went back to sleep.

29

I woke around six. Tess was lying next to me snoring gently. Not grossly, but just a soft inhalation. I poked her in the ribs and she rolled over. 'Don't snore,' I said.

'I don't,' she replied, and went back to sleep. After a moment I heard the faint snoring again. I grinned and got out of bed.

I pulled on yesterday's clothes and rinsed my face in Teresa's bathroom. I tried to shave with a stupid little disposable razor. I guessed she used it to shave underneath her arms. It felt like she used the blade to sharpen pencils as I dragged it across my face and winced at my reflection in the mirror set at least six inches too low for me.

I used her toothbrush too, then went and made some coffee. She only had instant and it tasted like hot iron filings. I took Tess a cup. She didn't want to wake up so I left it on her bedside table. She surfaced just enough to say goodbye. I kissed her briefly and she held my arm tight and asked me to stay.

'I can't,' I said. 'I'd like to, but I can't.'

'What are you going to do?' she asked.

'Get to the bottom of this mess. I hope,' I said.

'I'd rather you came back to bed and get to the bottom of me.'

I could tell she was beginning to wake up properly.

'There's nothing I'd rather do.'

'I know,' she said. 'But you've got to get out on the streets and right all the wrongs and be a man.'

'Something like that.'

'You're a fool, Nick.'

'Maybe.'

'There's no maybe about it.'

I shrugged and pulled a face. What could I do about it?

'You'd better take care,' she went on.

'I will, and I'll see you soon, at Emerald's place.'

'I'll be waiting.'

'Make sure you are.'

Then I left.

The morning was already warm, moving towards hot, but huge storm clouds were banked on the horizon. They sat high and still and threatening. In a way they reminded me of the way my life was going.

I walked down to Stockwell tube and caught a deserted train through to Balham. The storm clouds were closer when I came out into the street. I picked up a cab at the rank outside the station and took a short ride up to Clapham Junction. The Trans-Am was still parked at the back of Arding & Hobbs on the yellow line. It had been ticketed. I took the plastic bag from under the windscreen wiper and dropped it into a bin down by the Wimpey. Keep Britain Tidy.

No-one seemed interested in the car as I drove it back to my office. No-one seemed interested in the office either, or me for that matter. I kicked the chairs around the room in temper. Then picked them up and sat on one. I sat for a long time waiting for something to happen. Then it did. The phone rang.

When I answered it I found myself speaking to a man with a cultured voice that contained just a trace of a foreign accent that I couldn't identify. The voice asked to speak to Nick Sharman.

'This is he,' I said. All those years of schooling hadn't been wasted.

'I believe you are looking for a Miss Patricia Bright,' the voice said.

'Nearly everyone who calls me believes that,' I replied.

'Is it true?'

I agreed that it was.

'May I ask, in what connection?'

'On behalf of her father.'

'Alas, she has no father.' I had to admit he was very polite. I wasn't.

'Look,' I said. 'Don't fuck me around, I'm not in the mood today.'

'I'm perfectly serious,' the voice said.

I paused for a moment. He sounded as if he meant it. 'Who are you?' I asked. 'What do you want?'

'My name is of no importance now, but I think we should meet and I can introduce you to Miss Bright,' he replied.

'The last time someone told me that I ended up with severe scalp abrasions, and almost got nicked for manslaughter or worse, and she wasn't even there. So why should I believe you?'

'It is of little concern to me, what happened to you previously.'

The voice said again, 'But I can certainly produce the girl. If you do not want to take up my offer of a meeting, so be it. If you wish to stumble around like a blind man in a maze, that is your prerogative. I am an honourable man. When I say something will happen, it will. I promise you will come to no harm with me, if you conduct yourself in a civilised way.'

I decided I had no choice. 'Where and when?' I asked, all businesslike. He interrupted me. 'We will come to you. I will call you again within the hour with full instructions.' The phone went dead in my hand as he cut me off.

I sat and waited, and did all the things private detectives are supposed to do when they think a case is about to break. I thought about what the man with no name had said about Patsy not having a father. What the fuck was all that about? I quickly dialled George Bright's numbers. The answerphone was on at the warehouse again and there was no answer at his home. I didn't dare make any more calls in case my line was busy when the stranger called back with his instructions. If he called of course. I sat and worried about my ex-wife and child. I looked at the people outside in the street going about their business. I decided that maybe being normal wouldn't be so bad after all, and wished I'd gone into insurance. I felt the metal of the .38 boring into my back and fought off the temptation to check the load again. I wondered what had gone wrong with my life. Forty five minutes after his first call the man without a name called again. 'I am using a car-phone,' he said. 'We are waiting for you at Norwood Cemetery. We are parked next to the rose garden, beside the crematorium. Park your car at the bottom of the hill and proceed on foot. Come alone.'

'I hope you're not kidding me,' I said. I could hear the exasperation in my voice.

'Mr. Sharman,' the disembodied voice said. 'Please do not force me to constantly repeat myself. I am not in the habit of kidding anyone. We will wait for precisely twenty minutes. Do not waste time.'

The call was abruptly terminated. I did exactly as he had told me. I locked up the office and drove the Pontiac up to the cemetery. It was only five minutes from my office. I passed through the massive gates and drove slowly up the road that meandered between the gravestones. It is a beautiful place, although not one I'd choose to spend my leisure hours. I used to walk through it as a child holding my grandma's hand to visit the graves of my family who are buried there. The place always filled me with fear and awe. That morning was no exception. I parked the car next to a signpost that pointed to the crematorium and walked up the hill towards the single storey, red brick building. There were several cars parked outside, and I guessed that a service was taking place. The morning was cool again and a light breeze tugged at the coats of a mourning party attending a burial at the foot of the hill. Other people carrying flowers were visiting the graves of their late loved ones. I wondered briefly if anyone would ever bother to visit my last resting place, then realised self pity was a stupid emotion.

I walked up the gradient towards the old part of the cemetery. At the top of the hill, just past the crematorium building was parked a car. Not just any old car at that. It was a black Rolls-Royce stretched limousine. The bodywork shone like a mirror and the thin sunlight picked out the chrome trim and reflected back into my eyes. When I got closer, I saw that the side windows were tinted nearly as dark as the bodywork itself. The car sat square on the road, as big and silent as the tombs that surrounded it.

When I reached the vehicle, the driver's door opened and a heavyset man with a face set like concrete, wearing a grey chauffeur's uniform stepped out. From where I was standing the uniform fitted him well. In his right hand was a Colt .45 US Army issue automatic. In retrospect, I realised that the gun fitted him better. The driver pointed the gun in my general direction and opened the offside passenger door. A tall dark skinned man emerged. The chauffeur closed the door before I had had a chance to look inside. The tall man was dressed in a navy blue, double breasted suit, that I estimated wouldn't have left him a lot of change out of a thousand pounds. I would have been willing to bet he was the toast of South Molton Street. His shirt was blindingly white, with a tabbed collar, at which was knotted a slim black tie. His feet were shod in polished black boots, fastened with discreet gold buckles. He wore a snap-brim black trilby and wrap-around shades. His outfit was tailor-made for the bone orchard in which he stood. In his left hand he held a lightweight machine pistol. It was a small, snub nosed weapon, not much longer than the driver's automatic, but with massive fire power. From the grip a short magazine protruded like a thick, obscene metal tongue. I recognised the make and model. It was an Ingram MAC M10 9mm sub-machine gun. It was finished in matt-black. Instead of the usual webbing belt, which was used to hold the gun steady when firing, a custom made leather strap was attached to the gun. Any urban terrorist worth his salt would love to find one in his Christmas stocking. The magazine held 32 rounds that the gun could spew out in less than two seconds when on full automatic. It was a very, very sexy designer death all wrapped up like a pretty toy. It would never have surprised me to see a diamond cluster on the safety catch.

I could feel the tall man watching me through the black lenses of his glasses. After a moment he spoke.

'We meet at last, Mr. Sharman. I have been observing you for the last few days with great interest. You appear to be a very inquisitive man.' As he spoke he leant against the car, the machine pistol drooping lethargically in his grasp.

'That's my job,' I replied.

'Not when it interferes with mine.'

'Which is?' I enquired politely.

You can take my word that when the business end of a MAC 10 is less than three feet from your belly-button, everything you do is polite.

'Commerce, buying and selling. Finding a demand and filling it. The very stuff of life, you must agree.'

'If you say so,' I said.

'I do say so. And I can meet your demand to see a certain young lady. You seem determined to locate Patricia Bright. However, you appear to have met with little success in your search. I must confess that your powers as a detective do not fill me with particular admiration. But your meagre talents seemed to have set a few cats amongst certain pigeons, as it were.' He smiled coldly. 'Some of the demi-monde have become quite agitated about your interest in the girl. I must admit a certain puzzlement as to why. Now you're bumbling appears to be encroaching on my interests. So I intend to put you more into the picture regarding the Bright family. This, I hope, will lead you to cease meddling in my affairs.'

I was frankly puzzled and I told him so. 'I hate to say this,' I said, 'but I have no idea who you are, or what you do. And I might add, I rarely, if ever, meddle with people who carry sub-machine guns.'

'I do not intend to tell you who I am,' he said. 'I have many names, you may call me David. It is of no importance. It can be another mystery for you to solve. After all, you are the detective. Find out for yourself if you can. Many people better than you have tried and failed. But you are looking for Patricia. I have certain interests in her. Ergo, you interfere with me.'

I loved his vocabulary. 'Ergo', 'Demi-monde'. David must have had a classical education, or pretended that he had. So had I, so I wasn't impressed, but I must admit a certain fondness for his suit.

'Can I see her?' I asked.

'Of course. That's why I invited you here,' he replied.

'When?'

'Now, I think,' he said, and with that he opened the rear door of the Rolls again. That time I had a clear view into the car. On the back seat sat Patsy Bright.

I could hardly believe I was seeing her at last.

'Patricia,' said the tall man. 'Come out and say hello to Mr. Sharman.'

She climbed out of the car and into the daylight. Her face was even more beautiful in real life than the photo which I had looked at so often, led me to believe. But when I looked closely I noticed that her skin was slightly puffy and there were dark shadows forming under her eyes. And when I looked into her eyes, there was something that belied her beauty. A knowledge of life that no girl her age should have. The eyes that looked back at me were a million years old.

She was taller than I had expected, although by then I knew her measurements better than my own. She was wearing a blue mini-dress, white tights and flat heeled blue pumps that matched her dress exactly. On her left arm she wore a dozen or more plastic bangles in rainbow shades that rattled slightly when she moved. In her left hand she held a single long-stemmed rose. It was hardly more than a bud. I tried to recognise the type. I was sure that I'd once grown similar myself. I felt it was very important for some reason to identify it. But I couldn't.

Patsy wore pale make-up and bright pink lipstick, which contrasted with the sooty mascara that coated her eyes. Her hair was longer than it had been when the photo was taken, and hung down to her shoulders like two golden wings framing her face. She looked as though she had just stepped off the set of 'Blow Up'. In her left hand she carried a pair of red framed Ray-Ban sunglasses.

I was relieved when she put them on.

I wondered what to say to someone I had never met, yet who had dominated my life for more than a week that seemed to have lasted a lifetime. Someone I was in love with for all the wrong reasons.

'Hello, Patsy,' I said after a moment.

'Hello,' she replied dutifully.

'I've been looking for you.'

'I know.'

'Your father asked me to, he's worried about you.'

'My father died fifteen years ago,' she said.

I looked from her to David, as I was supposed to call him, then back again.

'What do you mean?' I asked in a confused way.

'What I say. My father is dead,' she replied. Although her accent was good, South London was teetering on the edge of it.

'Who's George Bright then?' I asked no-one in particular.

'Perhaps, I can explain,' said David. 'George Bright is Patsy's adoptive father. He is also the man who managed her career as a prostitute.'

I couldn't believe what I was hearing.

'He started fucking me when I was twelve,' interrupted Patsy, a bitter edge to her voice. 'Then when I was broken in, he started selling me around.'

After her brief outburst, she went back to admiring her rose. 'It was soon after George Bright's wife died that it started,' David explained. 'Like George, a lot of men like young children. He was happy to furnish Patsy's services to them. Then he discovered that at the places he sent her to work, there was a great demand for expensive drugs. So he started to cater to that need also. It turned into a most lucrative business, and quite a safe one. Apart from the fact that some of the clients were highly placed in the establishment of this country and thus well protected. In order to fulfil precise functions of the fantasy, Patsy was expected to wear her school uniform whilst engaged in certain sordid practices. So she was free to travel around London with a satchel full of merchandise. Who would bother to stop and search an angelic child like her?' David smiled again. 'I must admit it has a certain diabolical humour about it.'

'If you think that's funny,' I said 'I feel sorry for you. Anyway, where do you come in? What does your taste run to, little boys?'

The Ingram twitched in his hand. 'My taste is not your concern,' he said evilly. 'Do not set yourself up as a moral arbiter. Just listen.'

I shut up and listened.

'Bright was basically small time,' he continued. 'To increase his turnover, and ultimately his profits, he had to take on certain partners.' He made a moue of distaste with his lips. 'They had little or no imagination. No flair. Patricia was beginning to outgrow the particular market she was in. The partners were only interested in the drug side of things. However, I learnt that when she visited her clientele she often picked up certain items of, how can I put it, a sensitive nature. These items were eminently saleable. I approached Patricia with a view to marketing her for the nineteen nineties. She has, believe it or not, an unusually keen memory for names, faces and places. She is also an accomplished thief. There are men, powerful men, in this city who are prepared to pay dearly for their particular pleasures. Some of them are still paying.'

'Blackmail?'

'An unpleasant word, Mr. Sharman. But use it if you must. Do you realise that you are out of your depth in shark-infested waters?'

'Why did George Bright pick me, I wonder?' I asked without expecting an answer.

David looked at me strangely for a moment. 'Who knows?' he asked. 'Perhaps for more reasons than either of us can guess.'

I ignored him and turned back to the girl. She couldn't even see me. She was on her own private trip. I knew the feeling well. I'd been there often enough myself.

I looked back at David. 'What about the Brixton connection?' I asked. 'The punks and the squatters, where do they come in?'

'Patsy is still a child,' he replied. 'She needed friends of her own age. She wanted to see her beloved musical groups. We all crave peer acceptance. She did not choose her friends wisely. She gravitated towards an unfortunate social set. She could and did supply them with drugs, without George Bright's knowledge. It was an easy way to obtain popularity. Unfortunately it brought tragedy in its wake, and notoriety. She has now been weaned away from that particular episode in her life.'

'So she did supply Jane Lewis with the pure heroin that killed her?'

'No, Mr. Sharman. How could she? She'd been away from George Bright and his drug sources for over two months when the Lewis girl died.'

'Patsy could've got them from you. You told me that she's an accomplished thief. She's obviously high right now. You must be involved in drug trafficking too. You didn't get this motor with Co-op stamps.'

'I must disappoint you again. Patricia has absolutely no access to drugs at all. Any that she receives from me are in carefully controlled doses and administered in a clinical way.'

He really was a cold hearted bastard. If I hadn't had two guns pointed at me, I'd have administered him a clinical broken arm.

'So what was the tragedy then?' I asked.

'Why. Your friend Southall of course,' he replied.

'You killed Terry?'

'No again. I can see I must let some more light into your life. Let us go back to the afternoon you were lured to the house in Brixton.'

My head was spinning. David seemed to know everything that had happened to me recently. 'How the hell do you know about that?' I asked.

He shrugged. 'May I continue?' he asked.

'Go ahead,' I replied.

'The three men you met there worked for George Bright's partners. They pose as staff at Bright Leisure. I believe you missed them when you paid a visit to the warehouse earlier today.'

I felt like a berk. I'd believed George Bright when he told me there were only two of them. I'd believed the descriptions he had given to me. I'd believed far too much without substantiation. It was going to get worse before it got better.

'The yellow haired one is called Lynch,' he went on. 'The negro is known as Winston and the other's name is Michael Grant. You may need these names, so I suggest you remember them.'

I hoped I didn't look as confused as I felt.

'Lynch was sleeping with Jane Lewis,' David continued. 'If the euphemism is acceptable. From what I understand, very little sleeping actually occurred. Lynch was introduced to Lewis by Patricia. Sometimes Lynch accompanied Patsy when she visited clubs to listen to the music, and he obviously met her friends. To be blunt, he was paying the Lewis girl for her favours with drugs he had stolen from Bright and Company.'

'It seems that everyone who works there, rips off drugs,' I commented.

'Of course,' he said, 'it's the nature of the beast.'

He stopped and thought for a moment. 'The one thing I'm not sure of,' he went on, 'is if he murdered her for reasons of his own, or if he did not realise the quality of heroin in that particular batch.'

I was glad to hear that he wasn't infallible.

'In any case,' he continued, 'he used the body to try and convince you that Patricia was dead. When you saw through that, he decided to incriminate you by leaving you with it. Not very clever, I'm afraid. Lynch is not the most intelligent of human beings.' David shook his head sadly. 'He should remain what he is, an efficient strong arm man.'

'Who was the other man in the house?' I asked.

'What other man?' he asked back.

'I thought you knew everything.'

'Some things I know, but prefer not to divulge. You must do some work for your income.'

My income, that was a joke.

'Why do you think they didn't just kill me like they did Terry?'

'Ask the elusive fourth man.'

'Was it you?' I was stabbing in the dark.

He smiled his cold, hard smile again. 'I can assure you that if it were,' he said, 'they would certainly kill me out of hand. I am no friend of Bright and his cohorts.'

So there I stood, with my mouth open, none the wiser. I felt I had to keep probing, asking questions. 'What about Terry? Who killed him?'

'Surely, even you must have worked that one out.'

'My friends from the squat?'

He nodded. 'Well two of them anyway. The blonde man Lynch, with the help of Winston.'

'Why haven't I heard any more about it?'

Once more the smile flashed as warmly as a refrigerator door opening. 'No one has,' he said. 'The investigation is making very little progress. I wonder why?'

That smile again.

'But why did they have to kill him?'

'I think that Southall was probably a better detective than you are. I know that he was trusted by the young drug users in the neighbourhood where he worked. Obviously someone talked to him that night. Someone else must have contacted Lynch. Drugs can buy much. Sex, information, power,' he shrugged again. 'Lynch and Winston went to the club that Southall was visiting. I assume they followed him home and killed him.'

'How do you know so much?'

'I told you drugs can buy information. What I'm not told, I deduce. Why don't you try it some time?'

I felt just like the fool I'd proved to be, unless he was lying. But why should he bother? For that matter, why should he bother to tell me so much right then. I knew he wanted to use me to clean out the Bright firm. He obviously had me well sussed. Stupid I might be, but I was tenacious. If he knew half as much about me as he pretended, he knew nothing short of killing me was going to stop me getting to the bottom of the matter. He was going to aim like a gun and walk away from the mess, clean and green. What was worse was that he was right. We both knew it would work.

'What about the threats to my family?' I asked.

'Not guilty again,' he replied. 'I think Bright has started to panic. The organisation is beginning to fall apart since you began poking around.'

'So I've done some good in my own blundering way?'

'You have unwittingly helped me up to a point, I must admit. But that point is past. The Bright organisation had been tainted by it's own corruption. Soon I will be able to pick up their business. You are of no further use to me, and besides, people are apt to die when they come into contact with you. That is why I am telling you all this. I do not want you meddling further with things that concern me. Do you think I'd waste my time otherwise?'

Liar, I thought. Of course you would. Especially if the pay-off was me getting George out of your hair for good.

'What happens now?' I asked.

As I spoke, with the corner of my eye, I saw a dark coloured car pulled up and join the others outside the crematorium.

Talk about being late to someone else's funeral.

I looked back to David as he spoke again.

'Now, Mr. Sharman. You forget everything you know about Patricia and me. You return to your seedy little life and pick up the pieces that remain. I go onwards and upwards.'

'I meant to Patsy.' I said.

'She will be very rich,' said David. 'Travel the world, have loves and adventures. She is a very privileged young woman.'

'Bollocks!' I cut in. 'She'll be dead within a year. Just look at her.

You have to keep her as high as a kite, or else she'll blow it. I bet she can hardly function now. What happens when she gets so high the only way is down?'

I grabbed her by the wrists, and pushed the bangles up her arm. She didn't resist. I guessed she was used to being pulled about by men. David moved slowly towards me and the barrel of the Ingram dug painfully into my side. I didn't stop. I checked both arms. They were clear of tracks.

'Where are you injecting her?' I demanded. 'Between her toes or under her tongue, to keep the meat fresh for the punters?'

Patsy looked from one of us to the other.

'I spoke to Steve, Patsy,' I said, addressing her now. 'Your friend the punk from Brixton. You used to go to gigs with him, remember?'

'Steve,' Patsy said dreamily. 'He's nice. He never tried to touch me.'

In her world that probably was her definition of nice.

'Yes, Steve,' I said. 'He told me you never took heroin. Come with me Patsy. I'll get you clean and you can start again.'

The machine gun twitched in David's hand against my body and I could feel the presence of the chauffeur behind me.

'Sharman,' David hissed. 'You've been lucky so far, but don't push your luck beyond its endurance. We're going to leave now, Patricia and I. Your argument now is with George Bright. Leave us out of it.'

He bundled Patsy into the car. I could feel the Colt hard against my back in the waistband of blue jeans, but I knew I had no chance against the M10 in a gun-fight. Let alone the back-up gun the driver held.

'Move away from the car,' David ordered.

I backed away slowly.

He began to get into the car himself. Then he turned and looked at me. 'Remember,' he said, 'the machine always demands a sacrifice.'

Then he climbed into the Rolls-Royce and sat next to Patsy. I saw him tuck the Ingram neatly under the passenger seat. Then the rear window hummed up, hiding the pair from my view. The chauffeur was still eye-balling me. He ducked in behind the wheel, started the car, put it into gear and let it glide silently away from me. I stood in the driveway and watched it go.

As I stood, the left hand passenger window slid down again and I saw Patsy's hand emerge. She threw the red rose back towards me. The driver kept his window open and the barrel of his pistol rested on the frame of the door as he drove one handed. That's the only problem with bullet proof glass. It works both ways.

On one side of the narrow tarmac, just before it turned into the main road, stood an old chestnut tree. Its branches swept low towards the ground, and its trunk was thick and covered with gnarled bark. On the other side, set slightly back on a grassy knoll, stood a family mausoleum. It had once been white but was now weather-stained and falling into disrepair.

As the Roller slowed to make the turn, all hell broke loose.

From behind the tree stepped the blonde man, Lynch, who had knocked me unconscious in the Brixton squat. He tossed something heavy and hard through the driver's window. From where I stood it looked like a cricket ball. Then I heard a muffled explosion, and smoke and flame billowed from the front of the car. I realised with true horror that it had been a hand grenade.

I estimated that the car weighed nearly two tons, and it only shook slightly on its heavy suspension from the blast. It rolled across the road and stalled against a gravestone depicting a heavenly host of angels, Victorian style, heavy and ornate. The gravestone was pushed out of the earth, but held the weight of the car.

The other white man from the squat, Flared Trousers, or Grant or what the hell his real name was, ran from behind the mausoleum. He was carrying what I assumed to be the sawn-off that had raised a scar on my head. I decided that they really did take turns with the weapons.

He poked the shot-gun through the open rear window of the car, from where Patsy had thrown the flower, and fired twice in quick succession. The sound of the shots echoed through the cemetery and a murder of crows flapped from the trees where they had been roosting. I had frozen in the act of picking up the rose from the ground. Grant reloaded the sawn-off, carefully picking up the spent cartridges that ejected. Lynch drew a pistol from his jacket pocket and fired at me. I heard the bullet zip through the air close to my left hand side. I stood paralysed with horror. I wanted to turn and run but couldn't move. Lynch fired again and the bullet dug a groove in the roadway behind me. I couldn't let him keep shooting at me without retaliating. I pulled my .38 from the belt of my jeans and fired back three times, snap shots, double action, hardly taking aim.

I saw no sign that I had hit anyone. I expect that my hands were trembling too much. The doors to the crematorium burst open and three men in dark suits and black ties burst through, then stood teetering on the steps. Lynch and Grant looked at each other, and made a beeline in tandem to the car that I had seen draw up to the building whilst I had been talking to David. One of them had obviously ducked through the building, out through the rear exit, then round to lay deadly ambush with the other, who must have been dropped off in the road.

I should have taken more notice, they must have followed me from my office. So much for Leicester, George. That was another one I owed him.

The three men from the crematorium remained standing on the step as Lynch and Grant made their tyre-squealing escape.

I raced towards the Rolls. As I ran I gestured for the three to stay where they were. I used the hand with the gun in it. I think they got the message, because they backed through the doors again.

I checked the front of the car first. I didn't want to know what had happened to Patsy, not right away. I could guess only too well.

The driver's compartment was carnage. The grenade had exploded in the chauffeur's lap. Through the smoke, I could see that it had ripped out of most of his stomach, and all of his groin. I could also see his thigh bones poking whitely through his shredded uniform trousers. He was sitting in a pool of blood and guts. I had to turn my head aside to stop myself vomitting at the sight and smell. I cursed the murderers and myself, and George Bright.

Reluctantly I opened the rear passenger door. I knew what I was going to find, but it didn't make it any easier. The bodies of Patsy and her companion were huddled together on the wide leather seat. I placed the rose I had picked up off the ground onto the roof of the Rolls, and put my gun in my jacket pocket. I gently separated the bodies. I assumed that David had been hit first, because Patsy's corpse covered the massive chest wound he'd sustained from the point blank blast of the shot-gun. Patsy had been hit in the head and most of her face had been blown away. Blood, brains and blonde hair were coated over the back window. The rear compartment stank of cordite and the coppery odour of freshly spilled blood. There was nothing I could do for any one of them.

I suddenly remembered the Ingram. It was still under the seat where David had placed it. I checked that the safety was on as I picked it up and slung it over my shoulder by its leather strap. I looked towards the crematorium, a priest was standing on the steps now, staring at me.

When they realised that the shooting had stopped, someone was going to be brave enough to come and see what had happened. I didn't want to be around to answer any questions. I retrieved the rose, then ran away across the graves in the direction of my car.

30

I was limping by the time I reached the car. My foot had started to play me up. I scrambled behind the wheel and prayed that the car would start right away. It fired up at the first turn of the key in the ignition, and I screeched back down to the main gates. I sped past visitors and mourners staring up the hill towards the crematorium, from where the explosion and gunfire had come. I sent the car into a power slide onto the main road and accelerated into the one-way system. My hands were shaking on the steering wheel and I could feel the dampness of my palms against the slick leather. I was down to the wire with fear and tension, mixed with an elated relief that I had escaped unharmed. The killer's car was long gone. As I drove away from the carnage. I guessed that they had lost themselves in the maze of backstreets that crisscrossed the area. I drove as fast as I dared southwards, away from central London, down into the outer suburbs.

I wasn't thinking too clearly, I just needed to get away from the horror that I had witnessed and put together the information that had been disclosed by Patsy and the tall man named David.

When I thought of the girl and what had happened to her, I literally felt a stab of pain inside. I should have stuck to my commitment of non-involvement. Falling in love with a photograph was stupid. I might have guessed that when the image became flesh, she would let me down and do something dumb like getting killed. Ultimately people always disappoint you. It must be something to do with being human. I looked at the rose that Patsy had thrown to me, where I had tossed it on top of the dashboard and tears stung my eyes.

I was the only person left who knew everything, or nearly everything. The only person on the side of the angels that is. It was up to me to expose the whole sorry mess to the light, and identify the killers to the authorities. As such I was a marked man. Too many people had been killed with me in close proximity. I'd been an eye witness once too often now. Someone at the cemetery must have spotted the registration number of the Trans-Am. If the police traced the car, through Charlie, back to me, I was the prime suspect in a bunch of brutal slayings. It didn't matter that I'd been shot at myself. There were no witnesses to that fact as far as I knew, except for the killers themselves. I had been there, and that was that. Tie those latest killings in with the decapitation of Terry Southall, and of course the death of Jane Lewis, accidental or not, and I was public enemy number one. David had told me that the machine demands a sacrifice. He was right, and it could be me.

There was every reason to bang me up in Brixton nick, to await trial at the Bailey. A bent ex-copper, drugs, and now five deaths in as many days. I couldn't see anyone buying coincidence on that. I had to find one of the gang who would talk, tell the truth and let me off the hook. It would be easier said than done. There were at least four of them still at large, possibly more, and all with blood on their hands. The weak link had to be George Bright. David had told me George was beginning to panic. I'd seen it myself for that matter. I had to get him to the police alive. As for the rest of the villains, they'd be well pissed off that they hadn't topped me already. They'd had enough chances, God knows. Only being armed and the intervention of the mourners had saved me in the cemetery. I'd bet that the bad guys were kicking themselves that they hadn't finished me off at the house in Brixton, or when they were chasing me through Waterloo. I was living on dumb luck and that wasn't good enough.

So there I was, in a car that was getting hotter by the moment, fleeing from a mass murder, wanted by both the law and the lawless. It was a classic 'B' movie scenario, only it was real and scaring the shit out of me. Whichever way I turned was a dead end, and it looked like being me that ended up dead.

I found that I had driven mechanically as far as Croydon. I checked my watch and discovered it was ten to two. I needed a drink badly. My mouth was dry and tasted bitterly of fear and defeat. I had to stop soon. If I didn't, I knew that I'd pile the car up and I didn't need that on top of everything else.

I drove around to the market, and even though the town was as busy as ever, I found a parking meter straight away. I stashed the Ingram under the driver's seat, hoping that no juvenile delinquent would bust into the car and lift it. But I could hardly carry it around the shopping centre at port arms. I ducked out of the car and into the first pub I saw. It was crowded with shoppers and market workers, but I welcomed the noise. I bought a beer and fought my way into the back bar where I found a seat. I took stock of my assets. I had my driver's license, banker's card and about thirty quid in cash on me. I could get more money from a dispensing machine using my bank card. But from here on in, I had to assume the worst about my immediate future. Eventually I was bound to be tied into the cemetery murders. That would put me amongst the most wanted in London. It figured that I had to get further out of town. I couldn't chance going home for the shotgun or a change of clothes, but I did have the sub-machine gun and a full magazine of ammunition, and a pistol, and where I was going, I didn't think anyone would be worried if my undershorts were a bit grubby.

At that point I didn't know if the police had the details of the Pontiac or not. Assuming the worst, I had to believe they did. I didn't want to hire a car, as the personal details from my license would go on file and the law could get the number of any new car I was driving within a very short time. Once again, and until the whole business was cleared up one way or another, I had to keep taking a paranoid, pessimistic view. That way, I might come out of my first case all in one piece. I considered stealing a car, but ignored the idea. Firstly I was no great shakes at vehicular larceny, and secondly it would be just my luck to get picked up for taking and driving away, and find myself explaining the situation to some uniform who would eventually put two and two together and end up getting a bit of promotion out of nicking me. Even if I did get away with it, the registration could be on the air within a couple of hours and I'd be fucked up again. So I was stuck with the Pontiac. Not exactly the most discreet car on the road, but that was tough. Next I decided I needed somewhere to get some rest. My nerves were shot. I needed some peace, if only for a few hours, but preferably for the night. I'd frozen with panic at the cemetery when the fire fight had started. I needed some time to psych myself up for whatever was to come. I knew exactly what kind of place I wanted.

Somewhere I could jump in and pull over myself.

When somebody started playing 'A Whiter Shade of Pale' on the juke, I went off to find a bank. I withdrew £100 in cash and went back to the car. On the way I stopped at a chemist and bought a toothbrush, some paste and a shaving kit. Even in times of adversity I wanted to have clean teeth and a smooth jaw. I also stopped at an off-license and bought a bottle of good scotch. By the time I reached the car, I felt that everyone in the street was watching me.

Right by where I'd parked the motor was a hi-fi store. Inside they were demonstrating a new compact disc player. The record that was being played was 'Carmen'. I stopped to listen as I checked if the Trans-Am was being bugged. There were no squads of marksmen wearing flak jackets, ready to riddle the car and me with M-16 rifle fire. Not even a traffic warden in sight. I relaxed when I found that the Ingram was where I'd left it. I rolled down the window and listened to the music as I sat in the car deciding where to go next.

I drove out of Croydon and headed south again. The sort of place I was looking to hole up in would be large and anonymous, full of transients. The last thing I needed was a nosey landlady. I drove down in the direction of Gatwick airport, avoiding the motorway. I struck lucky almost immediately. I was just about a mile from the airport when I came across a single storey motel. It had a huge carpark shadowed by the giant oak trees. I mentally thanked the architect who had landscaped the outside. I drove to the furthest corner of the lot, and parked the car close up under the leafiest tree. It must have been a car thieve's paradise, when I left the car I couldn't see the motel at all.

I found an old Nike sports' bag in the boot of the Pontiac. The canvas was scuffed and grubby, but passable. I wanted to look like a rep on his way to his sales area having a night in a hotel on expenses. Into the bag I put the toilet gear that I had purchased, the bottle of scotch and the machine pistol. I kept the Cobra in the waistband of my jeans. Then I went to see if there were any rooms available. I got a single, with shower en suite with no problem. The girl on the reception was totally disinterested in me. It did my ego no good, but bolstered my sense of safety. I checked in with a fake name and car registration. I paid cash in advance, and trusted that no-one would bother to look around for the non-existent Ford Sierra, that I claimed to drive.

There was no porter, so I had to find my own room. That was another plus.

The room was small and smelt of dirty socks, used ashtrays and old sex. But the bed was a fair three quarter double, the bathroom was clean and the room contained a colour TV that showed recent movies on a special channel, twenty four hours a day. At least I didn't have to think if I didn't want to. On the way to the room I saw an ice making machine in the corridor. I went and filled one of the tooth glasses from the bathroom with ice. Into the other I put the rose from the cemetery to keep it fresh.

I turned on the TV and watched 'Back To The Future' on video and drank scotch on the rocks. Not that I particularly like scotch, but I figured that a private eye in a scruffy hotel room should do just that.

Now the taste of scotch always reminds me of that night, I don't drink it often any more. It also helped my hands to stop shaking and blocked out the memory of how terrified I'd been under fire. When the booze made me feel brave again, I checked the M10 over to familiarize myself with its workings. The magazine was fully loaded with thirty two brass jacketed slugs. I wondered if I'd have the nerve to pull the trigger. I'd only fired a machine gun once before, on a special anti-terrorist course when I'd been on the force. All I could remember about them was, they had a tendency to pull upwards whilst firing, they were very noisy and stank of gunpowder.

When half the whiskey was gone and I'd watched two more movies on the tube, I ordered a steak and baked potato from room service. I asked them to bring along a bottle of red wine with the meal because Patsy's face was beginning to creep into the corner of my mind as I stared at the TV set. I knew it would take a lot of alcohol to keep her out of my thoughts.

While I waited for the food to arrive, I switched the TV over to the evening news. The cemetery killings were the main story. Thank God there were no detailed pictures. The cameras had only been allowed to film the Rolls-Royce from a distance. No names were mentioned. The news people obviously had very little hard information to work from. They tried to flesh out the report of the triple murder by interviewing one of the witnesses who'd been in the crematorium when the killing took place. He'd seen nothing of the actual explosion and shooting, but managed to give a fairly accurate description of me. I was described as the third gunman. Charming. I was reported to have escaped in a large American car. The witness also described Blondie and his partner. They'd fled in a black car. That was all. When an item about Princess Diana opening a kidney unit appeared on the screen, I switched back to 'The Terminator' on the movie channel. It seemed an apt choice.

I could hardly face the meal when it arrived. The steak was dry and the potato undercooked. The salad that accompanied the food had surrendered to old age long before it reached my plate. I ate what I could and chased the rest around my plate for a while. I drank the wine straight from the bottle. It looked like blood and tasted slightly of decay, but I was getting too drunk to care. Finally I fell asleep with the TV still playing, my revolver lying on the bed next to me. That night I had the first of the awful recurring dreams that have haunted me ever since. I dreamt that I was walking through a garden filled with rose bushes. They were all the same variety as the one Patsy had held at the cemetery. The perfume that rose from the flowers was thick and heady. I knew that danger lurked in the garden, that people were hiding from me amongst the bushes. And I knew who they were, they were the people I had seen dead over the past few days. I was desperate to avoid them. I was sure if I spoke to any one of them I would die myself. I could feel the eyes of the cadavers upon me and smell their putrescence through the scent of the roses.

I awoke with the .38 clutched in my fist, the hammer drawn back. My finger was twitching on the trigger, a bare fraction of an ounce of pressure from pulling it. The gun was aimed at the TV set, where 'Back To The Future' was playing on the screen.

I carefully eased the hammer back and stuck the gun under my pillow. I dried my sweat on the sheet and fell asleep again.

Finally the morning insinuated itself through the thin curtains of my room and squeezed beneath my eyelids. I woke up sweating again in the overheated atmosphere. I was repulsed by my own stale smell. I dragged myself out of bed and staggered into the tiny bathroom and showered in the cramped stall. Then I shaved and cleaned my teeth. I dressed in two day old crumpled clothing and demanded coffee from room service. It was only warm when it arrived twenty minutes later, but after a potful I began to feel half human. I left the detritus of my stay to the maids and went and returned my key to reception. I was ignored again by the new blonde at the desk. I looked at myself in the mirror in the reception and decided I looked surprisingly respectable. I was only a little ragged around the edges. My eyes were slightly pink, but not so as anyone would remark upon them. Luckily I wasn't hungover. There must have been so much adrenalin in my blood it had neutralised the alcohol.

I went out and found my car in the morning mist. It hadn't been touched and started immediately. I drove down to Gatwick Airport. Suddenly, all I wanted to do was catch a plane. Any plane, anywhere. I'm sure if I'd had my passport on me I'd have buggered off to Spain. I fought back the urge to flee and parked the Pontiac in the long-term car park. I locked it up and pocketed the keys. I hoped Charlie would get his car back. It had been invaluable to me, and I'd grown rather fond of the beast. But for now it had outlived its usefulness. I walked from the car park to the BR station. There was a through train to Victoria due in just under five minutes and I bought a ticket.

I also purchased a newspaper from the newsstand. The murders were front page news. No arrests had been made so far. The paper had sussed out that international drug dealing was behind the crime. I was mentioned again but with little detail. However, they'd identified the Trans-Am even if the registration number printed was two digits out. Perhaps the police would find it parked up at the airport and assume I'd jetted off to the Costa Del Crime. I guessed that within a few hours, one way or another they'd know I hadn't, but by then it would be too late. I caught the train and travelled back up to town. The compartment was nearly empty as it was a weekend. I sat and looked at the country turn to suburbs and then city proper with the bag of massive firepower resting on my lap. When I got to Victoria I ate a proper breakfast in a back street cafe, and then got lost in the West End. I wandered around the familiar streets for hours. I knew that time was running out, but I couldn't bring myself to face whatever was waiting for me south of the river. I found myself in Soho at lunchtime. I went into a pub, but drank only fruit juice. I caught an early showing of a porno film in Brewer Street. I sat in the deserted cinema and stared at the naked bodies on the screen and felt nothing. I felt cold and emotionless. I had cut everything out of my mind except for the need for vengeance. I left the cinema after twenty minutes and found a call box. I tried George Bright at his warehouse. Surprisingly he answered after the first ring. I said nothing just gently replaced the receiver onto the cradle after he spoke. I left the telephone box and hailed a cab.

31

The cabbie dropped me off at the gates to Brockwell park. I crossed over the road and walked under the railway bridge. When I got to the warehouse, there were lights burning on the ground floor. The mesh gates were open and I went round to the back of the building. The loading bay was closed up tight. The outside steps leading down to the basement looked promising so I crept down them on tip-toe. I couldn't see any sign of life, and with luck George would be on his own on a weekend afternoon. The basement area smelt of cats and was piled with garbage. Underfoot the ground was slimy. I picked my way as quietly as possible through the junk and tried the windows, one by one. All of them were bolted and barred. Down at the end of the entry, around a blind corner was a door. I tried the handle. Of course it was locked tight. I felt sick, after all my brave intentions, I couldn't even get into the place.

I leant back against the wall and tried to concoct a plan. As I was thinking, I heard the rattle of the loading bay door opening. I peered up from the basement, through iron railings and saw the door rolling up into it's mounting. Standing in the opening was the fat man from the Brixton squat, who I'd subsequently seen pump two shots into the back of the Rolls-Royce in Norwood Cemetery. The man that David had told me was named Grant, now dressed in khaki fatigue trousers and an Iron Maiden T- Shirt.

I unzipped the sports bag and took out the Colt Cobra, which I tucked into the waistband of my jeans, at the back, out of sight again. I carefully removed the M10 and wrapped the leather strap around my forearm. I left the bag amongst the other rubbish in the entry. I walked back through the muck and climbed the stone steps slowly back to ground level. Grant was carefully man-handling a giant juke-box onto the edge of the loading bay.

So it was business as usual at George's. The box was probably full of A.1 pink Peruvian flake. The sort of stuff that makes it a pleasure to need a new septum. Grant seemed to be alone. I pussy-footed round until he was clearly in my view, but facing away from me.

'Turn around,' I said quietly. He stiffened, and let the juke-box tilt back gently onto its feet, then slowly turned his head until he could see me.

'Hello again,' I said. 'Now turn around like I told you to and keep your hands where I can see them.' The words sounded stilted and overdramatic. But coupled with the machinegun I was holding, pointed at his back, they seemed to work. He turned on the balls of his feet and stood with his arms raised from the sides of his body. All at once I heard the sound of an engine from behind me. Without thinking, I turned my head and saw a Hi-Ace truck with the words 'BRIGHT LEISURE' painted on the sides turn beneath the arch directly behind me and pull into the yard. At the wheel was the Heavyweight. The Ingram was no longer covering Grant, and he took his chance and ran back into the shadows inside the warehouse. Heavyweight, meanwhile, seeing me standing holding the machinepistol hit the brakes of the van. It skidded to a halt on the damp cobbles. When it stopped, he tried to put it into reverse, but only managed to stall the engine. He was desperately trying to restart it when I ran up to the vehicle and stuck the barrel of the M10 through the open window of the van.

'Leave it,' I ordered. He immediately took his hand off the ignition key. 'Get out,' I continued, and stepped back from the cab door so as to allow him room to do so. He opened the door slowly and stepped out of the truck. 'Face down on the ground,' I said, jamming the gun into his side. He dropped to the muddy ground as if to start a series of press-ups. 'Spreadeagle,' I shouted. He concurred. Just as I was going to frisk him, I heard heavy footsteps from within the darkened warehouse. Through the gloom I saw Grant running towards the loading bay door. He was carrying the sawn-off I'd already seen him use to great effect.

'Get up,' I said to the black man lying on the ground. 'Get behind the truck, quick.' He sprang to his feet and I pulled him out of Grant's firing line, behind the van. I kept the Ingram poking into the negro's spine, with my left hand twisted into the material of his shirt. I peered out from behind the protection of the bodywork of the Hi-Ace. We were so close I could smell his sour odour.

'This is on full automatic,' I hissed into his ear. 'If I pull the trigger, your guts are down the road.'

Grant slid to a halt behind the juke-box which he had abandoned on the loading bay floor. I saw him stealing a glance towards us, using the box as a shield. My hand was greasy with sweat on the pistol grip of my gun. I was scared again. I didn't want to die in a muddy yard in a South London slum . I wanted to live and would do anything to make sure I did. I hammered the muzzle of the Ingram into the Heavyweight's kidney and whispered into his ear. 'Walk slowly in front of me.'

'Fuck off, Blood,' he said. They were the first words he'd spoken since driving into the yard.

'I'll shoot you in the back if you don't, now move,' I said threateningly. I let go of his shirt to check that the magazine of the machine-pistol was pushed securely home, and he took his chance to make a break for it. He powdered himself around the side of the truck, shouting as he went, 'Don't shoot, it's me.'

Grant took no notice, perhaps he was as scared as me. Obviously he'd identified the Ingram for what it was. As the black man left the shelter of the van, Grant stepped from behind the juke-box and fired his shot gun. Immediately he ducked back. The shot hit the Heavyweight in mid-stride, across his upper arms and chest. The force of the sawn-off's load snapped his head back. A gout of blood, skin and material from his shirt fountained from his body, a good deal of it splashing onto me. His legs kept pumping, but the punch from the blast knocked his body backwards. He did a lazy half-flip and landed in a puddle of dirty water by the front bumper of the truck. I squinted through the side window of the van, and saw through the windscreen, Grant, half hidden by the juke-box. He was desperately trying to re-load his gun. In the excitement he must have discharged both barrels. It was all the edge I required.

I moved out from my cover and pulled the trigger of the Ingram. The tiny gun burped noisily in my hands, and I felt the kick reverberate up my arms. I'd aimed too low, but the muzzle velocity pulled the gun upwards as I'd remembered it would. The shells hit the juke-box, shattering coloured glass, plastic and chrome which flew in all directions. At that range, it was as if there was nothing in the way. The bullets zipped up Grant's chest, throwing him backwards onto a work bench which collapsed under his weight in a cloud of dust. He lay in the debris, blood pumping from his wounds. The shot gun lay by his side. I paused to draw a shakey breath. The shooting had taken less than twenty seconds to occur. It felt like a lifetime. For two out of three of us involved, it was.

I checked the Heavyweight's body. He was dead. The mass of

pellets from the shot gun had nearly ripped one of his arms off. The puddle in which he lay was stained a deep red colour. I didn't feel a thing. I remembered what he and Lynch had done to Terry Southall.

Next I ran over and jumped up onto the loading bay. Grant was still alive, but only barely. His heart was still beating, but there was nowhere for the blood to go. His chest was a mess, blood and fluid ran across the concrete floor of the bay. I breathed deeply to retain my equilibrium. I left him where he lay. I'm no doctor, and even if I was I'd have done nothing.

I checked the magazine of the Ingram. There were twelve bullets left, which meant I'd pumped twenty shots into Grant's body. I was quite happy, he'd deserved it.

I picked up the sawn-off that he had dropped; it was empty. I found the two fresh cartridges he'd been trying to load on the floor. I finished the job. I could feel the presence of more people in the warehouse and I needed all the firepower I could muster, besides I wanted the shot gun for evidence. I hung the M10 by it's strap from my shoulder and, shot gun at the ready, I moved deeper into the building. I walked slowly through the loading bay and into the dimness of the warehouse proper.

Juke-boxes, arcade video games and pin tables lined the walls. Pool tables filled the middle of the windowless storage area looking like great coffins under their cloudy plastic wrappings. The mezzanine gallery that ran close under the roof was in darkness. The only light in that place came from weak flourescent fitments that hung down at the end of rusty chains and tied into the power system by thin, snakelike cables. I prowled between the equipment, looking from left to right. Everything was quiet until I heard the squeak of a rubber sole on the metal walkway above me, and to my right.

I saw a muzzle flash in the gloom of the mezzanine and heard the explosion of gun-shots. The first two bullets smashed into the slate top of a pool table in front of me. The third hit me in the meat of my upper left arm. I felt as if I'd been smacked by a length of 2x4 timber. The bullet spun me round and dropped me into the aisle formed by the rows of pool tables. As a reflex, when I fell I pulled one of the triggers of the shot gun. The pellets bounced harmlessly against the concrete walls of the warehouse.

Whether or not I actually passed out, I don't know, but I found myself lying on cold stone clutching the sawn-off. The Ingram was lying by my side. I heard footsteps descending the metal stairs from the gallery. Through slitted eyes I watched the blonde man, Lynch, peering through the bannisters in my direction. I fired the other barrel of the shot gun. He ducked back out of sight, firing the pistol in his hand as he went. The bullet raised sparks from the stone floor on which I lay, and splinters cut into the skin of my face. I reached for the machine pistol with my right hand as I lay face down on the cold floor. Time dragged by and my arm began to throb from the bullet wound. I could feel blood collecting in the sleeve of my jacket. It felt warm against my chilled skin. I guessed that five minutes had passed, but it might as well have been five hours, when I heard soft footsteps coming towards me. I kept my head down and prayed that Lynch wouldn't just put a bullet into my skull to confirm I was out of the picture. With my eyes still half closed I saw his feet in their white sneakers moving closer. Apart from an echo of the gun-shots in my ears, everything was quiet.

He walked slowly up to me. The combination of the splashes of blood from the Heavyweight's fatal wound, plus that from my injured arm, together with the trickles of blood I could feel running down my face as a result of being hit by the concrete splinters must have convinced him I was dead, or at least badly wounded. I tried not to breathe as he came even closer. He allowed his gun-hand to rest down by his side. The empty shot gun was in clear sight but the Ingram was in shadow. He stopped and kicked the sawn-off away from me. Whilst he was momentarily distracted, I lifted the M10 and pointed it up in his direction. He tried in vain to bring his revolver round to bear on me.

'Bad idea motherfucker,' I said as I squeezed the trigger and watched the bullets cut him down. My gun emptied in less than a second. At point blank range the slugs tore into his body and tumbled him back down the aisle, screaming wordless screams. His pistol flew from his grasp and landed somewhere in the darkness. He lay, kicking his legs spasmodically until he was still. I climbed to my feet, feeling like a whipped dog and wiped the blood of my eyes with my sleeve. Still carrying the empty machine gun I went to look for George Bright in his inner sanctum.

32

I walked down the short flight of stairs to the basement carrying the Ingram like a talisman. I'd given up any idea of being quiet, as the noise from the gunfight would have awakened Sleeping Beauty in the close confines of the concrete building.

I could feel the sticky ooze of blood running down my left arm and I left a trail of crimson spots on the uncarpeted steps as I descended into the bowels of the warehouse. Lights burned, but there was no sound. I pushed open the door to George's office. He was sitting behind his desk. His expression could have been carved from wood. The surface of the desk was stacked with long, transparent packets of what might have been icing sugar, but I knew weren't. Behind him the safe was standing with its steel door slightly ajar. My arm was beginning to stiffen up and I felt a little dizzy. George didn't acknowledge my presence. I looked around the office. There was a tea towel draped over the handle of the electric kettle standing on the filing cabinet. I tossed the Ingram carelessly onto the desk and went over to fetch the cloth. There was a single edged razor blade in an ashtray beside the kettle. All the better to cut the lines out with, I thought. I picked up the blade and sliced the edge of the cloth. Using my right hand and my teeth I ripped off a length of rag. I tied the thin material awkwardly around my arm just above the bullet wound. I knotted it into a rough tourniquet as tightly as I could using my teeth again. It reminded me of the preparation for shooting up, but I put the thought out of my mind. My little piece of first-aid had been conducted in perfect silence. I felt just a little freaked out at being so studiously ignored.

'Well, George,' I said to break the silence. 'Is this how it ends?'

'She's dead,' he said bluntly.

'I know, I was there,' I replied. I sat down on the chair on my side of the desk and let my left arm hang limply at my side.

'Wasn't that what you wanted?' I asked.

'Me?' He looked at me for the first time. 'Me, you bastard? Of course it wasn't. I loved her.'

'Enough to turn her out as a whore?'

From somewhere above I heard a faint noise. Perhaps it was a mouse, or a rat, or any one of the noises that can be heard in an old building as it settles on its foundations, or perhaps it wasn't.

I ignored the sound.

'Why me George?' I continued. 'Why pick on me for your bloody scheme?'

'I wanted her found,' he replied.

'You succeeded, but why me?' I asked again.

'You'll never understand,' he said. I was the first to agree.

'I loved her,' he said again. I was getting more and more pissed off with him.

'Love!' I spat out the word. 'For Christ's sake don't bring love into it.'

'Why don't you just go?' he said after a moment.

'Just like that George, just go? You must know I can't do that.'

'Take one of these.' He gestured at the packets that littered the desk top. 'You know what they are, don't you? And you like it, he said that you did.' I didn't bother to ask who 'he' was. George picked up a scalpel blade from the clutter in front of him and split a packet from end to end. 'Try it,' he invited. I dipped my finger into the powder that spilt from the cut in the plastic. I tasted the bitter dust on the end of my tongue and immediately felt the freeze turn my mouth numb.

'Top grade, George, supreme even,' I said. 'Connoisseur's coke, no-one's walked on this batch yet.'

'Take one, and go,' he said. 'Any one of these bags is worth close to eighty grand.' He turned in his chair and looked at the open safe. 'Or cash,' he said, his voice rising. 'I've got plenty of cash.' He got up from his chair and went to the safe. He pulled the door all the way open. The interior was stacked with neatly bundled bank notes.

'I heard you were small time, George, but I heard wrong,' I said. 'Keep your drugs, I don't dip into that bag any more. As for your money, it wouldn't get me far. Too many people are looking for me. No, my friend. It's you I want. I need you to tell everyone how I was set up.'

'No,' he said, turning from the safe. He walked calmly back to the desk and picked up the Ingram that I had dropped onto it.

'Put it down George, I'm not impressed,' I said gently.

He swung the machine gun round and pointed it at my chest.

'I'll kill you,' he said.

'No George,' I said tiredly. 'You look about as happy holding that thing as a nun caught changing the batteries in her vibrator. You're used to other people doing your killing for you. Besides it's not loaded.'

'Don't try that one on me,' he sneered.

'You are a prat, George,' I told him as I got up from the chair on which I was sitting.

I was wrong about the killing part. He was prepared to pull the trigger and did. There was a metallic click from the firing action of the M 10 and nothing else. George looked down at the weapon in pure frustration. I snatched the gun from him with my good hand and busted him on the side of the head with the butt end. He fell to the floor, knocking his chair over as he went. I flung the Ingram into the corner of the room, knelt beside him and felt for the pulse in his throat. It was weak, but regular. The last thing I wanted to do was top him. I righted his seat and slumped into it on his side of the desk. I heard another noise, this time from directly outside the office, and the door began to open slowly inwards. 'Come in John,' I said. 'I was beginning to wonder where you were hiding yourself.'

33

John Reid slid into the room like a dangerous little snake. He was wearing his cream Burberry mackintosh again. It was hanging open over a pink Lacoste shirt and baggy blue jeans. The outfit was perfect, regulation, off-duty copper's casual wear. He could have been going for an afternoon's shopping down the Arndale with his old woman, if it hadn't been for the automatic pistol clenched in his right hand. He looked so neat and tidy, so respectable, so ordinary, standing there, that it pissed me right off. I sat and fixed him with what I hoped was a killing look. We surveyed each other. Him all tarted up, me covered in blood, filth and dried sweat, smelling of cordite and death, and trembling because of what I'd done. Him, still official with a warrant card in his pocket and me, facing God knows what charges. If ever I hated anyone in my life it was then, but I had to talk to him. Had to communicate. Had to dig the last vestige of truth from someone who treated truth like an old cigarette end to be discarded, as and when he pleased.

'Surprise, surprise,' I said, 'of all the drug dens, in all the towns, in all the world, you have to walk into mine.'

John regarded me, and sneered.

'Still the jokes, Nick, you silly cunt. You're lucky to be alive, do you know that?'

'Yes,' I replied irritably, 'your little firm has done its best to see me off again today.'

'And it looks as though they nearly succeeded. I should've let them do it when they wanted to, days ago. It would've saved me a lot of trouble.'

'You mean at the house in Brixton,' I said, 'or when they chased me around Waterloo, taking pot shots at my car?'

'Either time would have done,' he retorted.

'So you were the fourth man at the squat?'

'Very good, Nick,' he replied sarcastically, 'how long did it take you to work that out?'

'A lot longer than it should have, and even then I didn't want to believe it. Why didn't you let them finish me off? I don't get it.'

'Because I felt sorry for you. You looked so fucking pathetic lying there, that I thought I'd leave you for the force to take care of.'

'I suppose it never occurred to you that I might do some hard time in the Scrubs?'

'It did as a matter of fact,' he said with a humourless smile, 'and you know how they treat ex-old bill inside, don't you?'

I knew and it wasn't pleasant knowledge.

'I think you're lying,' I said, 'I think you couldn't resist facing me down. I think you wanted to tell me everything before you topped me. You wanted to let me know how clever you were. How you didn't give a fuck about the law. Well it was a big mistake, John, leaving me alive to carry on.'

By the look on his face, it seemed he was well aware of that.

'I know,' he said, 'that's why I let them have a second go. I forgot what kind of driver you are, but even when you got away from them on Thursday, I never thought you'd take it this far.'

'It was forced on me.'

'Why didn't you just quit when I told you to?' he asked.

'Because I always quit, and I'm getting sick and tired of it,' I replied.

'The funny thing is,' he said, 'that even when you don't quit, you're still fucking useless.'

'But it's funny how everyone that's said that is either dead or out of the game.' I looked over towards George Bright lying unconscious on the floor.

'Except me,' said John.

'Precisely, except you,' I said, 'and me,' I added.

He looked at me in a way that hinted that the arrangement might only be temporary. 'Well, what now?' he asked.

'Now John,' I replied. 'We all take a trip down to the local nick and tell your mates in blue exactly what has been happening under their noses for the last couple of years.'

'Just like that,' said John. 'Just like in a story book. Remember I'm the one with the gun. You expect me to go quietly and confess everything. Well, bollocks to that. I'm not giving up everything I worked for because of you.'

I sat and looked at him, and he stood and looked at me. The automatic was pointed at my chest, he had the winning hand and he knew it. With his left hand he reached into his coat pocket and pulled out a packet of cigarettes and a lighter. He threw them down onto the desk top in front of me.

'Get one out and light it for me,' he ordered.

'I've given up,' I said.

'Just do it', he snarled.

I did as I was told, rather awkwardly, using only my right hand. The smoke bit into the back of my throat. It was the first cigarette I'd tasted in over a year. It felt good. I put it down on the edge of the desk. John motioned for me to sit back and I slumped down into the chair. He picked up the cigarette and took a deep drag.

'You are a bastard, John,' I said. 'After all we've been through together. I never thought it would turn out like this, I thought we were friends'.

'Friends, you've got to be kidding,' he said through a cloud of smoke. 'I never even liked you. You had all the breaks. All the advantages, and you couldn't hack it. Just look at the state of you. And then,' he continued bitterly, 'you lost me the chance of promotion away from all this shit, you selfish bastard. You stole evidence that was down on me, you didn't care if I suffered. You never gave a toss for anyone but yourself. I would've been Inspector at least, by now. You cost me, you slag, and you talk about friendship. Well fuck your friendship.'

There was contempt in his eyes, but I didn't flinch. It was true I had failed him, and a list of others that it would take me a week to remember, but that was past. I'd paid for that shit in hospitals, and during long sleepless nights, and the final payment had been made with the MAC M10. Or maybe the total bill hadn't been settled yet. But it wasn't going to be paid with apologies to a renegade copper.

'What happened to you John?' I asked.

'I've been getting rich.'

'Congratulations. You used to be happy just being a good copper.'

'Don't give me that sanctimonious shit,' he spat. 'What do you know about being a good copper? You were never any good at the job from the start.' All the compliments were getting tiresome.

'Maybe, John, but at least I never pretended to be anything I wasn't. You sat and listened to my story the other night as though you gave a damn. I told you about my wife and kid and you took it all in. You phoney son of a bitch.'

Then something terrible struck me.

'Where are Judith and Laura?' I asked, with a terrible dread grabbing at the pit of my stomach. 'You left that bloody note, didn't you? Just so I'd tell you where they were.'

I half rose from my seat. He must have been able to see the murder in my eyes.

'Relax, will you,' he said, gesturing with the pistol in his hand. 'Don't worry about them. It was just a wind-up. I wanted to make you squirm. I wanted you to concentrate on something else apart from the Bright case. Your pal Louis took them both off to Scotland. They'll be back in a day or so. I don't make war on women and children. They're safe and sound. Which is more than I can say for you.'

'Are you crazy?' I interrupted. 'You don't make war on women? Yesterday I saw Patsy Bright with half her head blown off. What was than then? A game?'

He was silent for a long time.

'She had to die,' he said, 'otherwise, that lunatic,' he gestured towards George, 'would never rest. He was obsessed with her. That's what all the cash was for. He was going to get you to find her, then do a runner to South America.'

George could have saved the effort, I thought. Half of South America was on the desk in front of me already.

'But why involve me? That's what I don't understand. Of all the people in the world, why me? I came back to town to earn a few bob and live the quiet life.'

'I saw your stupid advertisement in the paper,' John replied. 'I mentioned you to George. I laughed when I told him about you. How was I supposed to know he'd get a hard on for you and hire you?'

'But I still don't understand,' I said.

'You don't understand much, do you? Still, I suppose you never did. I was in charge of the investigation into her disappearance. I just didn't do anything about it. George couldn't go to a big firm of investigators. Anyone half way decent would have sussed him out in no time. That only left losers like you. When I told him you were bent and into drugs, he obviously thought there was no-one better to find his precious little fuck.'

'You must've made me sound good,' I said.

'I only told the truth.'

'Only it wasn't the truth, was it John? I'd been through changes. I'm straight, you're the bent one now, aren't you?'

He didn't answer.

'But why wouldn't you look for Patsy?' I asked.

'Because I knew where she was all the time. I knew she'd been sucked in by that bloody Arab poof she was killed with yesterday. I wasn't about to tell Bright and have him start a war to get her back.'

'But you got one.'

'That wasn't war. That was assassination. They had to be got rid of. Especially when the Arab latched onto you and spilled the beans about everything. He did, didn't he?'

'Not quite everything. He never mentioned you. I wonder why that was?'

'Because he wanted to team up with me. He wanted Bright out of the way, and for us to form a consortium. He knew my contacts are the best.'

'That's not what he said to me. He told me that your mob were on the way out. George was panicking and he'd pick up the business easily.'

'He was lying, he thought you'd get rid of George for him. But he needed me. Admittedly Bright is the weak sister, but I had the Arab's number. I took him out just when I needed to. His blackmailing game with Patsy Bright was making too many waves'.

'So you just killed them, just like that?'

He shrugged.

'By the way,' I said. 'Who's idea was it to send the letter to George? The one that said Patsy would be home soon.'

'I let it be known that it would be a good idea. The Arab got Patsy to write it.'

'So here we are,' I said. 'We've come to the big crunch.'

'It doesn't have to be. I've got no troops left now. You've seen to that. But you could come good. Together we could carry on the trade, pick up where Bright and I left off. Jesus you'd be a millionaire inside three months. You could handle sales and I'd look after security.'

I couldn't believe what he was saying.

'What are you talking about?' I asked incredulously. 'Don't you know what the body count is this week? Eight, John. Eight people have died. Do you expect to just erase that from the records with no questions asked?'

'I can handle it with a little help,' he replied coolly.

'How high up does this thing go then?' I questioned. 'You're talking almost government level here.'

'It goes high, Nick, very high.'

I remembered the tall man at the cemetery. The Arab, as John called him, or David as he'd called himself, and what he'd told me about powerful men with strange tastes. Obviously John was moving in exalted circles these days.

'So answer me just one more question,' I said, although by then I was heartily sick of talking. My throat was dry and it hurt to swallow and my left shoulder hurt like hell.

'Why did George kick me off the case, if he wanted Patsy back so badly?'

'Because I told him that, if by some miracle you did find her, I'd kill the pair of you.'

'You're a real sweetheart John, do you know that?'

He gave me that kind of look, usually reserved for something you've found sticking to the sole of your shoe, but said nothing.

'I bet Fox isn't involved,' I continued.

'That bastard,' said John. 'He's so straight, he can hardly turn corners.'

'Well, thank God someone still is.'

I knew then to whom to take my story if I could get out of this.

'Straight,' John said. 'What do you know about being straight?' It was you that got me into this in the first place.'

'Me?'

'Yes, you. I saw how easily you'd got the coke away from the station lock-up. I gave it a try and sold some heroin. It was simple.'

'A nice little bit of private enterprise for you,' I said.

'Too true, and now you can have a slice of it.'

'No thanks. It's too rich for my blood.'

'You have no choice.'

'I always have a choice.'

'Not this time Nick. If you don't want in with me, I'll kill you.'

I climbed slowly to my feet. I wanted John Reid to think I was in even worse shape than I looked.

'Not so fast,' John said threateningly.

'Relax, John,' I retorted, 'you've talked me into it. I accept your offer. How can I refuse? Just get me somewhere I can get cleaned up and have my arm looked at. I feel like hell.'

I could sense from the look in his eyes that he didn't trust me completely. But at least his gun was no longer pointing directly at me.

I pretended to stagger and put my hands on the desk for support. Under my fingers I felt the bag of cocaine that George had split open. Slowly and carefully I gripped the slick plastic. I looked John straight in the eyes.

'Well, are we going?' I asked.

The barrel of his gun moved even further from me. It was my one and only chance.

I flipped the bag of cocaine at his head.

Everything went into a kind of slow motion.

I remember clearly watching the plastic bag arching through the air. A thin mist of powder flew from the cut in the side. I saw John's left hand rise slowly to his head level as he tried to deflect the missile from his face.

He was too late. The packet hit him on the forehead and burst open. A cloud of dust exploded around his head, it must have filled his eyes and blinded him immediately, but he still managed to swing the barrel of his pistol back in my direction. He clawed at his eyes with his free hand to clear his vision.

As soon as I had thrown the bag, I went for my revolver. I pushed the material of my jacket back and felt my hand smack onto the rubber grip of my Colt.

I knew then, that if the metal of the gun snagged in the baggy cloth, I was going to die. There was one heart stopping moment when something caught, then the .38 was free.

I pulled back the hammer with my thumb as I brought the gun round to aim at John. Meanwhile, the business end of his pistol was looming closer to me. I could see the bore-hole of the automatic as it swung in my direction. It seemed to be as big as the Blackwall Tunnel as it moved. I watched as I sluggishly brought my gun up to arms' length and pulled the trigger.

Immediately everything jumped back to normal speed.

The first shot took John Reid in the chest on his right hand side. The impact of the bullet smashed him back against the door of the office, slamming it shut.

He fired his pistol. The bullet went wide and gouged a lump of plaster from the wall behind me.

I kept the Cobra at arm's length, but changed my aim slightly. Before I fired again, I saw John open his eyes wide and realised that he could see clearly again. His face contorted into a look that held hatred, mixed with fear, and something else that I could only construe as love in equal quantities.

He opened his mouth to speak, and said just two words:

'Nicky, don't.'

I didn't want to hear anything further from him. Not then, not ever.

I squeezed the trigger of my gun again and aimed at his heart. I kept firing, trying to keep a tight cluster of hits, just like I'd been taught on the firing range. I pulled the trigger until all six chambers of the Colt contained only empty cartridge cases.

I fucking loved it.

John Reid was only kept standing by the force of the bullets slamming into his chest.

As I fired I could feel tiny bubbles of sweat on my trigger finger mixing with the droplets of oil from the mechanism of the gun forming a sticky suds that seemed to bind my skin to the metal.

The explosions from the firing cracked in my head until I thought that my eardrums would rupture.

I felt like I was on an acid flashback. I was actually tripping out on death. I knew in the small, sane part of my mind that it must stop soon or I would go completely mad.

When the gun was empty, and no more bullets entered John's body, he slowly slipped down the door on which he was leaning into a sitting position. He left a long, thick, red smear of blood on the paintwork. I dropped my gun to the floor and then fell back into George's seat, cradling my head with my arms onto the desk in front of me.

'No more. Please God let there be no more,' I said aloud.

I had terrrible visions of non-stop streams of people coming through the office door to be killed by me, like some kind of horrific hydra. But the killing ground was finally silent.

I sat in the same position for quite a while, slowly pulling myself together.

I knew I had to get hold of Fox. He was the one last straw I had to cling to. With George Bright in his custody, I knew that the truth would, at last, be allowed to emerge.

I reached for the telephone which was half buried under the packets of drugs. With a sweep of my good arm, I cleared a space on the desk sending a small fortune in cocaine onto the floor as I did so. I looked at the soda scattered across the carpet and pondered that once upon a time I would literally have killed to possess a fraction of it. It was ironic. Now that I had killed, I had no desire at all for the drug.

I wondered how many people who knew me in the old days would actually believe that, surrounded by all that coke, my strongest craving was to smoke a cigarette. A regular, low tar king size cigarette. I looked at John's packet in front of me. He wouldn't be needing them now, I reached for it, took one out and poked it into my mouth. I picked up his lighter and lit it. I inhaled deeply, it tasted wonderful. Then I remembered George's brandy. I opened the desk drawer and took out the half filled bottle. I managed to unscrew the top with my good hand. I took the bottle and placing it against my lips, swallowed a mouthful. The cool heat of the liquid seared my throat. Placing the bottle on the desk, I went over to the open safe and stared at all the cash stacked neatly in it. I picked up one brick of notes. The denominations were fifties. Each package contained five thousand pounds.

I looked over at George slumped on the floor. His breathing was regular and he was snoring slightly. Then I looked at John Reid, lying dead against the door.

I remembered George's promise to pay for the repairs to my car, and a bit on top for myself. A bit, I thought, the conniving shit owed me more than mere money could buy.

Every death I'd participated in had destroyed a part of my soul, and every lie I'd believed had lessened my capacity to recognise the truth. I picked up another packet of currency, hefted the two in my hand, and put one in each of my inside jacket pockets. What the hell, I thought, the law would probably confiscate them, but nothing ventured, as my old mum used to say.

I felt no twinge of conscience as I hid the money away. I delved further into the safe. Right at the back, behind the stacks of cash was a cardboard envelope box about 10" x 12" and maybe six inches deep. It was heavy and I lifted it out and onto the cold metal top of the safe. I lifted off the top and struck pure gold. The box was full of photographs and papers. The photographs, some in colour, some in black and white were sexually explicit. They had been taken in several locations, all indoors. Some were shot in bedrooms, others in living rooms. The photos were taken at strange angles and I guessed that the cameras had been hidden. The participants were either very young or middle aged to elderly. Some of the children looked to be only six or seven, although it was hard to tell. It was all pretty sickening, but the older men were evidently enjoying themselves. It was disgusting sleaze, made even worse by the ordinariness of the backgrounds. Old men fucking young girls and boys in every position imaginable and some too weird to contemplate. The photos slipped between my fingers like shiny corners of hell. The only reason I kept looking was that I recognised the identities of some of the elderly subjects. I'd seen a few of the faces before the TV or in newspaper photographs. Now I saw them again frozen in filth. Taking their pleasure with little children. After a while, I found I couldn't take any more. I closed the box and placed it by the door. With the evidence

I was holding, I was in the position to operate a little blackmail scam myself. After what I'd done I needed all the help I could get.

I went back to the desk and sat for the last time in the executive chair. I reached for the brandy again, and had another long drink. Reality was fading fast. The memory of the horrors of the last few days were beginning to blur at the edges. Whether it was the liquor or the loss of blood from my wound, I didn't know.

I remembered my promise to Teresa. Things had worked out for me, at least so far.

She'd read about me in the Sunday papers, and know that very soon I'd keep our five o'clock appointment.

Then I stopped smiling.

I could only hope that with all the laws I'd broken recently I'd be able to keep any appointment in the next ten years, apart from those with my brief.

I had to sharpen up my act. I could imagine how I looked right then. Covered in blood, drinking brandy in that sordid little office, that stank of gunpowder and blood, with two big time drug smugglers lying on the floor. One dead and the other unconscious, surrounded by money, drugs and guns.

What could I do? That's show business.

It was going to be a long night.

Finally, I reached for the phone and dialled three nines.